BOYS DON'T CRY

J.K. HOGAN

Copyright

Cover Artist: KHD Graphics
Editor: Labyrinth Bound Edits
Boys Don't Cry © 2017 J.K. Hogan
Publisher: Euphoria Press
First Edition April 2017

All Rights Reserved:

Warning:

Intended for an 18+ audience only. This book contains material that may be offensive to some and is intended for a mature, adult audience. It contains graphic language, explicit sexual content, and adult situations.

ISBN: 154673306X
ISBN-13: 978-1546733065

DEDICATION

To Rachel, for always being there when I need milk.

Tina, Kathie, and Posy, my GRL Nerd Herd, you ladies keep me going.

And special thanks to all the members of my YOI group – this fandom gives me life and y'all brighten my day.

ONE

Notice of Eviction…

I had found the official-looking notice taped to my door the day before, and I was staring at it where it lay on the kitchen table. I felt like I'd suddenly forgotten how to read, and if I gazed at the document long enough, the letters might eventually coalesce into something I could understand.

When I confronted my landlord about it, he told me the entire apartment building was being torn down. The whole area was being renovated and rebuilt as part of some kind of urban gentrification project. In my mind, the definition of gentrified was somewhere I couldn't afford to live. I didn't want the neighborhood to be gentrified; I wanted to still be able to afford my rent-controlled dump of an apartment. But alas, it was not to be. Mr. Bardo, the man who owned the building, had essentially taken the money and run to avoid getting shivved in a forced sale, à la eminent domain. He needed all the residents to clear out as soon as possible so he could complete the transaction.

That was how, two months before my college graduation, I, Mackenzie Pratt, became homeless.

Knocking my forehead repeatedly against the heavy oak table in my favorite restaurant didn't seem to remedy the situation. My best friend Taylor had accompanied me to Serrano's—an odd combination of Italian restaurant and raw bar that somehow just worked—so I could drown my sorrows in a pitcher of beer. "I literally—" *Bonk* "—have nowhere—" *Thunk.* "—to fucking—" *Thud.* "—live."

With an irritating calm, Taylor refilled my glass from the pitcher, seemingly oblivious to my *dire* circumstances. "I'm sure you'll find something."

"There is nothing out there. There is not a single apartment for rent in the entire city of Baltimore that I can afford right now. Might I remind you that I also don't have a *job*? I have a little bit put aside for emergencies, but that won't last very long without an income."

In six weeks, I would be collecting my degree in early childhood education from Morrell College in Towson. I'd interviewed with several schools in the area, but I'd yet to hear back from any of them. My chances of getting something were fairly good, but until then I was—just to recap—jobless and homeless. I looked at Taylor with his shiny blond hair, shiny white teeth, shiny fucking life, and hated him just a little. But since I also loved him like a brother, I swallowed it down. "Sure I can't stay with you?" I asked, only half kidding.

He raised a manicured eyebrow. "Oh yeah, in my parents' basement? How would that work?"

I groaned and thunked my head again, nearly toppling my beer. "Ugh. Forgot." Taylor had moved back in with his folks so he could save money for med school. After our graduation, he would go to med school, then he was surely headed straight for Johns Hopkins. And I was headed straight for…a park bench, apparently.

"What about River?" he asked, referring to my estranged brother.

"You know him, too hipster to be tied down by life. He's off on another adventure. I think it's Prague this time. Or Budapest. I can't remember. He'll send me a postcard after he's already moved on to the next city." My brother was an editorial photographer. He took care of me for a few years after our dad passed away—my mom left before I was even out of diapers—but once I was old enough to go it alone, he let his free-spirit flag fly.

"I'll ask around at work, see if anyone knows of a place for rent. I'll have Karla check too."

Letting out a sigh so heavy it hurt my chest, I gave him a shaky smile. I had my doubts that either he or his girlfriend would come across a place I could afford, but I appreciated that he was trying to look out for me. "Thanks, man." After draining the dregs of my beer, I stood up, wobbling just a bit. "I'd better get home—while I still have one—and keep searching. Need to compose some follow-up emails to potential employers too."

Taylor stood too and tossed some cash on the table for our waiter. "Hold on there, Champ. I'll drive you." He'd cut himself off ages ago, electing to be the DD so I could wallow in self-pity, for which I was eternally grateful.

I stopped moving, but my momentum carried me on until I had to brace myself against a column. "Good call."

He clamped a hand on the back of my neck, guiding me through the restaurant so I didn't fall on my ass. "I just remembered, I've got to run a quick errand for work on my way home. You'll just have to tag along."

"But it's like…almost midnight."

"It's ten thirty, Grandpa. Besides, it's for one of our freelance developers. He works from home and keeps odd hours. I basically courier stuff to and from the office for him. The glamorous life of a help-desk operator at a tech company. All the shit errands get foisted off on us."

"Whatever you say, man. As long as he isn't going to call the cops on us for showing up so late."

"Trust me. This guy never sleeps anyway. Because of that, he's kind of a bear, so just let me do the talking and stay out of the way."

"Sounds like a laugh a minute," I said as I sank into the supple leather passenger seat of Taylor's Mercedes SUV. The car had been a birthday present. While his parents were well off, they believed in teaching Taylor the value of a dollar, hence the living in the basement and helping to pay for his own tuition. *Still, it must be nice to come from money.*

I couldn't believe that was the last thought I'd had before falling asleep and waking up parked in front of an honest-to-Christ mansion. I didn't even know there *were* mansions in Baltimore, but there it was, looming from its perch on a perfectly groomed grassy hill. A circular drive surrounded the house and grounds—a drive that was named after the house, according to Taylor—and there were no other houses on that street. They all would have paled in comparison, so it was just as well.

The architecture wasn't overly impressive, not that I was a connoisseur by any means. It was just a brick rectangle with a stately entryway held up by Corinthian columns, but the sheer size of the place just oozed money. I was instantly and irrevocably jealous. "Christ on a bike."

With a snort, Taylor threw the car in park and climbed out. "Don't let the outside fool you. His place is a sty because he never leaves. I force him out with the other guys from work once or twice a month, just to make sure he gets a little fresh air."

I followed him up the walk, wondering what kind of guy lived in a giant mansion he never left unless his coworkers dragged him out. Taylor pulled out a crumpled piece of paper and looked at it while punching a series of numbers on a keypad underneath the doorbell. When the lock disengaged, he pulled the door open and held it for me to step into the foyer, then followed, shutting the door behind us. "Don't let him scare you. He can be a broody mess when he's in the middle of a project, but he really is a nice guy deep down. Deep, *deep* down."

The house was dark so I couldn't see much, but what I could see was immaculate, contrary to what Taylor had said. The hardwood floors gleamed in the moonlight, the furniture looked expensive and perfect, and there wasn't a dirty dish or dust bunny in sight. "I thought you said it was a sty," I whispered.

"Oh, this? Not this. He only uses a fraction of the house, the suite with his bedroom, living room, library, and office. All of this is just for show," he said with a sweeping gesture toward the big empty parlor we were facing. "And why are you whispering? He knows I'm coming."

"I don't know. It seems so quiet and…undisturbed."

Taylor's chuckle had an evil ring to it. "You want disturbed? Follow me." He cupped his hands around his mouth and yelled. "Mr. Beaudry! It's me, Taylor. Morrison. From Mindstream. The place you work."

He made his way down a dark corridor with me dogging his heels. "He doesn't remember who you are? Where he works?"

"Oh, he knows. But when he's been staring at code for hours on end and not sleeping, sometimes basic stuff slips his mind. Details like that can be hard for geniuses like him."

Genius? I didn't think I'd ever heard that term used to sincerely describe someone. "What does he do again?"

"He's a mobile app developer. Highly sought after, but right now he works exclusively for us. That was a huge coup for the company." He stopped in front of a heavy, ornately carved door made of some kind of dark hardwood. He rapped his knuckles on it three times before barging on in while I hovered in the doorway.

So *this* was the suite. Taylor had been right. What a mess. We stood in what I assumed was the living room, but it was hard to tell because every available surface was covered in wrinkled clothing, pizza boxes, and empty dishes. A huge fireplace was installed in the far wall, surrounded by shelves and shelves of books. More books than I'd ever seen in one place outside a library. The fire blazed in the hearth, and I was honestly surprised there wasn't any garbage close enough to it to catch fire. As beautiful as the house was, the mess made my skin crawl. I usually lived in shitty apartments, so I was a bit of a neat freak to balance the universe.

"Beaudry? You in here?" Taylor called. There was no answer. "He must be in the bedroom suite." He headed to a door on the left like it was no big deal.

"*Wait!* You're just going to barge into the guy's bedroom?"

Pausing in his tracks, Taylor looked over his shoulder. "This is no ordinary bedroom. Just because there's a bed in the corner doesn't mean it's some intimate setting. It's just a giant workspace." With that parting shot, he burst through the door, once again calling the man's name.

Trembling from too much alcohol and not enough nerve, I stepped inside the room. I was stunned speechless by the scene before me. Taylor had one thing right—it was no ordinary bedroom. It was the size of three average rooms lined up in a row and probably had double the square footage of the apartment I was getting booted out of. There was indeed a bed, a California king canopy bed off in one corner of the room. A fire was blazing in this suite as well, only I realized that it was the same fire in the same fireplace, which apparently connected the two rooms.

Taylor stood next to what had to be the man's workspace. There was a giant U-shaped desk adorned with four widescreen computer monitors and various other gadgets typical of an office. However, on one leg of the U, there was a collection of what looked to be every tablet, PDA, smartphone, and any other mobile device known to man. I supposed he had to test his software on each gizmo that was likely to employ it.

Behind the office area was a ginormous TV screen—at least seventy inches—that looked like it would be more at home in a movie theater. Several fluffy couches were set up in a semicircle facing it. It would be amazing to have a movie marathon in this place. And of course, there was every gaming console imaginable to go along with the screen yardage. But…despite all the cool stuff, there was some very *weird* stuff about the place as well. Besides the office setup and the movie area, all the furniture in the suite looked like it had been bought from a garage sale at Versailles. It was expensive-looking, obviously, but very gilded and frilly. There were also several racks flanking the giant TV that displayed the man's sword collection.

And then, the murals. The murals were creepy. On at least a couple of the walls above the wainscoting, there were huge, garish wall paintings of nudes in various scenes. Men and women, sometimes in sexual situations, sometimes just hanging out or whatever. But they weren't like Renaissance or fine art nudes or anything; they seemed to be done by just some random modern artist. I had no idea how the guy could manage to look at them all day every day. Though if it weren't for those, I'd never leave a place like this either. Speaking of the guy, though, there was no sign of him.

"Where is he?" I was whispering again. It just seemed like the thing to do when you snuck into someone's bedroom at night. Not that we were *really* sneaking, but still.

As if in answer to my question, we heard a toilet flush, and a door to my right that I hadn't even noticed swung open, startling me. The person who came through was pretty much just as unbelievable as the house he lived in. He was tall—very tall—and lanky, but with wide shoulders and well-defined musculature. His hair was just a little too long, like maybe he'd forgotten his last couple of haircuts, and very dark, shot through with a tiny bit of gray. It had to be premature because I doubted he was much more than ten years older than me. His facial features—though thrown in deep shadow because of the low light in the room—were chiseled and angular, too handsome to be fair to the rest of the world. Wire-rimmed glasses perched on the tip of his straight nose, slightly askew. Despite the handsomeness, he had dark circles under his eyes and frown lines around his mouth, as if he hadn't slept in weeks. And he was wearing Angry Birds pajamas.

When he saw me, his deep-set blue eyes widened and he flinched like I'd snuck up on him. "Who the hell are you?"

I let out a squeaky gasp and backed away toward Taylor because the guy looked fucking scary when he turned on the full force of that scowl.

"Jesus Christ, Beaudry, relax," Taylor said. He picked up his briefcase and pulled out a legal-size envelope. "This is my friend Mackenzie. I was driving him home, and I just popped in to drop off these contracts from Harrelson."

Beaudry grunted and crossed the room to sit at his desk. He waved a hand in the vague direction of a stack of shelves. "Just put them in the inbox. I'll deal with them later."

"If you look them over now, I can take back any questions or return them…"

He glared at Taylor over his shoulder, and Taylor wisely shut his mouth. Then the man's gaze settled on me. It wasn't the scowl he'd given me earlier, but it wasn't exactly a…nice expression either. It was more of an assessing glare than anything. "Welcome to Chatham House, Mackenzie. What do you think?" he asked.

8

I had no idea what he meant. What did I think of the house? The room? Him? "It's…impressive. The artwork is…unusual."

He let out a belting laugh I hadn't been expecting, so I jumped, but then the rich baritone of it made my toes curl. It was an odd reaction, as I wasn't usually affected by such things.

"Unusual is a kind way of putting it. The artwork came with the house, along with much of the furniture. I just haven't gotten around to redecorating."

"Oh, that's…" *A relief.* "How long have you lived here, then?"

Beaudry turned back to his computer and began typing furiously. "About five years," he answered without turning back around.

I choked on air, and Taylor snorted. "I think by 'haven't gotten around to it,' you mean 'just don't give a shit,'" he muttered.

"Touché, Mr. Morrison. Is there anything else you need?"

Taylor sighed, probably realizing that the man was not going to look at whatever was in the envelope while we were still there to relay any messages back to Mindstream. He clamped a hand around my wrist and started dragging me toward the door. "All right, we're going. Remember, drinks at the King's Shield next Friday."

"I don't think I'm going to be—"

Taylor spoke right over Beaudry's muttering. "You already said you would. No backsies. I can pick you up."

"I think I'd enjoy driving my shiny Lotus instead, but thank you very much for the offer," Beaudry growled. "Nice meeting you, Mack," I heard him call through the open door.

"Nickname basis already?" I laughed to Taylor.

"That has nothing to do with nicknames and everything to do with your name being too long for him to remember."

"I heard that, Morrison!"

"I didn't stutter, Beaudry!" Taylor rolled his eyes as he

opened the door that spilled out into the hallway. "Don't forget, Friday night!" he hollered over his shoulder.

Taking the silence as agreement, Taylor kept pulling me until we were out the front door, into the crisp air of the spring night.

"What just happened?" I asked to no one in particular.

"Oh, just a typical visit to Chatham House. Welcome to my life."

TWO

Orchard Grove Apartments left everything to be desired. It was ridiculous because nowhere in the Baltimore area was there an orchard. But bad names notwithstanding, the place was an absolute dump. The building had popped up on one of my searches for rentals in my price range, but the truth was, I'd gotten incredibly lucky with my current place. It was becoming increasingly obvious that anything I could afford was going to look like… well, *this*, unless I just happened to get lucky again.

Baltimore was unusual in that (in my opinion) it didn't have a "good side" of town and a "bad side" or anything like that. It was more like a checkerboard of affluence and squalor. You could be walking down the street on the block that your dorm was on, and when you set foot on the next block, you were right in the slums—not *actual* slums… Sadly, I was prone to hyperbole. Anyway, so I basically had no idea what I was dealing with until I got there. And what I was dealing with were cockroaches and mouse droppings…just sayin'.

When the landlord let me in to take a look at the place, he just walked off and left it wide open. Not that there was anything in there that *anyone* would want to steal, but it still didn't bode well for the security of the building. The apartment was only a one-bedroom studio, about seven hundred square feet of dingy, drab sadness. The dark wooden wainscoting and the beige wallpaper that was peeling in a dozen places gave it this gross, monochromatic brownness that I just could not handle. I could already feel myself getting depressed.

Unfortunately, the aforementioned mouse droppings were in the kitchen, so a massive cleanup would be in order to even use it. Several of the cabinet doors were hanging off their hinges, and there was an...odor...that I wasn't eager to find the source of. The bedroom came with a bed, which should've been a plus, but the bed literally filled the entire room, and if I slept in it, I'd feel the need to set myself on fire to cleanse my body of the bedbugs.

The only redeeming quality to the place was that it had what looked like possibly a walk-in closet, which I would need because the apartment wasn't big enough to hold all my stuff. I tried opening the door, but it was stuck, so I yanked on it for a couple of seconds until it finally flew open and banged against the wall. The closet was decent-sized and workable until the pile of trash bags on the floor moved. Then something furry and aggressive, about the size of a schnauzer, lunged at me, making this creepy chittering noise—it looked like maybe a raccoon but I'm not entirely sure it wasn't a gremlin—and I peaced the fuck out of that place. In other words, I ran screaming from the room, out of the unit, down the hall, away from the building, never to look back. If I wanted to sleep with raccoons, I could do that on any park bench in the city.

I calmed down once I was outside on the sidewalk and had put a fair distance in between me and the hell-monster in the closet. Once my thundering heart slowed, it sank in that my one prospect for a place to live was literally unlivable. I was back to where I started, two days from being homeless. Feeling the need to drown my sorrows but unable to afford any beer, I decided to call Taylor. Just as I picked up my phone, it rang in my hand, nearly causing me to drop it.

"Hey, Tay. I was just about to call you."

"How'd it go?"

"Hazmat."

"That good, huh?"

"I'm literally going to be homeless, Taylor. I'm getting desperate."

"Don't worry, man. We'll figure something out. I can squeeze you into the bathtub in my parents' basement for a few days if worse comes to worst."

"It probably will, just warning you now."

"You sound like you could use a drink."

"You just get me. I don't have any money, though."

"Relax, I'll spot you. I still owe you a few rounds from the Christmas break drink-a-thon anyway."

I groaned in remembrance of the epic hangover. "Don't remind me. So where do you want to go?"

"Just come to the King's Shield with us."

"Us?"

"Yeah. You know, the guys from work. We're doing our monthly thing."

"Oh, I totally forgot. You sure it's okay if I tag along?"

"Positive. These guys never meet a stranger."

I felt better already. Even if I had no job and nowhere to live, at least I had a good friend in my corner and some nice people to drink with. It would have to be enough.

"Walking over to your place. I'll be there in fifteen minutes."

13

The King's Shield was a run-of-the-mill tavern in the Inner Harbor. It had the same wood, brass, and neon décor you could find in any other watering hole. Really, its only unique quality was that it was right on the waterfront, which made for some decent views. We had chosen to take a cab from Taylor's house so neither of us would have to be the designated driver.

We entered through the patio door, and Taylor immediately spotted some of his work friends, who'd already commandeered two tables in the back near the picture windows facing the harbor. He waved to them and motioned for me to follow. There were already four guys and one woman sitting at the tables when we sat down, only two of whom I recognized. There was Henry Ashland, one of the in-house web developers with Mindstream, and the woman was Shayna Kepner, one of the IT techs.

"Hey, guys, what're we drinking?" Taylor said.

"His highness ordered a bottle of Lagavulin for the table. It'll be here in a minute."

"His highness?" I asked.

"Ah, Mack is back," said a voice from behind me.

I flinched and turned around. Laurent Beaudry again. He was ensconced in a shadowy corner, and I hadn't even seen him until I was practically on his lap. Blushing and sputtering, I scooted my chair over so I wasn't blocking his view of the group, although I had no clue why he chose to sit in the corner booth beside us instead of at the table. Maybe it was just part of the broody, antisocial nature that Taylor had told me about.

"Hello, again. I see Taylor was able to drag you out after all."

"He threatened to call Dr. Phil on me to stage an intervention." He smiled slightly. He was looking much more put together than when I'd seen him in the midst of his work. Wearing a suit that likely cost more than my car, he had this aura of expensive refinement, but in an understated way. All it did was draw more attention to how handsome and mysterious he was.

"I'd do it too," Taylor said through a mouthful of bar peanuts, interrupting my embarrassing thoughts.

"I know you would," Beaudry said in that silky-rich voice of his. "Hence my being here."

Shayna gave me a bright smile. "Weren't you looking at an apartment today, Mackenzie? How'd that go?"

I sighed, swallowing down the legitimate urge to burst into tears. "It was awful. They had rodents—and not just the fun-size kind. One of them lunged at me. I almost died."

"Aww, you poor thing. I told my sister to ask around at her job—she works with an urban development group, so I was hoping she'd heard of any new units going up for rent. No luck so far, sorry, hun."

My gut clenched, but I forced a smile because it had been kind of her to ask. "Thanks anyway. I appreciate all the help I can get."

"Wait, so what's going on?" This came from Henry, who was across the table facing me. I'd been picking up a weird vibe from him, but I couldn't figure out if his questioning glances were for me or the quiet man to my right.

"My apartment building is being torn down, so we've all been asked to move out with much less notice than I would've liked. I'm graduating in a couple of months and I'm between jobs, so anything for rent within my price range seems to be…well, infested."

"That's tough, man," said Brian, one of the guys I hadn't met before. "The housing market has been ridiculous all around lately. Everyone always talks about mortgages, but they don't really think that it affects renters too. I hope you find something soon."

We paused when the waitress showed up with the expensive scotch Mr. Beaudry had ordered. She poured us all two fingers and then melted back into the chaos of the dining room. Scotch wasn't my favorite drink—I sure as hell could rarely afford it—

but even I could appreciate the dark, smoky taste of the amber liquid. It went down smooth, even with the burn. Breathing in the scent through my nose, I sighed and closed my eyes, trying to enjoy the delicacies wherever I could because they were few and far between.

I tipped my face toward the window, intending to lose myself in the view of the harbor lights, but I found Mr. Beaudry watching me. His face was again completely unreadable. What was he thinking? What was it about me that he found interesting?

When he spoke, it was so quiet it almost didn't register. "I have room in my house."

I gasped and promptly inhaled the hundred-dollar scotch. "What did—?" *Hack, wheeze.* "What did you say?"

He shrugged and fiddled with his cufflink, not meeting my eyes. "I said, 'I have room at my house.' You know, if you're desperate and all. I'm an absolute horror to be around most of the time, but it's there if you want it."

"But—but you don't even know me."

"I know Taylor and these two," he said, indicating Henry and Shayna. "So if they vouch for you, that's good enough for me. You saw that Chatham house has plenty of space that isn't being used."

"That's…very nice of you to offer, but I couldn't—I mean, I don't really have any money. Just a little saved up, and that's going to run out fast if I don't hear back about my job interviews soon."

Again, he shrugged, as if it was all inconsequential to him. "It wouldn't cost you anything. Those rooms are just sitting there. But if it's like a pride thing, you can just help out around the house. You know, clean up, cook a few meals. I kind of live off takeout right now."

Was this guy really offering to take in a total stranger out of the goodness of his heart? I cast a helpless glance at Taylor, who looked just as dumbstruck as I felt. His mouth opened and closed like a fish as he struggled to find something to say. "Maybe..." He rubbed the back of his neck. "Maybe you could just crash for a little while. Surely something's bound to come available soon." *I should politely decline. I should.* I didn't know the guy at all. But as scary as rooming with a stranger might be, I was more scared of literally being homeless, so I was pretty sure I'd already made up my mind the moment he'd mentioned it. I gave him a shy smile. "Um, well, if you're sure... You've got yourself a roommate. Tenant. Whatever."

When he smiled back at me, I got the feeling it was a rare sight. My heart raced, and I could feel my skin flushing all over. It was an unusual reaction for me. I hadn't thought I was attracted to him, other than aesthetic appreciation—I'd never been notably attracted to other men either, and rarely to women. I'd had a bit of an isolated adolescence, despite always having my brother, and I'd thrown so much energy into doing well in school and making something of myself, I never really put much thought into dating or sex. And two months from graduation definitely wasn't a good time to start. Mr. Beaudry definitely stirred up *some* kind of feelings—I just wasn't sure if it was attraction, anxiety, or straight up fear...or maybe a combination of all three—but I wasn't going to give it any more thought.

"Glad to help. You can move in whenever you like. There's another suite across the hall from mine that should suit you. And of course, you'll have the full run of the kitchen, laundry, grounds, and any other thing you need." His voice was formal but deep and rich, like whisky poured over ice. After hearing him talk more, I noticed that it was also very faintly accented. My brain itched to find out where he was from, but there didn't seem to be a polite way to ask. I was sure to find out while I was living with him. *Staying* with him, not *living* with him. Jesus Christ, what was I doing?

THREE

The day I moved in, I was already in a terrible mood. I'd gotten a call from one of my interviewers; I didn't get the job. There were still a few schools I was waiting to hear from, but getting a rejection right out of the gate was really demoralizing. Coupled with the fact that I'd stuffed all my worldly belongings into my old Toyota and driven away from my apartment building for the last time, it was just a shitty day in general.

Since I was headed there anyway, Taylor had given me some work stuff to take to Mr. Beaudry. It was the least I could do, considering I never would've met the guy who was giving me a place to live if it hadn't been for Taylor. Pulling into the driveway, I keyed in the code I'd been given for the three car garage. Once the door came up, I parked next to—*Christ*—Mr. Beaudry's shiny black Lotus that was worth more than my life.

Too tired from all the packing and moving, I left most of my stuff in my car, only taking my laptop bag and the envelope from Taylor. The door from the garage into the house had the same key code, only backward. This door opened up to a kitchen that could've served a Michelin Star restaurant. I wasn't an expert at cooking by any means, but I liked to do it, and my previous kitchen had been woefully inadequate. I couldn't wait to try out a meal in this one.

The security system in the mansion was state-of-the-art, so I was pretty sure Mr. Beaudry would know I was there. It surprised me that he hadn't come out to greet me, considering I didn't know where I was going to be staying. I noticed a piece of paper on the butcher block, so I went over to check it out. Turned out it was a note to Taylor.

Morrison—
I pulled an all-nighter last night, so I've gone to bed. Just leave the files in the kitchen.
Thanks.
—LB

Okay, so my reaction to this was completely irrational. I'll say that upfront. After the day I'd had, the idea that this guy, who'd invited me into his home, not only wasn't around to greet me but didn't even bother to leave me a note like he'd done Taylor completely set me off. What the hell was I supposed to do?

My illogical anger was consuming, causing my heart to thunder in my ears and my vision to swim. It had just been one goddamn thing after another lately, and this was the proverbial straw that broke the camel's back. Based on the proximity of the garage to the front door, I was able to find my way to that massive foyer. From there, of course, I knew the way to Beaudry's suite, so I stomped my happy ass down the hall and burst through the door, ready to give the jerk a piece of my mind.

All right, so I stormed into an empty room. Because of course the guy was sleeping, so he wasn't in the living-room-library part of the suite. Once again, I was struck by the cataclysmic *mess* of the place. It occurred to me that he'd said I could do some light cooking and cleaning in lieu of rent, but I wondered if that included *this*. On the one hand, ew...but on the other, it would be good to get it cleaned up because...ew.

I wasn't going to let the state of his rooms deter me from my mission. I had a good head of steam worked up and I needed to release the valve. Shoving my way through the next door, I found the space shrouded in darkness. He'd drawn the heavy drapes, so the only light in the room was what little that streamed through the open door behind me. Sure enough, there was a lump in the middle of that enormous canopy bed. "Hey!" I said. It wasn't exactly a shout, but it was close.

The lump didn't move. I passed the workspace and the media area and finally made it to the bed. Suddenly I realized just how cold it was in there. March in Baltimore could sometimes be chilly in the evenings, and it seemed like the heat hadn't kicked on. Who knew what possessed me to care, but I took a detour over to the fireplace and located the remote for the gas on the mantle. When I turned it on, the room was filled with the dull glow given off by the flames.

Back at the bed, I tried talking again. "Hey! What gives? Did you forget I was coming?"

This time the lump shuddered and a groan rose up from beneath the duvet.

"Look, Mr. Beaudry, I don't want to inconvenience you any more than I already have, but I don't know where to put my stuff. Isn't it a little rude to not even be awake when I get here?"

The duvet came flying off, slapping me in the face before pooling back on the mattress. He rose up halfway, propping himself up on his elbows. God, he looked awful. The dark bruising under his eyes that had been absent that day at the bar was back in full force. His hair was sticking up at all angles, and he had a couple of days growth of beard on his jaw. He was still probably the most handsome man I'd ever seen, but it was obvious he'd had a rough time. I instantly regretted my tirade.

He blinked rapidly, then squinted at me. "Huh?"

"I'm sorry for barging in, I just… It's been a rough day and I'm tired. I just need to know where to put my stuff."

"Wha—who?" His brow furrowed in confusion.

You've got to be kidding me. "Mackenzie Pratt. Your boarder for the next few weeks, remember?"

He pinched the bridge of his nose, shook his head hard, then sat up straighter. "I know who you are. What are you doing in my bedroom?"

"I-I-I was just… I didn't… I was surprised that you weren't around, is all. Didn't know where to put my stuff."

"I told you the other night at the bar."

"Huh?"

"I said there was a suite across the hall from mine. You obviously found your way *here* just fine."

"Oh, I…guess I forgot about—"

"You know, usually when a man comes into my bedroom and wakes me up, he wants something very specific from me."

"*What*—?"

He didn't give me a chance to finish my squeaked question. Grabbing my arm, he pulled me down so suddenly that I face-planted onto his bed. Before my brain even had a chance to send the signal to my extremities to move, he was on me. He dragged my arms up over my head and clenched my wrists together in one big hand.

"Is this what you need?" he purred in my ear.

I couldn't help the full body shudder that racked me as a result of hot breath on my neck and a hard body pinning me down. I never would've thought that'd be something I'd like, but, then again, I'd never spent much time finding out. Still, the audacity of the man to ambush me in such a way…

He slipped a hand underneath my shirt, his large palm slid

across my stomach and up to my chest while I remained frozen with shock. When his thumb grazed my nipple, my whole body tightened and reverberated like a plucked violin string. My brain kept trying to feel appalled, but it was no longer in control, as all my blood had gone rushing south. Much to my embarrassment, I felt myself hardening.

I didn't want to give him the satisfaction of drawing a reaction from me, so I bucked underneath him, trying to throw him off. My efforts had little effect, but he loosened his grip enough so I could flip over and glare at him. That...might've been a mistake. He was hard as well; I could feel his erection against my thigh, and I couldn't stop thinking about it. His eyes were dark and dangerous, and I was unable to look away. "What are you *doing?*" I asked, using my legs to try and dislodge him.

He let out a hearty laugh, that deep, dark sound that shimmered under my skin, and then he grinned, but with his face appearing so predatory, it looked more like a sneer. "You're blushing like a virgin." He rolled his hips, and my pulse pounded so hard in my brain that I was sure I would have a stroke.

Such an idle remark. I tried to keep him from seeing the truth of it, but my pale skin hid nothing, even by firelight. He dipped his head, bringing his face closer until our lips were mere inches apart. But he just stared, that measured appraisal that he'd given me the day we met and again at the bar. Then his eyes widened, and he scrambled off of me, backing up against the headboard in the far corner of the bed. His bare chest heaved as he panted through parted lips. Even though his lowered brow threw his eyes into shadow, I could see light glinting off of them like...like he was near tears.

"I-I'm so...," he stuttered. "It's probably best if you go to your suite. I get weird when I'm woken up after a marathon work session. I'm not always...aware."

"O-oh, okay." Why did I feel the urge to comfort him? He was the one who had jumped me with little provocation. But I *had* barged into his room in a snit when I knew he was sleeping. Maybe we should just call it even and start over the next day.

He decided for me, rolling over and pulling the duvet over his head. That, apparently, was that. I climbed off the bed and tiptoed out of the room in search of my place.

The suite he'd indicated for me wasn't quite as big as his, but again, it could've fit my whole apartment inside of it. It had a huge main room, filled with empty bookshelves on the far end for a library like he had, and the area closest to me had some barebones living room furniture—a couch, love seat, coffee table, and a "normal-person" sized TV. There was a small kitchenette in the right corner with a mini-fridge and a wet bar, but I knew I'd be using the fancy main kitchen as often as he'd let me.

I was surprised to see a queen-sized bed made up with robin's-egg-blue bedclothes, stacked with fluffy pillows. There was also a large bureau, a desk, and a walk-in closet—*without* a raccoon. This all came as a huge relief to me, as all of the large pieces of furniture I'd used had come with my apartment. Mr. Bardo had offered to sell them to me since the building was getting torn down, but of course I couldn't afford them. Honestly, I was so relieved to have furniture that my eyes pricked with tears. I'd brought a sleeping bag thinking there would be nothing but bare walls and floor. Mr. Beaudry must've used this suite for guests, lucky for me.

With renewed energy, I quickly and quietly hauled all of my belongings in from my car. I loaded myself up each time, so I was able to do it in four trips. By the time that was done, I was exhausted. I dug some sweats and an old T-shirt out of my suitcase and flopped down on my new bed. My body sank into the luscious mattress, and I was asleep before I could form another coherent thought.

I was awakened by the sun streaming into the room through the bare windows. I'd have to ask Mr. Beaudry if I was allowed to put up shades. It felt pretty early, but when I checked my phone, I saw it was just after eight. It still felt like I was just crashing on someone's—really nice, fancy, expensive—couch, so I wasn't exactly sure what to do. Because we'd sort of agreed that I would do some light housework in lieu of rent, I decided to take the initiative and go make breakfast.

The granite and stainless monstrosity of a kitchen appeared to be fully stocked. Mr. Beaudry didn't strike me as the grocery-shopping type, so I imagined he had some kind of service take care of it. Finding the door to the pantry, I opened it and was shocked to find that it had multiple hinged shelves that folded out to create even more storage. The massive Sub-Zero refrigerator had similar hidden shelves and doors, and the whole thing was camouflaged to look like it was part of the cabinets. It was yet another thing Beaudry owned that cost more than my car. If I was going to live here, I was going to have to get over my hang-ups with how much stuff cost. The guy was obviously rolling in money, but that didn't mean he was happy.

Taking down some pans from the hanging rack above the center island, I scrounged around until I found some eggs, bacon, cheese, peppers, and a few other vegetables. I decided to make some simple omelets because I wasn't even sure if Mr. Beaudry had any dietary requirements. I sure as hell wasn't going back into his suite to ask. My cheeks heated at the mere memory of what had happened the day before.

I was facing the stove when I heard the shuffle of bare feet behind me. I turned around to see Mr. Beaudry slide into one of the stools that accompanied the island. His hair was rumpled, barely contained by the reading glasses he'd pushed up on the top of his head, and his face was a storm cloud. He was also wearing Batman pajamas. I did not understand the fascination with cartoon character PJs, but the guy was eccentric, so whatever.

He folded his arms on the marble countertop and rested his head on them with a grunt.

"Good morning, Mr. Beaudry. I didn't expect to see you up and about so early."

"You cooked. Least I can do is show up to eat." His voice was muffled by his sleeves. He suddenly raised his head and blinked at me like he'd just woken up. "You can quit it with that Mr. Beaudry business. Makes it feel like you're my butler or something."

I pursed my lips to keep from saying I *was* kind of a servant, only for rent instead of money, but I didn't want to sound ungrateful. "What would you like me to call you?"

He paused, staring off into space for a moment before answering me. "You can call me Laurie."

"Laurie?"

"Yes. My name is Laurent, so I guess it's like a nickname."

"All right, then, Laurie. I made omelets. I don't know what you like so I just took a guess."

I plated up two omelets, set one in front of him, and held my own plate while leaning against the counter and dug in. I'd always gotten some weird domestic pleasure out of feeding people, and I loved seeing them enjoy my food. When Laurie closed his eyes and let out a groan that could've found a home in a porn flick, my stomach got all fluttery and warm.

"This is fantastic, Mackenzie. You'll make someone a fine wife someday."

"That's offensive," I deadpanned.

He swallowed a mouthful. "Wouldn't be the first time, won't be the last."

Well, at least he's honest. I studied him like I would an animal at a zoo, trying to figure out what made this odd man tick. "You know…," I began, cursing my lack of a brain-to-mouth filter, "most people would be embarrassed about having basically molested a man they barely knew. And maybe feel the need to apologize."

Unconcerned, he savored another bite of omelet. "Most people would probably be embarrassed about having burst into the bedroom of a man they barely knew while he was sleeping."

Touché...

"Apologies indicate regret, which indicates indecision. I am never indecisive, therefore I never apologize unless I have hurt someone. You weren't hurt. Were you?"

I gave the question the thought it was due. Had I been hurt? Physically, no. I wasn't too proud to say it hadn't felt bad at all. What about emotionally or psychologically? I'd been indignant, embarrassed, maybe a tad bit frightened, but I hadn't actually felt like he wouldn't let me go if I'd really asked. So there was my answer. "No, I wasn't." I turned away from him and started washing the dishes.

He sighed, and I heard his fork clatter on his plate. "I will say, as a means of explanation rather than excuse, I'm just recently out of a relationship that I thought was going...somewhere. It didn't end well. So I haven't been myself lately. Plus, as I said, I get weird when I'm woken up after a long stint of working and no sleep. Take that however you will."

I faced him again. "I'm sorry. About your relationship. Did she—?"

"He." His dark blue eyes locked onto my face and he raised a brow as if to challenge me to say something derogatory.

"Did *he*...break up with you?"

"It's complicated. I started to get the feeling that he didn't actually like me very much. I'm not an easy man to be with and...I guess I just expected too much."

I frowned, not entirely sure I understood. "You're a very cryptic person."

"It's a personality flaw. Everyone says so." He shrugged and stood up to take his plate to the sink.

He didn't quite make it. He just set it on the counter beside the sink. I glared at the side of his head for a moment before I remembered our deal. I took the plate, rinsed it, and put it in the dishwasher.

"What about you, Mackenzie? Or is it Mack?"

"Usually Mackenzie, but either one, really." I shrugged. "What about me, what?"

"Tell me about your life. Do you have a girlfriend?"

"No."

"Boyfriend?"

"No. I've been focusing on school for the last eight years, basically since starting high school. I didn't want to get distracted."

He watched me silently for a few seconds. "You said you were job hunting. What are you looking for?"

"My degree's in early childhood education. I graduate in May, so I'm looking for jobs at preschools and elementary schools in the area that hopefully could become permanent positions once I'm done with school."

"Do you have school today?"

"It's Sunday."

He scratched the back of his neck. "Really? Oh. I usually sleep for a couple of days after a marathon of coding. Must be your fault."

"Of course it is," I said dryly.

"You might prove to be something of a distraction."

I just rolled my eyes and finished drying the dishes and pans. Once I'd put everything away, I wasn't sure if I should just leave or if it was okay to stay and chat with him without the pretense of cooking, eating, or cleaning.

"So that's what you want to do with your life then? Be a teacher?"

I whirled on him, angry even though I hadn't really heard any derision in his tone, just curiosity. "Hey, it's a good profession! I may not ever become a zillionaire like *some* people, but I'll have you know Maryland *is* ranked eighth in the nation for teacher pay."

Yes, I was aware that I sounded like the five-year-olds I was trying to get a job teaching. Laurie watched me have my tantrum with a slightly amused smile on his face. With a laugh, he stood up and ruffled my brownish-blond hair in a gesture befitting the aforementioned tantrum.

"No, no, I don't care about money. It's just...*children*." He gave a delicate shudder. "They're cute to look at from a distance—like tiger cubs or something. Doesn't mean I want to get in the cage with them."

I chuckled, calmer once I realized he wasn't looking down on me for my career goals. "Yeah, liking kids is sort of a job requirement to be a teacher. Well, usually. I had a couple in high school that were questionable." His hand was still on my head, just sort of resting there, and I wasn't doing anything to stop it. Why wasn't I making him move?

"Thank you for breakfast, Mackenzie. I'm starting work on a new app today, hence the documents Taylor had you bring over. I'll probably be holed up for quite a while, so just make yourself at home." *Finally*, he moved his hand, trailing his fingers through my hair before removing them.

"Ah. Okay. Should I...? Do you want me to make you food at mealtimes? I can bring it to you."

"That's very thoughtful, but we can eat our meals together. You just might have to let me know when it's time." He looked down at his feet and I swear he blushed just a little. "There's an intercom beside the door to my suite if you...don't feel comfortable coming in."

Strangely, I wasn't worried about going into his room, even after what had happened last time. "I'm fine. Whatever you prefer."

He smiled brighter. "How about you buzz me first and come in if I don't answer. When I get in the zone, sometimes I don't hear the 'com."

"Oh. Okay, then. See you at lunchtime."

He'd already headed back toward the hallway, but he looked over his shoulder at me. "See you later, Mackenzie."

I didn't see him for the rest of that day. I ended up leaving both lunch and dinner in the outer room of his suite, which he requested over the intercom. I was beginning to wonder at what point I should start to worry about his health until I remembered he was a grown-ass man who'd obviously survived on his own before I showed up to make sure he ate.

I was finishing a modest breakfast of homemade oatmeal with fresh strawberries and blueberries when he finally emerged from his cave. When he slumped onto one of the barstools, I gasped because he looked like hammered shit. I didn't know anything about mobile app development—or about programming…or about computers much at all, really—but it was obviously hard work because he was pretty much a zombie when he was in the middle of a project.

"Thank you for the meals yesterday. I'm sorry I couldn't eat with you. When things are flowing, I have to keep going so I don't lose the thread." He squinted when he realized he was still wearing his reading glasses, then pushed them up on his head, pulling his hair back from his face. It made him look younger somehow, but then I realized I didn't actually know how old he was.

"It's okay, I figured you had a lot of work. I wouldn't expect you to eat every meal in here with me. I hope you don't mind a simple breakfast… I've got school this morning, so I had to do something kind of quick," I said as I placed a bowl in front of him.

"It's just fine, thanks. If you're worried about getting to school on time, I can drive you. I'm on a forced break right now anyway." I was starting to notice his accent, wherever it was from, came out a little more when he was deprived of sleep.

"You don't have to do that. I've got my car, and Towson's not that far."

He looked up and gave me a crooked smile. "The Lotus is faster than whatever rattle-trap you've got. You'd have a little more time to eat breakfast. Please? I'd like to."

I blinked at him, confounded by his dichotomous personality. "I don't understand how you can be such an asshole yet strangely kind, all in the same breath."

"It's a gift. So, how about it?"

I didn't know if I should be spending more time with this man, but I'd probably never get a chance to ride in an Esprit in my entire life. I couldn't bear to pass it up. "Well...if you're sure it's no trouble, I wouldn't mind having a ride in that car."

"Atta boy," he said with a grin, then hurried to scarf down his breakfast.

Before long, we were flying down the road, and he was not wrong. That monster *was* faster than my car could ever dream of being, and he pushed the speedometer as far as he could get away with. Honestly, he'd probably be able to talk his way out of a ticket even if he did get pulled over.

Being inside the Lotus was like riding in a tank—at least, how I imagined that would be—with the car being so low to the ground and the door panels coming up so high. I melted into the supple, plush leather bucket seat like warm buttercream. I'd never been in a car this nice before. Or loud. I could hardly hear myself think over the rumbling of the V8 engine. I wasn't going to let that stop me because my curiosity about Laurie had reached a boiling point.

"Hey, so I keep hearing this slight accent when you talk.

Where's that from?"

He glanced over at me, brows raised, before turning his attention back to the traffic on York. "Oh? I thought it had mostly faded. No one ever picks up on it. I'm originally from Quebec."

"Really? I've never been to Canada. How long have you lived in the States?"

In profile, I could still see his jaw clench and his lips purse. "A long time."

Sore subject, apparently. I desperately wanted to know more, but I didn't press him. I was dying to figure out how he'd become so wealthy—shallow, yes, but nosiness had always been my downfall. I was pretty sure he got paid a lot for the apps he developed, but that mansion, this car...he must've had some other source of cash flow to supplement. But I didn't exactly know the guy well enough to ask to see his tax returns.

"So what classes do you have today?"

I wasn't oblivious to the redirection, but I decided to humor him for the moment. "Um, Monday, Wednesday is curriculum building and principles of language arts. Tuesday, Thursday I have problems in education and teaching math to primaries. I'm really glad I got my internships out of the way last semester, so I didn't have to deal with that on top of the whole eviction thing."

"Mmhmm," he said, the conversation trailing off. I didn't know if he'd ever actually been interested in my classes or if the subject of teaching children was just so distasteful that he had nothing else to say. I guessed probably the latter.

Either way, we stayed silent until he pulled through the main entrance of the university. Taylor, who was supposed to be meeting me there so we could walk to class together, stood out front by the curb. He'd fixed us with an open-mouthed stare— whether he recognized the car or was just surprised to see a Lotus in person, I had no clue. It was pretty hilarious the way his eyes bugged out when he saw *me* get out of that car.

When I turned to shut the door, I leaned down so I could see Laurie. "Thanks for the ride. See you at dinner."

"Anytime, Mackenzie."

I shut the door, and the jet-black sports car thundered away.

"Lucy, you got some 'splainin' to do." Taylor hooked an arm around my neck and used it to drag me in the direction of our classes—the buildings were adjacent, so we could walk together. "What, that? Laurie just offered to drop me off because I was running late after making breakfast."

"*Laurie?* Seriously? Do you have a thing going on with your new landlord? I guess he's a lot better than Bardo, but Jesus, you move fast. And here I didn't even know you swung that way."

My heart skipped over itself from a sudden attack of nerves. "Wait, *what?* No, there isn't...I don't... For fuck's sake, he just gave me a ride to school."

"What was all that 'see you at dinner' business then?"

"Nothing! You know I'm cooking meals as part of our agreement. He just likes to eat together if I've cooked something."

"Hmm..." was all Taylor said in response. He was infuriating.

Class went by in a blur. It was disconcerting how often my mind drifted back to Laurent Beaudry and the mystery that surrounded him. Surely that was all it was; I was curious about him, and it consumed my thoughts as such things usually did. Unfortunately, what I needed to be focusing on were my classes. I couldn't afford to make any mistakes so close to graduation.

My friend Emily and I exited Hannigan Hall and walked over to the psych building where Taylor's pre-med classes took place. He was just coming out the front door with his former roommate Charles when we got there.

"You guys want to grab some food?" Taylor asked.

Everyone did, so we headed across the main quad to the student union, where the best food courts were. Emily, Charles, and I decided to go to the deli, while Taylor got in the pizza line, nutrition-conscious med student that he was. We grabbed a table near the large picture windows that overlooked the trees that surrounded the union. I was starving. The oatmeal from that morning had long since worn off.

While we ate, I gave Charles and Emily the rundown on my housing situation. They'd known I was being evicted, but I hadn't talked to them much since then... I may have been wallowing in self-pity, just a bit. I paused when Emily interrupted with a high-pitched gasp. "You were saved by an eccentric billionaire. You realize you're actually in a Harlequin romance novel, right? Do you want to go ahead and get fitted for your bodice now, or—?"

Blushing to the roots of my hair, I jabbed a finger in her face. "You're dead to me." This only served to dissolve her into a giggling mess. The guys were laughing at my expense as well. *Great.*

"Yeah, yeah, enough from the peanut gallery." I turned to Taylor. "So what's his deal anyway? You work with him, you've gotta know something about him."

Taylor shrugged and took a bite of his pizza, chewing thoughtfully. "I only work with him tangentially. He's *way* above my pay grade. His background is kind of a mystery around the office."

"He said he was from Quebec, but he didn't seem to want to elaborate."

"Yeah, he was born there. His parents were über-rich, but I'm not sure what they made their money from. I think his parents had some kind of consulting firm—at least, that's the prevailing theory. Anyway, they died when he was pretty young. I heard he came to the States with his uncle as his guardian. The rumor is that they didn't get along at all, and Beaudry was basically raised by servants. Most people in the office take that to mean he had a pretty lonely childhood, hence the...lack of social instinct he seems to have."

Something snapped inside my brain when I heard the sad story. "Oh my hell... It's Bruce Wayne. I'm literally living with Bruce Wayne."

"Maybe he'll show you his bat cave," Emily said.

I tossed a balled up napkin at her face. It caught her right between the eyes.

FOUR

A few days later while I was driving my own self home from school—*thank you very much*—I got some really bad news. The worst news since the eviction notice. It started with a phone call. I tried not to talk on the phone much while I drove, considering my own father had died in a car accident, but when I recognized the number of my top-choice school from all my interviews, I took a chance and answered it.

"Hello?"

"Hi. Could I speak with Mackenzie Pratt, please?"

"This is Mackenzie. What can I do for you?"

"This is Anita Jeffries, the director of Sunnyvale Early Learning Academy. I'm calling in regards to your recent application and interview with us."

My heart leaped into my throat, almost strangling my voice. "Oh, yes! How are you?"

"I'm well, thank you. I don't want to take up too much of your time…"

My heart plunged into the depths of my gut.

"But I just wanted to let you know, while your CV was impressive and you did well in your interview, we have decided to go with another applicant. We'll definitely keep your application on file if a position comes available that we believe you'll be suited for. And please, feel free to reapply once you've gained some more work experience."

"Oh..." *Speak. Move your lips. Make sounds. A responsible professional would politely thank the woman and move on.* "Right, well. Thanks so much for letting me know."

"Of course. Have a nice day, Mr. Pratt, and good luck."

"Thanks...you too," I muttered, but she had already hung up. After checking my mirrors and putting on my blinker, because I wasn't an idiot, I pulled the car over to the side of the road. I could no longer see because unshed tears were clouding my vision. One more blow...one more...how many more could I take?

I pounded my fists on the steering wheel until they ached, and then I scrubbed my eyes, trying to wipe away the offending tears, but they just kept coming. No one gets their first choice on the first go round, right? But still...

"...once you've gained some more work experience..."

"How am I supposed to get work experience if I can't *get a fucking job!*" I shouted into the stuffy emptiness of the car.

Tears had started streaming down my face in earnest, but through the blur, I picked up my phone and typed a short text. I'd been on my way home to cook dinner, but I just... That man—that successful, rich, "has everything he'll ever need" man—I just couldn't face him with failure written all over my face. I needed to get myself together before I went home.

held up at school. wont make it 4 dinner. so sry. i can call for tkout 4 u.

I was normally a stickler for proper grammar even when texting—hello, *teacher*—but I could barely see the screen, and I just didn't care at that moment. My phone chirped back almost immediately.

No problem. School is top priority. Don't worry about dinner, I'll take care of it. Be safe, Mackenzie.
-LB

Despite my misery, I laughed. He had a tendency to sign his texts as if I wouldn't know who it was. I usually found it hilarious, but it wasn't enough to cheer me up. Why had he said "be safe" if he thought I was just at school. I shook my head because my brain couldn't handle Laurie's eccentric ways right then. I had to focus on getting myself together so I could drive.

After I took a few deep, cleansing breaths, I was able to get the tears to stop. My hands were still shaking, but it couldn't be helped. It might've been my first choice, but Sunnyvale was one of the many schools I'd interviewed with. Something would come along. I wouldn't be a bum working as a freaking servant in a rich man's home forever.

I was immediately ashamed of myself for thinking that. Laurie had never treated me like a servant. He'd been incredibly generous to cut me a deal for lodging, and I'd be forever grateful. I'd just much rather be paying rent. Then I thought back to how bad things could've been if he hadn't made his gracious offer, and I felt even worse.

Finally, I calmed down enough to drive. I cruised around the city for about an hour, then I went to Federal Hill Park to watch boats putter in and out of the harbor until the sun went down. It was hard not to dwell on the rejection from Sunnyvale, hard not to feel like a failure, like nothing would ever get better. I knew my luck would change eventually, but I felt like a night of wallowing was well within my right.

I was only a college student for a few more weeks. After that, I'd be expected to handle my problems like a responsible adult. Until that point, I thought a great way to wallow was to go home and get faced. And I just bet silver-spoon Laurie had some decent booze I could convince him to lend me.

When I finally came back to Chatham House, it was like walking into bedlam. The kitchen was hazy with smoke, even though the windows had been opened. The room kind of smelled like a skunk burning tires in a landfill, and there looked to be a...black hunk of something simmering in the sink. Laurie was nowhere to be seen.

Running the risk of being accosted again, I stomped down the hall and burst into his suite without knocking. He looked up from where he sat on the couch in the library, where he'd been reading.

"Christ, you startled me. What's going on? All finished up at school?"

"*What*—?" I took a calming breath. It didn't work. "What in the ever-loving hell happened in the kitchen?"

His mouth formed an *o* of surprise, as if he'd forgotten about it entirely.

"Oh... I'd forgotten about that entirely."

Lord, give me strength not to strangle this man.

"I ordered a gyro from that place I like. You know the one with the cannibalistic logo—with the chicken eating chicken? Anyway, the office called and needed me to troubleshoot something, and by the time I was done, it was cold. So I stuck it in the microwave."

There was a lot of information in those couple of sentences...

"Those gyros come wrapped in foil."

"Yes."

"Tell me you took the foil off." I already knew the answer. I wanted to hear him say it.

"Ah, no."

"For the love of Thor, you can't put metal in the microwave! It sparks. It can catch the whole damn thing on fire!"

"Yes. So I learned."

I slumped down onto the adjacent sofa and rubbed my face with both hands. "How on earth did you survive this long without a keeper?"

"Dumb luck, apparently," he said with absolutely no remorse. He was completely comfortable with his domestic incompetence."

"You know, I'd be really mad if you burnt down that nice kitchen."

"I do know that. So burning kitchen aside, how are you? Did you get your school stuff finished?"

Doubling over, I folded my arms over my knees and smothered my face in my sleeves. "I wasn't at school." My voice was muffled through the fabric, and that was just fine with me.

"I know."

Huh? I sat up straight and faced him. "Huh?"

He gave me a slight smile, didn't look pissed off in the least. "Even over text, you're a terrible liar. It's adorable."

I gave him a scowl I hoped conveyed how I felt about being described that way.

"What happened?"

His soft, kind voice was almost my undoing. "I got some bad news. My first choice from the schools I interviewed with rejected me. I just…I had to drive around for a while, be alone. I'm sorry."

"No need to be sorry. For what it's worth, you could've said exactly that and it would've been fine, but I understand. Is there anything I can do to help?"

"Actually… The reason I finally came back is to see if you

had any alcohol you need to get rid of. I honestly can't afford any, and I could sure use some liquid distraction."

Laurie assessed me for a moment before rising and walking over to a bank of cabinets. He rummaged around in the one to the right of the fireplace, which actually turned out to be a liquor locker and wine fridge. He came back with a bottle in each hand and plunked them down on the coffee table with a dull thud.

"My donation to the cause."

I let out an unmanly squeak when I saw what he'd brought. Two bottles of Dom Pérignon perched on the table, and he set a glass beside each one. "But these—these are too much. I was just thinking crappy bottom-shelf stuff."

His face hardened and his jaw flexed. "You're not the only one who's had a rough couple of months. Trust me, these are from the bottomest of shelves. I want to be rid of them. Am I drinking alone?" he asked as he popped the cork on one dark green bottle.

I straightened my spine, determined not to let my pride keep me from accepting his generosity. "Thank you," I said when he handed me a glass full of golden bubbles.

"Shall we toast?" he asked, picking up the second glass.

"To what?"

He sighed and looked down at his hands that gripped the champagne flute. "To missed opportunities. And to new ones."

I knew I was blushing by the time he clinked his glass against mine. I watched him as he drained the fizzy liquid in one long swallow. He'd pulled his too-long hair back into a half-ponytail, and he was dressed simply, in thin sweatpants and a black fitted Under Armour shirt. As I looked at him, I had the sudden urge to see him in a suit again. I could feel my blush intensify as soon as the thought crossed my mind.

"Are you just going to stare at me all night or are you going to drink?" he growled.

I flinched at the sound of his voice, knowing I'd been caught.

In answer, I took a deep swallow of the expensive champagne. Normally, I hated the stuff. To me, it tasted like someone tried to make a soda out of rotten grapes. Then again, I'd never had the good kind. This was…fantastic. I closed my eyes and hummed in my throat as the fizzy, tart liquid slid down. When I opened them, he was the one staring, a slight frown marring his perfect features.

"What?" I asked, rubbing my face like maybe he was staring at a smudge or something.

"Nothing." He looked away and took another swig of champagne.

We drank in silence pretty steadily for about an hour. I'm not exactly proud to say we finished off one of the bottles and a quarter of the second. My limbs had grown warm and loose, my head fuzzy, and my thoughts as fizzy as the champagne. My problems no longer seemed quite so dire. I was…comfortable, even with the big, silent presence next to me. In fact, having him there made me feel sort of…safe. Like it was okay to let go and mourn for a moment before I had to pull myself together.

Unfortunately, the alcohol also loosened my tongue, my filter, and my ability for tact. "Why did you want to get rid of this champagne?" I asked, knowing it was not at all my business.

His throat worked as he swallowed the sip he'd just taken. His eyes were a bit glazed, but I wasn't drunk enough to miss the fact that he'd slowed down way more than I had, probably to make sure I didn't get into any trouble. "I bought it for an anniversary. One that didn't happen."

I waited, assuming he'd elaborate. He didn't. "Are you ever going to tell me what happened with your ex?"

"No."

With a sigh, I slumped back against the couch and pouted—I might have actually poked my lip out, because I was an immature drunk, apparently. "You're no fun."

"I have been told that, yes."

There was such sadness in his voice at that moment that I whipped my head around to look at him. But his face remained impassive. I had the sudden ridiculous yet overwhelming urge to crack through that shell, to find out everything about him. I couldn't figure out why, but I wasn't typically prone to introspection, so I just went with the flow.

Before I could get back to prying, he asked, "This job you didn't get, it was that important?"

I narrowed my eyes at him. "Of course it was! Would I be this upset otherwise?" I was only slurring a little bit, so I helped myself to another glass.

He held up his hands as if to soothe a growling animal. "Calm down. I meant are you...will you be okay? Do you have other prospects?"

"I do, but that one was the favorite by far. It's not just the rejection—it just seems like it's been one hit after another for a while now. I just wish I knew when my luck was going to change."

"Maybe it already has," he muttered in that cryptic way of his.

I kept on ranting. "I mean, when my dad died and my brother agreed to take care of me so I wouldn't go into the system, I wanted to do everything I could to make sure I wasn't a burden. So I've been concentrating on nothing but school for the last eight years of my life so that I could make something of myself. It kind of stings that it's not working out, and I have no other life experiences to fall back on."

Talking about it made my head hurt, and my brain felt swimmy with alcohol. I pinched the bridge of my nose, and much to my embarrassment, my eyes started to fill again. God, I was such a sorry mess. I nearly jumped out of my seat when a warm arm slid around my shoulders. With a shuddering sigh, I let him pull me into a hug as the silent tears began to fall.

I knew it was wrong. I shouldn't be hugging this guy I barely knew or burdening him with my problems, but it just felt so good to share the weight of it all, just for a minute. I leaned into his chest, breathing into the hollow of his neck while stray strands of his hair tickled my nose. He squeezed me tight, and I let out a couple of quiet, hiccupping sobs.

Suddenly his arms banded tighter around me, and he hauled me all the way into his lap, so I was basically straddling his hips. In that position he could get a better hold, so he tucked my head back onto his shoulder and squeezed hard until I shuddered and pulled myself together. After a few minutes of breathing him in, I raised my head and sat up straighter—I was just drunk enough to not be weirded out by straddling a guy.

I rubbed the tears from my eyes and sniffled. "Sorry," I mumbled.

He brushed my hair away from my face and gave me this soft, unreadable look. "No need to apologize."

"Boys don't cry," I murmured, lost in a memory. It was something my brother used to say when he found himself out of his depth, dealing with an already overly emotional teen just out of puberty, who he didn't quite know how to handle. River eventually became more understanding about my tender-hearted sensitivity, but the words stuck with me, and I was still self-conscious about it.

"Who told you that?" Laurie grumbled. "That's ridiculous. Everyone gets to fall apart now and again."

"I bet you don't."

His eyes did that sad, faraway thing again. "I do. I just don't ever let anyone see it."

That made me wonder if he saw me as weak for letting myself lose it in front of him. I started to climb off of him, but he tightened his arms again.

"It's okay. Today you cry about it. Tomorrow you get off your ass and fix it."

I slumped forward again and mumbled into his shirt. "You're

mean."

"Yes. But I'm right."

"I know," I grumbled. Smug bastard. With a sigh, I sat back again, sinking lower into his lap.

"You said you've been focusing on *nothing* but school for eight years?" he asked, cocking his head.

I nodded, unable to look him in the eye.

"So the conclusion I came to about you the other night was spot on…"

I pretended not to know what he was talking about. No way was I going to admit to the fancy-eccentric-billionaire-romance-novel hero I was living with that I was a twenty-three-year-old virgin.

He grabbed my jaw in his big hand and lifted my head so he could see my face. "Bet you're all pent up, huh?"

I'd never really thought about it that way. I mean, I took care of myself every now and then—it was a biological need, right?—but that was probably an entirely different kind of release than sex. Hell, I had just had a crying jag while straddling my landlord's lap, and I was actually hard. Come to think of it, now that I was focusing on parts south, so was he.

He wrapped his arms around my waist, low, near the small of my back, and pulled me against him so that I could feel his erection nestled against my balls. He used the flat of his palm to push my face back into the crook of his shoulder and then squeezed me again, which caused my crotch to slide across his lap, rubbing…things….together.

I grunted, and heat crept up my neck to my ears and across my face. My whole body felt heated, and I could feel every drop of blood thundering through my veins. What was happening to me?

"Seems like you've been sorely deprived." His voice rumbled up through his chest to my ear, which was pressed against his throat. "Just let go. Do what you need to do."

I tried to pretend I didn't know what he was talking about, but my body called me a liar. One thing I always tried to be was honest with myself. And if I was honest, I *was* pent up. I couldn't remember the last time I'd had a release of any kind. Thus I chose not to think about what I was doing; I just widened my legs and rocked my hips so I slid along that hard ridge in his pants, chasing just the right friction. My reaction was instantaneous. Electricity sizzled up and down my spine, and my skin buzzed with the need for something just out of reach.

His big, warm hand was a welcome weight on the back of my head as I rubbed my face against his throat. The needy, broken sounds bubbling up from my chest were hardly recognizable as my own. His other hand dug into my side, keeping me from floating away entirely and pressing me down further into the delicious friction. My skin was on fire; I felt my pulse in every cell of my body, rioting and gathering until it finally culminated in an explosive release of pent-up tension.

My scream was muffled by his skin as I bucked through my orgasm. He made a sort of rumbling sound of—what felt like—approval that vibrated through my body and teased out some aftershocks. When it was all over, I slumped against him, a sated pile of mush, and rested my forehead on his sternum.

"Feel a little better now?" he teased.

"Mmmm," I mumbled. I was fading fast, exhaustion creeping in around the corners of my consciousness.

"You might have a hangover in the morning."

I might have let out a little half-asleep snore. Maybe.

"Mackenzie." He wiggled underneath me to try to shake me awake.

"Hmm?"

"You should get to bed."

"'M good."

"Mackenzie."

"Huh?"

"You cannot sleep here."

"Why not?" I whined sleepily.

"Because there are limits to my chivalry." His stern voice got my heart thundering again for some reason. "I'll help you to your room. Can you walk?"

"Nope," I muttered without even trying.

I let out a squeak when he stood up and tossed me into a fireman's carry and stomped down the hallway to my suite. I spaced out or dozed off at some point, because one minute we were in the hall—my face level with his ass—and the next minute, he was dumping me on my bed.

"You probably want to change out of those shorts. I'm sure you're a bit of a mess."

I wasn't going to think about it. *I'll think about that tomorrow.* "Yup," I said faintly, already drifting down the lazy river to REM. The last thing I registered was Laurie heaving a put-upon sigh and warm hands skimming my waist.

Hours later I awoke to the sunlight through the bare windows again with a massive headache and wearing clean pajamas. Then I remembered.

"*What the fuck?*" I was sure my shout rattled every window in Chatham House.

FIVE

As much as I tried to pretend the other night didn't happen, I couldn't stop thinking about it. I turned it over and over in my head so much that I couldn't remember anything that went on in my classes the last couple of days. That was unacceptable. I hadn't come this far, denied myself this much, only to blow it in the seventh inning over some…some…*guy*.

And what about that, anyway? Everyone knew at this point that I had zero sexual experience and I'd dated very little. After analyzing my social interactions over the years, I decided I'd never felt any particular inclination toward one gender or another. But I cringed at the thought of my peers, my friends—my *brother*—my future employers finding out that I'd messed around with a guy.

After drowning out the professor with my thoughts *again*, I resolutely decided to chalk up the experience with Laurie to too much alcohol and not enough sex, on my part. I wasn't sure what his excuse would be, but that wasn't really my problem. Besides,

I wasn't even sure I liked the guy, much less wanted to do it with him.

Something bounced against my temple, and I whipped my head around to glare at Emily. She'd thrown her pencil at me. "Would you pay attention?" she hiss-whispered at me. "The way you've been going, you'll probably forget to show up for graduation entirely."

I sighed because she was right. The professor had just wrapped up his lecture, and I remembered exactly nothing. It was annoying, and I blamed Laurie. I was going to have a talk with him about keeping his hands to himself when I got home—I was conveniently forgetting that there hadn't been many hands involved. So much for not lying to myself.

"Yeah, I know," I said to Emily as we emerged from the lecture hall. "I've been really distracted since losing out on that job I wanted." Charles and Taylor had walked up during the tail end of my sentence.

"If you guys are looking for teaching jobs, what about the new charter school in Highlandtown? My little sister just got in for this fall through the lottery," Charles said. "They probably have a ton of positions to fill."

"I didn't know about that!" I said.

"I thought about it, but it's kind of far away from where I live," Emily said at the same time.

I whirled around to face her. "What? Why didn't you tell me? I'll drive anywhere if I find a good job." I knew it wasn't her responsibility to share everything job related with me, but I still felt a little betrayed.

"Sorry! I guess I just assumed you'd heard about it."

With a sigh, I pulled out my phone. "It's okay. What's the name?"

"Forest Hills Charter."

Taylor clapped me on the back. "Well, what're you waiting for, Pratt? Drive over there and get an application! You need a paycheck like yesterday."

"Tell me about it. You guys go get food without me. I'll see ya later."

"Good luck. Oh, hey!" Taylor shouted after me. "Drinks next Thursday with the Mindstream gang. I'm putting you in charge of making sure *Laurie* shows up."

My brow furrowed as I felt an inexplicable surge of irritation at Taylor using the nickname, but I let it go. I had more important things to worry about.

Things had gone well at Forest Hills. They'd let me fill out an application on the spot and accepted one of the copies of my resume that I kept in my car. What little I saw of the place, I liked, so I was cautiously optimistic.

Once I arrived home, I dropped my stuff off in my living room and decided it was time to tackle a task I'd been avoiding: decontaminating Laurie's suite. It was, after all, part of our unofficial rental agreement. At least I thought it was. I went into the spacious laundry room in search of cleaning supplies, collecting industrial strength trash bags and a caddy full of cleaners. I was hoping for a hazmat suit or even one of those paper jumpsuit deals they used at crime scenes, but I found neither. Settling for a dust mask and some rubber gloves, I headed for Laurie's suite.

Pressing the intercom button outside the door, I waited for an answer even though I didn't think Laurie was home. Taylor had thought Laurie never left his house other than for their work outings, but I knew there were at least two things he would leave the house for. The first one was the gym—Chatham House had an exercise room, of course, but he said he worked harder when other people were around to judge him. The second thing was flea-marketing, which was kind of like antiquing but with flea markets. Laurie was always collecting weird little tchotchkes and bric-a-brac that no one else would see the value in. It was ironic, considering he could literally buy anything he wanted.

I wasn't sure which one of those things had taken him out of his rooms today, but I was grateful because, when I let myself into the main room, I cringed at the mess. It had only accumulated since the first time I saw it. I sent up a silent prayer to the gods that at least there wasn't a *smell*...other than Laurie's unique musky maleness. Donning my gloves and mask, I started by shoveling all the empty takeout cartons, paper plates, cereal boxes, and whatever other trash was lying around into the giant trash bags. I made a half-hearted attempt at separating the recyclables and vowed to go through it more thoroughly on trash day.

After that was done, I fetched an old five-gallon paint bucket from the garage and brought it back to the suite. I dumped all the used dishes into it so I could carry them back to the kitchen and put them in the dishwasher. Once that was done, I brought in a laundry basket and collected all the clothes that were lying on various surfaces. I didn't care if they were clean or dirty; if they were wadded up somewhere, they were going into the wash.

I repeated all the same steps in his bedroom, though luckily, it was slightly cleaner since his office was in there, and he was meticulous about organization when it came to his work. Giving his sheets a sniff, I deemed them clean enough and made the bed. The laden laundry basket was heavy as I picked it up and lugged it back to the laundry room. I dumped the clothes into the washing machine and started a cycle, then shoved the basket back in the closet. I'd do my own later—because at least I used a hamper rather than the floor.

When I was heading back into the suite to give the place a good scrub, I heard murmured talking. *Laurie must've come home even though I didn't hear him.* I started to walk through the open door but froze when I heard another man's voice.

Swallowing, I backed away, thinking maybe he'd brought home a lover. The idea made my chest burn with irritation, which seemed completely irrational even to me, so I turned to leave. I stopped in my tracks when I realized the second voice had an angry edge to it.

I'm not proud of eavesdropping but it happened—I've made peace with it. Laurie's voice sounded the same as always, but there was a thread of something else, almost like...pain.

"I've given you what you came for, Henry. I'm not sure what else you want from me." His voice cracked on the last syllable, and it tugged at my heart—there went my hair-trigger sensitivity again. This must be the ex.

"Same cold bastard as always, eh, Beau?"

Beau? So he had a little pet name for Laurie? And was still using it even though they'd broken up? That was kind of harsh. I waited for Laurie's response, and after a weighted silence, it came.

"I loved you, Henry. I'm not sure how you read that as cold."

Wait, *Henry?* I wondered if it was Mindstream Henry. That would explain the tense vibe I picked up from him at drinks the other night.

"You were always so closed off. Especially towards the end. It's unattractive."

"You know the reason for that." Laurie's voice was sad and gruff, which made me want to run in there and give him a hug—and tell Henry where to stuff it. I could already feel empathetic tears pricking at my eyelids, but I kept on listening.

"I told you I wasn't interested in telling people about us. Who I'm fucking is none of my co-workers' business."

"Fucking..."

Even I could hear the wealth of pain and anger in the pause that followed. Clothing shifted, someone sighed heavily—probably Henry, as Laurie wasn't prone to melodrama.

"I wanted to laugh. To have fun. To fuck on the balcony—"

"But not to tell anyone about us."

Henry sighed again. This time I was sure it was him. "You're just...so emotionally bankrupt. Is it the orphan thing? I've heard that can happen. You need to get over that shit because guys want a lover who can *feel*."

"I feel...," Laurie said in a quiet, broken voice he'd probably hate that I heard.

My heart was breaking. How could someone be so awful to someone they supposedly once loved.

"Not enough for me," Henry said.

I gasped softly. The shock of the words had me throwing my head back so I accidentally thumped it against the wall outside Laurie's suite. I froze. Silence pervaded on the other side of the wall.

So quietly I barely even heard it, Laurie growled, "You need to leave."

Henry huffed, and suddenly he was stomping past me, barely sparing a glance. "Watch out for that one," he said without looking back. "He's an absolute nightmare to deal with."

After staring at his retreating back for a few shocked seconds, I stumbled into Laurie's living room. He was standing behind the couch, shoulders hunched, facing away from me, and it seemed like his grip on the back of the couch was the only thing holding him up. I crossed to him but stopped a few feet away, unable to process what had just happened and formulate a response other than tears.

Laurie tensed when he heard my footsteps, and he turned around slowly. His tortured expression softened slightly when he caught sight of my face, blubbery mess that it was. "I really wish you hadn't heard that," he said in a hoarse whisper.

My breath rattled and hitched inside my chest until I doubled over with the force of my rage-sobbing. I tried to explain myself through the coughing and hiccupping that was my ugly cry, but I didn't think I got much across. "What an...guy... How could...be with...like that? What...the fuck?"

I gained control of my air intake and tried again. A little better. "You're someone who gave a near stranger...down on his luck...a place to live...for practically nothing. And the things...he said...I just... *I hate that guy!*" I scream-cried to the ceiling.

Laurie's eyes still held so much agony, but his lips twitched as he stepped closer. He carded his fingers through my shaggy hair in a fond gesture. "It's nothing to get so worked up over, Mackenzie, though I can't tell you how much I appreciate your fury on my behalf. I'm not used to having that."

"What?" I sniffled loudly. "A crazy emotional housemate who eavesdrops?"

The barest hint of a laugh rumbled in his chest, and it soothed my heart just a little. "A friend. Someone willing to go to bat for me. It's...new."

I frantically scrubbed at my face, trying in vain to get the tears to stop coming. I still had them closed when heavy arms wrapped around me, so I flinched before settling into the hug.

"What if it's true?" he whispered.

I didn't even have to know what part he was referring to. None of it was. "It's not."

"What if he's right, though? What if I'm dead inside?"

I squeezed him tighter, thinking that might make him believe me. "He's not right; he's an asshole. Maybe you see the world through a different lens than most people, maybe you express yourself a little differently, but you're not dead inside. Don't let him get to you."

I wasn't sure if he was crying, and I didn't check—no need to hurt his pride—but I could feel the fine tremors rippling through his body. Whether they were from grief or anger, I wasn't sure. His words from the night of my meltdown floated into my mind...

"Everyone gets to fall apart now and again."

53

"I bet you don't."

"I do. I just don't ever let anyone see it."

My heart broke for him all over again when I thought about how Henry had made him so vulnerable in front of me and how much I knew he hated that. I slid my hand up his back and stroked his hair, trying to give a little comfort, to let him know I didn't think any less of him for showing vulnerability.

As if reading my mind, he mumbled in my ear. "You're the only one who's seen me like this."

"You can be however you need to be with me."

He ruffled my hair again, making me blush. Then I remembered something that chilled my blood because of the new context. "Taylor told me to make sure you came to drinks next Friday with the work guys." I pushed him away gently so I could look him in the eye. "You're *not* going. I'll make an excuse."

"Oh, I'm going. We both are."

"But Henry will be there! Do you really want to see him again?"

"Yes. He caught me off guard when he came to pick up his things and went on his little tirade. I don't want that to be the last memory he has of me. So, we will go. We'll drink and have fun. Then we'll ditch his ass."

"If you're sure…"

"Only if you come with me." He pulled me into a hug again; this time it felt less like comfort and more like…he just wanted to touch me.

"Of course I will."

A couple of days later, Laurie had an unusual request. It all started at the kitchen table when I was dishing up my signature Bolognese. Laurie shoveled in a few bites, then took a sip of his wine and cocked his head at me.

"Where did you learn to cook like this? Isn't it unusual…for a twenty-three-year-old college student to be so good at cooking?"

"I'm not really that good, just proficient."

Laurie put another forkful into his mouth. "I beg to differ, but that's not the point. When I was in college, I could burn water. How come you can cook?"

With a sigh, I sat down in front of my own plate. "So, I don't know if I told you, but I was fifteen when my dad died. Since my brother kind of put his life on hold to be my guardian, I wanted to figure out ways I could help out, to keep from being such a burden."

Laurie's eyes softened. "I'm sure he didn't think of you as a burden."

I raised a brow. "You want to hear this or not?"

"Please, continue," he said with a sweeping gesture and a quirk of his lips.

"I asked a friend's mom to give me a few cooking lessons so I could make all of our meals. It just helped take some of the strain off of my brother."

Pausing with the fork halfway to his lips, Laurie blinked at me. "That's really…nice."

I shrugged. I hadn't done it for any kind of recognition. I'd just wanted to contribute since my brother had given up three years of his life to raise me. After that, we ate in silence until our plates were clear. I got the feeling Laurie was ruminating on something, but I couldn't force him to get on with it.

He cleared his throat and drained his wine glass. "Can I ask a favor of you?"

"You can ask," I deadpanned.

His lips curved into a rare smile. "Touché. I've got a project to finish; it's probably going to keep me up very late. But I also have a conference call at nine in the morning, which means I'll actually have to be awake that early."

"Funny how that works," I said, picking up the dishes and

taking them to the sink.

Laurie followed me. "I was wondering if you'd be willing to come to my room and wake me up. I know it sounds strange, but when I've worked most of the night and then I go to sleep, a simple alarm won't wake me."

I narrowed my eyes at him. "What did you do before you had a housemate?"

"I'd have one of the Mindstream guys keep ringing me until I'd finally get mad enough to get up just to make it stop. If I didn't eventually answer, one of them would come over and bang on the door."

"You're kinda high maintenance," I said.

"I guess that's a fair assessment. So? Will you?"

"I…I guess. As long as you do your best not to act like you did last time I woke you up."

He had the grace to look sheepish, an attractive blush riding high on his cheekbones. "Yeah…uh… I'm hoping I'll be better behaved now that I know you and since I'll be expecting it. If I'm not, though, just punch me. Seriously."

Drying my hands on the dishtowel, I sighed. "Yeah, all right. I guess I can do that." I froze when he engulfed me from behind, pulling me into a hug.

"Thanks, you're a lifesaver," he whispered in my ear.

I tried to pretend I shivered because I was cold. I wasn't cold.

At eight the next morning, against my self-preservation instinct, I let myself into Laurie's suite. He'd left it unlocked, just like he said he would. Light streamed through the gauzy curtains in the outer room, creating a sharp contrast to the heavily draped windows in the dark bedroom.

He didn't stir when I turned on the desk lamp, so I walked over to the bed. It was obvious that he'd indeed been working very late because his tablet and laptop sat beside him on the bed. His black long-sleeved T-shirt had ridden up when he slid down from where he'd been sitting, baring some impressive abs with a light smattering of hair just above the waistband of his Batman pajama pants. I jerked my gaze away when I realized I was noticing that detail.

His dark hair fell across his forehead, and his reading glasses were still perched on the bridge of his nose, slightly askew. I knelt on the bed, reaching out to snag them and put them on the nightstand. He didn't move a muscle except to breathe. I climbed onto the bed and gave his shoulder a gentle shove. "Laurie. Time to get up."

He grunted, his breath shuddering in his chest, but he didn't respond.

"I should've known you wouldn't cooperate. Because why should you be any different when you're asleep?" Leaning over him, I placed both hands on his chest and bounced him hard, like I was giving him CPR but just really bad at it. "Wake up, you giant manbaby."

I guess I shook him hard enough because he grunted and one of his arms flailed out, knocking me off of him. I rolled onto my back beside him, but before I could sit up, his big body rolled on top of me. He slid a hard thigh between my legs, burrowed his face into the hollow of my neck, and wrapped his arms around me. Tight.

A sound rumbled up from his chest, vibrating through me, and he chuffed and snuffled into my neck. I was pretty sure he was still mostly asleep and not trying…anything, so I just lay there for a moment, absorbing the feeling of him weighing me down. I'd never spent the night with anyone, so the sensation of being tangled up in bed with another person was new and somewhat exotic.

I knew it was wrong. He was asleep, and he didn't know what he was doing. I shouldn't take advantage of the situation, even if

I was slightly curious. But then... But then I felt a distinct hardness resting heavily on my thigh. Laurie getting hard didn't freak me out nearly as much as the fact that I didn't have the immediate impulse to move. That, more than anything, had me shoving at his shoulders until he pushed up with his hands and blinked sleepy eyes at me.

"Huh?" he grunted, a line forming between his brows. "What are you doing in my bed?"

I pushed him harder until he rolled off of me and I was able to sit up. "I just came in to wake you up like I was supposed to, and you sleep-tackled me again!" If I'd expected some kind of remorseful expression, I would've been sorely disappointed. Luckily or unluckily, depending on how you looked at it, I knew who I was dealing with.

He just gave me a dirty smirk and climbed over me to get off the bed. "How was I?"

"Nothing happened, ya jerk!"

"Pity."

I sprang up and hurried past him. "You're awake, so my job is done. I'm going to make breakfast. If you don't have time to eat before your conference call, I'll leave some in the oven for you. I have to leave early today."

"Sorry I can't give you a ride today." He looked genuinely contrite, unlike how he looked after he jumped me. He was such a strange guy.

"It's all right, I'll be fine. I have to go early to meet with one of my professors. Have a good day if I don't see you."

"You too, Mackenzie. Thanks for waking me up." His cheeky smile was completely unrepentant.

I rolled my eyes and shook my head. I had a feeling living with Laurie was going to threaten my sanity in a serious way.

SIX

At The King's Shield, we'd procured a long table in the back because so many Mindstream employees had come this time. Apparently I'd been adopted as an honorary Mindstream lackey since I'd unwittingly slipped into the role of Laurie's handler. According to Taylor, I was now expected at the Mindstream bimonthly drink nights henceforth and forever, plus it was my job to make sure Laurie showed up too. I couldn't decide if I felt flattered or annoyed, so eventually I settled on both.

Taylor and Brian were there already, along with a couple of the other contracted programmers, who I found out had been in Laurie's class at MIT. They also called him Beau like Henry had, and it irritated me. And then I got mad at myself for being irritated because it wasn't any of my business what people called him. It wasn't like he was my— *No.* I wasn't even going to let that thought form in my head. I couldn't be...

Situated with Laurie on my right, Taylor on my left, and my back to the windows, I had a good view of the room. That meant

I noticed the moment he arrived. Admiral Douchebag himself strolled over to the table like he hadn't a care in the world. Remembering the things Henry had said to Laurie made my leg twitch with impotent rage, accidentally brushing against Laurie's. He glanced over at me, his expression softening into something akin to fondness. I held his gaze for a moment before turning back to watch Henry pull up a chair.

Henry nodded vaguely in our direction. "Beau. Morrison..." His blue eyes narrowed on me. "I'm sorry, I've forgotten your name."

"Mackenzie," I muttered, even though he'd already turned to greet the rest of the group. Apparently Henry had been a freshman at MIT the year Laurie graduated, so they shared some of the same friends.

I jumped when Taylor elbowed me in the ribs. "Ow! What?" I whispered.

"Dude, if you scowl any harder, your face is gonna crack. Henry's a bit of a dick, but he's harmless. You shouldn't get so worked up about it."

I begged to differ, but I didn't want to tell Taylor about the scene between Laurie and Henry. I was pretty sure they'd kept their entire relationship a secret from their coworkers.

Laurie had turned our way, no doubt having heard what Taylor said. As usual, I could feel the tips of my ears turning red, but I forced myself to look at him. His lips curved up into an enigmatic half smile that I couldn't decipher to save my life. I was about to ask what the hell he was looking at me like that for when Michael, one of the MIT grads, pulled his attention away.

"So how goes life with Bruce Wayne?" Taylor asked in a voice low enough that only I would hear.

For some reason, I found myself reluctant to share the details of our arrangement with anyone. Chatham House was like our own little world, something I wasn't sure anyone else could understand without finding it strange. "It's fine. He's a little eccentric, but we get along pretty well." I took a swallow of my pilsner to cover my embarrassment over certain instances of exactly how we "got along."

Taylor leaned closer. "Has he shown you his Batcave yet?"

Somehow, he made it sound so suggestive that I nearly spit out my mouthful of beer. Instead, I choked on it, coughing and wheezing so hard I saw stars, and I couldn't pull in a good breath for the burning in my lungs. Shayna seized my left arm and lifted it over my head—like I was an infant—and Taylor pounded me on the back until I stopped hacking. The whole thing struck me as funny, so in between the coughs came barks of laughter, until Taylor and I were clinging to each other and cracking up.

When I was able to draw breath again, I happened to look over at Laurie. He was staring at me, not quite frowning, but he had this tightness around his mouth and jaw that he sometimes got when he was annoyed, along with that line between his brows. My smile slowly dissolved as I wondered what had happened to change his mood. Maybe Henry's presence was getting to him more than he'd let on, but he'd seemed fine to be casually aloof about the whole thing earlier.

Before I could figure it out, a few more Mindstream employees joined the crowd, and we all had another round of drinks along with several orders of nachos for the table. When everyone around us was engaged in their own conversations, Taylor turned to me again. "Have you heard back from that charter school?"

"Hmm? Oh, yeah, I actually got an interview with them next Wednesday. Let's hope I don't screw it up."

A heavy hand landed on my shoulder. I turned to face Laurie. "You have a job interview? Why didn't you tell me?"

Hurt flashed in his eyes, and I immediately felt bad, even though I didn't know why he assumed I *would* tell him. Besides, it was just a first interview, so it wasn't like there was really anything to tell.

"I'm...I'm sorry. I didn't want to make a big deal about it until I knew I had a shot. I'm not sure I'm a good interviewee since I've gotten either rejections or 'no-calls' up to this point."

"You should let me help you prepare," Laurie said. Taylor's arm was still casually draped over my shoulders because the guy had no sense of personal space. Laurie's gaze drifted to the loose embrace and his eyes narrowed.

Jesus, I hoped he wasn't thinking Taylor and I were a thing because that was...just... I suppressed a shudder. About as sexy as kissing my brother is what that would be. I honestly couldn't say why I cared so much about it, but I gently shook Taylor off while answering Laurie, hoping to distract him from whatever he was thinking about Taylor. "You'd do that?"

"Of course. I'd like to help. We could role play." He managed to make a completely benign idea sound so provocative that my face heated up.

"I don't know... You don't really know anything about teaching and don't even like kids, so wouldn't it be kind of hard to pose as an interviewer for a teaching job?"

Laurie shrugged, unconcerned. "Maybe, but I've had plenty of job interviews, and the basic questions are all the same."

"Well, I guess I could use all the help I can get. I really need this to go well."

Laurie treated me to one of his rare smiles, and my head got that hot, swimmy feeling that sometimes happened around him.

Taylor nudged me, and I had to shake my head to refocus on what was going on around me. "You want to come over to my place and game some? Karla's visiting her parents for the weekend, so I know I'm gonna be bored as fuck."

"Well...I've got some papers to finish this weekend, so I probably shouldn't stay out late tonight."

"Just stay over, then you can leave whenever in the morning to get your work done."

"Yeah, I guess that would wor—" I stopped when an iron

grip clamped down on my wrist.

"Sorry to interrupt, Mackenzie, but I've just remembered something that I need to do. I have to leave." His voice sounded much more casual than his hand felt on my arm. "Since I'm your ride, I guess you'll have to come too."

"Oh...uh...," I stammered, unsure of what was really going on.

"So sorry to cut your night short, but it really has to be now. Let's go."

"It's all right, I can give my boy a lift home in the morning," Taylor chimed in.

I could feel the tension rolling off Laurie in waves. I wasn't sure what was bothering him, but for some reason, I felt like me not leaving with Taylor meant something to him.

I gave Taylor a regretful smile. "Sorry, Taylor. I really do have so much work to do, so I probably should just leave with Laurie. If I get everything done, I'll call you and we can make plans."

"All right, man, no worries. Just remember what they say about all work and no play," Taylor answered, turning his attention back to his beer, unperturbed.

"Yeah, yeah, I hear ya." I had barely stood up before Laurie was half-dragging me through the restaurant and out to the car.

We rode home mostly in silence, Laurie still not mentioning what this mysterious "thing" he had to do was. I probably should've protested more when he insisted on chauffeuring me around, but... Well, let's be honest, I was a total whore for that car. *I can admit that about myself.* I laughed.

Laurie looked over, raising his brows. "What?"

"Oh, I was just thinking about how I didn't want to let you drive me around, but you could probably convince me to do just about anything if it involved getting to spend more time in this car."

His head swiveled back to watch the road, his throat working as he swallowed hard, but he said nothing else. *I wonder what that was about.*

When we got inside, I followed Laurie into the kitchen and stuck a bag of popcorn into the microwave. I was still hungry since I hadn't eaten many of the nachos at the bar. Laurie sank down onto one of the barstools at the kitchen island, propped his chin on his hands, and watched me. The microwave beeped, so I grabbed the greasy goodness and started tossing popcorn into my mouth. "Didn't you have to do something?"

Laurie's face registered surprise before shuttering completely. "Oh. Uh…yeah. I was just going to snag something to eat." He stood up, dug his hand into my bag of popcorn, and pulled out a handful before beating a hasty retreat.

Something was off. He'd been…blushing. That was usually my deal, all my feelings showing right on my face. I set the popcorn on the counter and hurried after him. I caught up with him in the hallway that led to our suites. "Hold it!" I shouted.

He froze in his tracks without turning around, his shoulders clenched up by his ears.

"What's going on?" I demanded.

He slowly turned around but wouldn't meet my eyes. He just stared at his feet. "Nothing's going on. I've got work to do."

I'd figured out what was happening, and I wanted him to own up to it. "No. You don't, do you? There wasn't any 'thing' that you forgot to do."

Saying nothing, he finally looked at me. Yeah, his cheeks were definitely red. "Uh… Well, not *exactly*. I mean, I guess it would've been fine if I did it tomorrow."

"Then what the hell? Why were you so insistent that we leave?"

Laurie surged forward fast enough to make me take a step back. He followed my motion, pushing me up against the wall with a hand on my sternum. "Because…he was…touching you."

"Huh? Who, Taylor?"

"*Yes*. He was hanging all over you like a bad suit."

"Um, so? He's my best friend. He just has no spatial boundaries. But why do you care?"

I gasped as he captured my wrists and pinned them against the wall above my head. He shifted so one of his thighs was between my legs, reminding me of being in a similar position that morning.

"What—what are you doing?"

He leaned in. "I don't want anyone else to touch you. I don't want you going home with anyone else. I've decided I'm in love with you."

Huh? Surely I was misunderstanding the situation. "You've *decided?* What does that mean?"

He didn't answer. Instead, he crowded closer and pressed his lips against mine. I was frozen in shock, and even though my arms were still pinned, I didn't think I could've made myself move if I was free. It wasn't my first kiss, but it was definitely my first one with another man. My pulse throbbed inside my head like I was underwater and running out of air. I opened by mouth to say…something, but he used the opportunity to slide his tongue inside.

It was like an electric current ripped through me when our tongues touched. I shivered as he lazily explored my mouth, sucking and biting my lips. I couldn't deny that it felt good— *amazing*—and if I closed my eyes and let my own tongue out to play, I could almost forget who was…

"Wait!" I freed my wrists easily and pushed against his chest until he stepped back. I couldn't think with him so close, radiating so much heat. "The hell are you doing?" I was out of breath, which made my face burn even more than before.

Laurie quirked an eyebrow. "I think it should be fairly obvious… I'm seducing you."

"You're *what?*" I squawked. "Oh, but… I'm not… I don't…like men…like that." The way I was panting and gripping his arms told me that maybe that wasn't entirely true.

Unfazed by my self-denial, Laurie chuckled. "You sure about that?" Then he ran gentle fingers up the inside of my thigh before cupping my traitorous dick, which I was pretty sure had gotten hard the second he'd pinned my arms. Yeah, I'd been unaware of *that* particular kink.

"Um..." No, no I wasn't sure about anything. But before I could formulate any kind of response, he dropped to his knees and started unbuttoning my trousers.

"What are you doing?" I squeaked again because I still didn't understand what the hell was happening— "Oh, *fuck!*"

He had freed my cock from my boxers and swallowed it to the root in one swoop. My brain stopped trying to make sense of things and shut down completely. Laurent Beaudry, eccentric billionaire, was sucking my cock like it held the meaning of life. Since I was helpless to do anything but writhe, I stared down at his aristocratic face. His dark blue eyes under severely arched brows, long, straight nose, and square jaw bespoke good breeding, but his lips... His lips were pure sin wrapped around my straining erection, causing all my thoughts to scatter.

He dragged his tongue up my length before sucking me down again, then swallowed around the head. Heat seared through me and my legs buckled. I probably would've dropped like a stone, if he hadn't braced me against the wall with a hand on my stomach. When he started up some fast and hard suction, I groaned and flailed around for something to hold onto. My hands landed on his head, and I started to pull away, but he hummed and leaned into my touch. His hair was surprisingly soft and silky. I sifted my fingers through it, enjoying the slide of it against my skin.

He hummed again, the vibration sending shockwaves through my body, and my balls pulled up tight. My first blowjob, and it was about to end embarrassingly fast. His rhythm was brutal, taking me higher and higher, hurtling toward release. I bit my lip till I tasted blood. I didn't want to make any noise because it felt like crying out would be an admission of…something.

The hand he'd been using to hold me down slid from my belly up to my chest, while he kept on sucking. Then he tugged on my nipple while swallowing around my cock, and I was toast. "Oh, fuck, oh fuck. *Laurie*, I'm… I'm gonna…" I tried to push him away but he only sucked harder. Sparks exploded behind my eyelids, and I doubled over as I shot down his throat. My body shuddered and twitched as he swallowed my release, and he didn't let me go until he had thoroughly licked me clean, until I was so sensitive that I could barely stand the soft rasp of his tongue.

My legs finally giving out, I slid down the wall and crumpled into a heap on the floor of the hallway. Laurie was still on his knees in front of me, a slight smirk playing at his mouth. He licked his lips and chuckled. "That was fast."

I glared at him, my face burning. "Hey! It's been a while, okay?"

He leaned in and gave me a dirty kiss, his tongue stroking the inside of my mouth. He tasted tart and salty, and when I realized that I was tasting *myself* on his tongue, my cock made a valiant effort to come alive again.

With another one of those infuriating chuckles, he pulled away. "Or maybe you were just into it." He stood up, then leaned down to ruffle my hair.

I scowled up at him, and his smile changed from smug to fond for a brief moment before his regular arrogant Laurie mask slipped back into place. "Get some sleep. You look worn out."

I huffed out a breath and ungracefully stumbled to my feet. I was at a loss for words. My mind was blown by what had just happened, and it looked as if he wasn't even going to acknowledge it with words. Helplessly confused, I stared at his retreating back, my body still buzzing with arousal.

He stopped suddenly and glanced over his shoulder at me.

"Goodnight, Mackenzie. I love you."

And then he was gone, leaving me gaping like a fish out of water. "How can you say that?" I yelled at the empty hallway. "You barely know me! You can't possibly love me! We've only known each other a few weeks! I'm a guy, and I'm not…" But I couldn't bring myself to finish that sentence because what had just happened raised some serious questions about the truthfulness of what I almost said.

SEVEN

"No way! I'm not answering that. They would never ask that!"

"Maybe not, but you have to be prepared for it to come up sometime throughout your work life. I'm waiting... Should I repeat the question?"

Laurie was helping me prep for my interview with Forest Hills, and the crazy train had gone off the rails, even for him.

He leaned toward me from his position beside me on the couch in his living room. "The question was 'How will your live-in *male lover* affect your work?'"

"I heard you the first time. They will *not* ask that. It's not even legal."

"Probably not," Laurie said, scooting closer, "but *someone* will. In an unofficial capacity. It's bound to come up eventually, so you might as well have an idea of how you want to handle it."

His words were bringing up all of my fears about what it would be like to actually...be with him and be in the education field. My stomach clenched and my brain shied away from the topic. "It won't come up because I won't let it. When kids are involved, people get weird about that kind of thing. I can't let anything interfere with getting a teaching position."

Laurie sighed, casting a pitying look my way. "You are *so* young."

It didn't sound like an insult—in fact, he'd said it rather fondly—but it also wasn't exactly a compliment. "Hey!" I shouted in indignation.

"But you are. It's 2017, Mackenzie. While there's still intolerance out there, and there's bound to be more with the way the government is changing, things are not the way they used to be. We have marriage equality and anti-discrimination laws—many places, anyway—and being 'gay' is no longer thought to be synonymous with 'pervert' like it was in the old days. There's no reason why you can't be in a relationship with a man and still be a teacher."

His words stirred the butterflies in my stomach, and they fluttered and tickled to the rhythm of my pulse. Why was I starting to want things? This wasn't me...was it? "You're—you're missing the most important point."

"Which is?" he prompted, dipping his head so his face was inches from mine.

"I am not— We are *not*...lovers!"

Faster than I could track, Laurie rolled over and straddled my lap, his long legs bent and hanging off the couch. "Really?" he asked, looking me in the eye. "That's not what it felt like the other night."

Our faces were close again. Too close. My heart ricocheted inside my ribcage as his lips neared mine. To be fair, he gave me plenty of time to get away, but I was frozen in place as he took my mouth in a gentle kiss. It was all soft brushes of lips and just the barest sweep of tongue. Shivers raced through my muscles and my skin prickled with goosebumps at the sheer sweetness of it. And then I remembered what I'd just said.

I broke the kiss and shoved at him. "What are you doing? Get off me, old man!" I said, bucking my hips to knock him off my lap. He rolled into his previous position beside me, and his rich laughter echoed throughout the room, throwing one more of his hooks into my already half-caught heart. He almost never laughed, and I was unreasonably happy to be the cause of it.

I was just about to ask him why it was so rare, why he was always so serious, when I was interrupted by my cell phone ringing. "Excuse me," I said, crossing to the kitchenette where I'd left it sitting on the counter.

I didn't recognize the number, but I had to answer it because there was always the possibility it was a potential employer. "Hello?"

"Mackenzie?"

The connection was tinny and filled with crackles of static, but I recognized my brother's voice. "River? Hey! Where are you?"

"I've been on assignment in the Congo, but now I'm in South Africa. How are you doing? That last message you left me said you were having trouble finding a place to live?"

I cast a nervous glance at Laurie, unsure of how much to tell my brother because it was a rather strange arrangement. Laurie had gone from laughing to scowling in the chirp of a ringtone. I swallowed down the impulse to ask him what was wrong. I rarely got to talk to River since he was always overseas for work, so I needed to focus on the call.

"Yeah, I worked it out. I'm staying with…um…a friend. Now I'm just focused on finding a job and making sure I pass my last classes so I can graduate."

"That's good. I was worried. I hate that I can't be there for you all the time."

"You don't have to worry about me, River. I'm getting by. I know your work is important. I just miss you, though." I eyed

J.K. HOGAN

Laurie as he stalked off to pour himself a drink at the minibar. "I miss you too, bro," River said through the staticky connection. It was getting worse, so I knew I'd probably lose him. "Hey, so speaking of graduation. No pressure or anything, but I have to order tickets for guests, so I was wondering if you thought you'd make it back stateside to come to it." I bit my lip and waited. As a sought-after photographer, River was constantly on assignment for various magazines, sometimes journalistic ones and some nature-related like *National Geographic*.

"I'll do my best, buddy, but I'm just not sure. I've been contracted to photograph the great whites when they migrate to Seal Island, and May is prime shark-spotting time." The phone connection began to break up. "Go ahead and get a ticket, but we'll just have to play it by ear."

"Okay," I said, heart sinking. "River, you're breaking up. Are you outside?"

"Yeah...should probably...soon... Mackenzie?"

"I'm here but I'm losing you."

"...breaking...too... Love you, br—"

"Love you too," I said. I was pretty sure the call had dropped before he heard me. I was swamped with a sense of emptiness, missing my brother like a phantom limb, but hearing Laurie shuffling around the suite helped me feel not so alone.

When I got a look at his thundercloud expression, I took it all back. The guy was a pain in the ass. "What?"

"What the hell kind of name is *River?*"

"Excuse me? What is wrong with you? Where the fuck do you get off talking about my brother like that?"

His eyebrows reached for his hairline, and his mouth fell open. "Brother?"

"Yes, brother. Who did you think it was?"

He looked down at his hands and his high cheekbones stained pink.

"You were jealous again, weren't you?!"

Seizing my waist, he dragged me into his lap, my back against his chest. He squeezed me tight and rested his chin on my shoulder. "What if I was? I can't help it if I want to be the one to make you smile, to hear you say—"

"Don't say it! I've already told you, we barely know each other, and I'm not—"

Grabbing my chin, he turned my head to face him and captured my lips. My brain couldn't keep up with the rapid change of pace, so I just froze, giving him the opportunity to slide his hand down my chest and belly and cup my groin. I let out that squawky noise he always seemed to draw from me, which of course allowed him to slip his tongue into my mouth. Before I could even think the word *stop*, he was tongue-fucking my mouth and rubbing my cock and balls through my thin athletic shorts.

And okay, it felt good. I couldn't deny that at the moment, I liked what he was doing and made no move to get away. As quickly as it had begun, the kiss ended, but the touching continued. While he kept lightly rubbing between my legs, his other hand explored my chest over my T-shirt.

His touch was so casually familiar that it stole my breath and made my heart ache. It wasn't like he was trying to get me off, or get himself off, or anything he'd done up to that point. It was like he just…wanted to put his hands on me.

He nuzzled his nose into the sensitive spot behind my ear. I arched my back slightly as tiny shivers prickled my skin. That was when I felt his hardness underneath me. Oddly enough, it didn't bother me that much, and I was distracted from it when his voice rumbled in my ear.

"Seriously, though, how'd your brother get a name like River?"

I didn't understand how he expected me to be able to make regular conversation while he was touching me like that.

73

Especially about my family. But I gave it a valiant effort.

"M-my mother... I guess she was kind of...a hippie." My voice was shaky because his barely-there touches were starting to make my body go haywire.

His chuckle vibrated against my back. "You guess? So then, how did you end up with a relatively normal name?"

I shrugged. "She already had one foot out the door when I was a baby, so I never met her. That's what's with the 'I guess' part. She didn't care about naming me, so Dad and River chose Mackenzie."

"Damn, I'm sorry. Didn't mean to bring up bad stuff."

His hands had frozen sometime while I was talking, and I was buzzing with the need for him to continue. I tried for a very subtle roll of my hips that sort of bucked into his hand. His smug laugh told me I hadn't succeeded with the "subtle" part, but I didn't care because he started up again without any commentary.

"It's okay, I mean... Well I had my moments, but mostly I couldn't miss what I never had. My family was enough."

My breath hitched. It was becoming increasingly harder to concentrate on the conversation.

"Why didn't you and River hire a PI to find her after your dad passed?"

Scoffing, I smacked him on the thigh. "You're such a silver-spoon baby! We were using our money for food and clothes and power, little things like that."

"Touché," he laughed.

My hand was still on his leg, and for some reason I left it there, feeling the heat of him seep through his clothes. "That's why River's so important to me. He's all I've had for a long time now."

"And now you have me too."

I groaned and leaned my head back onto his shoulder. How could he say things like that when we'd known each other for such a short time? His answering groan took me by surprise.

"You've got to stop turning me on like this," he muttered, sliding his hand up my thigh until it was inside my loose shorts and boxers. As he wrapped his long fingers around my hardened cock, he rucked my shirt up with his free hand. The dry friction he applied was maddening, and my body reacted without my permission, my legs falling open wider and my back arching. I felt feverish all over, like my insides were too hot for my skin, and my heart beat in every pore as he stroked me hard and fast.

I shouldn't be allowing it. I'd probably hate myself later. But it felt so good, and I *had* been pretty starved for physical attention. I moaned and twitched involuntarily when he plucked my nipple and twisted his hand over the head of my cock at the same time. My release was building in my balls, my cock swelling, but just when I was about to come, he let go, using both hands on my nipples until I was writhing and thrashing in his lap, humping the air to get some kind of friction.

"*Laurie*," I pleaded. Beyond all intelligent comprehension, I was no longer worried about what he was doing. I merely wanted him to *keep* doing it.

"Easy. I got you," he whispered in my ear. He shoved down my shorts and boxers, tucking the waistband below my balls. He wrapped both hands around my shaft and began to stroke fast and rough. My spine bowed immediately as my balls tightened.

I was shaking with the need for release, and the way he licked up the line of my neck didn't help. His voice was almost as tangible as a touch.

"One day I'll hear you say you love me, Mackenzie."

There was no time to formulate a response because my brain short-circuited when he bit down on the soft spot where my neck met my shoulder and sucked hard.

"Jesus!" It was like tugging a string attached to my balls, the way my orgasm exploded, painting his hands with my release.

Laurie groaned into my hair, and his arms tightened around me briefly before he relaxed. He gently tipped me off his lap onto the couch, then looked me in the eyes as he licked his hands clean. I was pretty sure my eyes crossed as a surge of lust rippled through me. God help me, I'd never admit it out loud, but despite my inexperience, I was definitely attracted to Laurie.

"Be right back." He stood up abruptly and disappeared into his bedroom. When he came back, he was wearing different pants. When I raised a brow at him, he just shrugged. Could it be that he'd gotten off just doing that to me? Surely not...

Once we were both clothed and sitting side by side again, awkwardness descended. I didn't know what to say to him after what had just happened, and he didn't seem to have any desire to fill the silence. I desperately cast about for something to say, but what I came up with was pretty stupid. "Why do your coworkers call you Beau?"

A muscle twitched in his jaw, but otherwise he seemed outwardly calm. "It's just a stupid college nickname that carried over from my rowing days." His voice was terse and kind of angry-sounding, though I had no idea why.

"Can I call you Beau?"

"No," he growled.

"But *Henry* does. And all the guys who knew you back—"

"Enough! No," he said in a tone that brooked no argument.

It seemed to me that he was making a pretty big deal out of a stupid nickname. Then again, so was I, so I shut up about it.

Giving me a sidelong glance, Laurie's expression softened. "Sorry... I just..."

"You don't owe me an explanation. I should've listened the first time. Don't worry about it."

He stared at me for a long time, like maybe he was working up to saying something. "Mackenzie, I— *Shit*." He was interrupted by his phone ringing. "Hang on, I need to answer this. It could be work."

"Sure." I watched as he fished his cell phone out of his briefcase and answered it.

"Beaudry." His mild expression melted into one of barely contained rage. "Uncle Theo. What do you want?"

Laurie stood up and began to pace the rug in front of the fireplace. I still didn't know anything about his childhood, but if Taylor's gossip was to be believed, Laurie and his uncle didn't get along. My stomach clenched in sympathy with the tension in his body.

"Why are you telling me this? It's got nothing to do with me," he barked, making me flinch. He listened for a few more minutes, his face growing more thunderous by the second. "Fine, send me the information, but I make *no* promises." He ended the call but stood with his back to me for a few seconds, breathing hard, fists balled at his sides.

"L-Laurie? You okay?"

He turned slowly, and it was obvious he'd schooled his features, as his face was carefully blank. "Yes, I'm fine. But I do have to get back to work now. I'll be in my office. You can just let yourself out whenever."

When he started to head to his bedroom, I was struck with a strange sense of panic, like somehow if I left things the way they were, words unsaid, something would change between us. "Hey, Laurie," I said as he passed me.

"Hmm?" He was already preoccupied with whatever projects he had to work on and maybe a little about the phone call.

"Thanks. You know, for helping me with the interview. And...other stuff."

One corner of his mouth quirked, and he ruffled my hair like I was a goddamn ten-year-old. "Anytime, Mackenzie," he said again. I was beginning to think he meant it.

EIGHT

"Dude, what is wrong with you?"

"Huh?" Surprised, I looked up from my tray of food and raised my brows at Taylor. "What do you mean?"

"You're so twitchy. You keep fussing with your clothes and shit. You're not having any issues with graduation, are you?"

"No, I've got plenty of credits. As long as I pass my two exams, it should be smooth sailing. I don't anticipate any problems."

"Then *what*, man?" Taylor had a chiding grin on his face, but his sea-blue eyes looked worried.

"Sorry," I said, forcibly holding my antsy limbs still. "I've got an interview with that Forest Hills school this afternoon. I'm just really nervous."

"Really? It's today? You should've told me. Couldn't tell from the way you're dressed."

"Yeah, I didn't want to sit through classes in my nice clothes and get them all wrinkled and sweaty. I've got them in my car."

"So are you ready for this interview?"

"About as ready as I can be. Laurie helped me prepare, quizzed me with sample questions."

Laurie. My other reason for being so antsy. After our interview cram session and couch extracurriculars, he'd taken that call from his uncle and then just...completely shut down. He'd locked himself in his office to work, only coming out for meals—when he bothered to eat—and he'd barely been speaking to me. He'd reverted back to the man he'd been when we first met. It was like we'd never been...friends. Or whatever we were. Something was obviously bothering him, but I couldn't force him to tell me.

Taylor hummed around a mouthful of sandwich, then swallowed so he could speak. "Well, things *have* been pretty crazy at Mindstream. Ton of releases this month. So maybe he really is just working a lot."

Huh? "Did I just say that all out loud?"

"Um, yeah," he supplied, chewing another bite rather obscenely. "To be honest, I was pretty surprised when you said he'd helped you, to begin with. Anyway, so the interview, are you going for a teaching position or an assistant?"

"I figured I'd apply for teaching, and if they felt like I didn't have enough experience, maybe they'd offer me an assistant position." The more we talked about it, the more nervous I got. The room was suddenly too hot, and it felt like my clothes were trying to strangle me. I hooked a finger in my T-shirt collar and yanked it to give myself some breathing room.

"Holy shit! The hell is that, Mackenzie?"

"Huh? What the hell is what?" I asked, wiping my face, thinking maybe I had food on it.

"Uh, that thing that looks like a bite mark on your neck!"

Oh, no. Not possible. He couldn't have... I picked up my phone, opened the camera app, and reversed it. Stretching out my shirt collar, I angled the phone to try and see what Taylor had seen. Sure enough, right where my neck met my shoulder, there was a dark spot—it looked like a very obvious hickey with very obvious but it also had little dots that were, indeed, teeth marks.

"Um... Uh, I don't..." *have any explanation for this.*

"Dude, did you finally get a girlfriend and not even tell me about it? Ouch!"

"No, no! I didn't. It wasn't... I just—"

"Just a hookup then?"

"I...guess?"

"That's cool, man. Wait. Did you finally get your cherry popped?"

"*Taylor!*"

"Oh, that's awesome. Finally! I thought for sure you were gonna die a v—"

I clamped a hand over his fat mouth because apparently that was the only way to shut him up. "Please stop. People. Can. Hear. You."

"Mfffph-mmm," he mumbled into my hand.

"Can you be trusted?" I asked with a pointed glare. He nodded, so I removed my hand.

"So, spill," he said.

"Not now, okay? I'm already worked up enough as it is. Besides, I have to go so I can make the interview on time. We'll catch up sometime after. I promise." I carefully did *not* promise that "catching up" would include any details about my sex life.

"All right, I concede. For now."

"You must be Mackenzie."

I looked up from where I was seated in the lobby of the preschool annex of Forest Hills Charter School to see a woman walking toward me. She was short, blonde, and invitingly plump, but the most striking thing about her was the sweetness of her face. It wasn't surprising that she was a director of a preschool. I could imagine kids really taking to her.

I stood up, discreetly wiping my sweaty palms on my slacks. "Yes, I'm Mackenzie. Pratt. Mackenzie Pratt, here for the interview." God, I was a mess. I shook her proffered hand and gave her a wobbly smile.

Her teasing laugh was kind as she gave my hand a squeeze. "I'm Angela Fiori. So happy to finally meet you in person. No need to be nervous, you wouldn't be here if we weren't interested in you."

I know she meant it to be reassuring, but all it did was put more pressure on me to perform. If they'd liked my resume, even with so little work experience, if I blew it now, it would just prove that I was crap at interviewing.

From the research I'd done, I knew that the building was long and rectangular, with a U-shaped hallway full of classrooms, and the gym and lunchrooms in the middle. Instead of taking me toward the classrooms, Angela led me into a small office across the lobby from the main door. There was a desk in there but also a couch and a couple of armchairs. She sat in one of the chairs and gestured for me to take a seat. I lowered myself onto the couch so that I could face her.

"Thank you for coming in today, Mackenzie. I'm sure you're very busy preparing for graduation."

"I have been, but I've gotten most of my work wrapped up now. Only a couple of my classes have final exams, so I'm mainly focusing on those right now." I clamped my mouth shut. That was probably more information than she needed to know.

Her cheek dimpled subtly as she smiled at me. "That's one thing I don't miss at all about being in school—those exams." She gave a mock shudder.

I laughed and relaxed a fraction. "Yes, ma'am. It's tough, but worth it. I can say that, now that it's almost over." I tried for a disarming smile, hoping I succeeded without looking creepy.

"I'm sure you're expecting all of the canned interview questions you usually hear, and we'll get to that, but I really want to get to know you. It's important to see the heart of someone to tell if they will be a good fit for our kids. Don't you think?"

"I do."

"So how's the job search been going? It can be rather discouraging, I know."

I searched for a response that would make me look smart, dependable—hell, I'd settle for even a little put together, but somehow I ended up just being honest. "It's been pretty tough, yes. Neither of my internships led to anything, so I've been applying and interviewing while finishing up school... And on top of that, my apartment building was being torn down, so I got evicted and... I am *so* sorry. I shouldn't have—"

She reached over and patted my hand gently before sitting back in her chair. "I asked because I really wanted to know. It can be pretty hard when everyone's hiring based on job experience, but you have to get hired to get experience, but if no one will hire you, how do you get the experience? Trust me, I remember starting out after college. That's awful about your apartment, though. I hope you found somewhere else to live."

I swallowed hard. I so wasn't getting into explaining *that* one. "I did. I ended up renting a room from a friend of a friend, who has a...big house."

"Oh, that's a relief. So why did you choose teaching as your career path? Because, God help us all, it's not a great time to be a teacher in this country these days."

"Well, if I'm being honest, it started after my dad died. Since my mom wasn't in the picture, my older brother stepped up to raise me to keep me out of the system. I was always grateful for that, but it didn't quite make up for having that adult, parent-like influence in my life. For that, I turned to a few of my teachers, who counseled me and filled in some of the gaps. My brother did the best he could but…" I shrugged. "As far as the age group, I've just always bonded quicker with younger kids. Maybe because I'm just a big kid at heart," I said with a laugh.

She smiled, but I could see the underlying pity in her expression, and I didn't want that.

"Not to give you some sob story, though. We had a lot of happy years with my dad, and my brother was my hero. Looking at the big picture, I had a really good childhood."

This time when she smiled, it reached her eyes. "That's a great story. It gives you a unique perspective on the importance of teachers."

I nodded, glad that "the crisis of the poor pitiful orphan who needs a job" was averted.

"How would you personally define success as a teacher?" she asked next.

"I try to focus on independence because I think the more young children learn to do for themselves, the more self-confidence they take away from school. I also like to celebrate diversity in the classroom, and I think with current events how they are, it will be important to emphasize including children from otherwise marginalized socioeconomic groups—whether it happens to be people of color, different religions or lack thereof, children of gay parents, or immigrants… I want to destigmatize those things by addressing them in the learning environment."

I broke off and thought for a minute, wanting to make sure I truly answered her question. "Mostly, if the kids come away happy, having learned something and enjoyed school, and also respecting their fellow students and teachers, I would consider that a success. No two children learn the same way."

Without saying anything, Angela wrote something down on the clipboard she was holding. Unlike before, her expression gave nothing away. Had I gone overboard with the veiled political references?

"So… What do you like the *most* about being a teacher?"

I blinked, taken aback because no one had really asked me that question in any of my interviews. "Um, well...I guess I just like being there when a child learns something new—seeing the way their eyes light up with understanding is just...phenomenal. And of course, at the preschool level, just seeing their personalities emerge, watching them become their own person literally in front of my eyes. It's the best. Sorry, I guess that was two things," I said, lowering my eyes and feeling my face heat.

"Two wonderful things," she said with a fond smile that I chose to take as a good sign.

We went through a few more questions, including rote ones like strengths and weaknesses, why I wanted to work at Forest Hills, and so on. After we finished up, Angela gave me a tour of the preschool. Since it was new, all the furniture was mint and top of the line, but the thing I liked most about the school was that it had a gymnastics gym because some of the teachers also coached gymnastics and cheerleading. So the kids got to have both indoor exercise and outdoor exercise on the playground.

In the lobby at the front door, Angela shook my hand and gave me a dimpled smile. "Of course, we have to go through all of our interviews before deciding, but I don't mind saying there's something about you, Mackenzie... I have a good feeling. Expect to hear from us within a week. Thanks for coming in!"

I was blown away by her words after all the bad luck I'd been having, that I couldn't help the goofy grin that spread across my face. "Thanks for having me." As I turned to leave, she stopped me.

"Oh, and Mackenzie? If you get any offers, make sure to give us a call before you decide."

My eyes widened because it really did sound like she wanted to hire me. Pulling myself together from my internal fist-pumping, I nodded and shook her hand again. "I promise. Thanks again!"

"Bye!" she called as I headed through the parking lot. I waved, then climbed into my car and thunked my head on the steering wheel. I squeezed my eyes shut against the adrenaline crash and tried some deep breathing to slow my heart rate.

When I was calm enough to drive, I turned the car on and buckled up. God, I was glad that was over. Though it had been nerve-racking, I thought it went pretty well. *I can't wait to tell Laurie about it. I'm sure he'll be proud of me...* As I started to pull out of my parking space, my thought echoed in my mind. My heart hammered painfully in my chest, and I slammed on my brakes. I stared at myself in the review mirror, seeing wide, shocked brown eyes looking back at me. What the hell was I thinking? Since when did I get so excited about seeing Laurie? On top of that, why did I care if he was proud of me?

My hands shook as I put them back on the wheel and continued carefully on my way. I didn't know what was up with my strange fascination with Laurie. Sure, we'd messed around a little when he initiated, but I wasn't...into men...like that. The voice in my head that kept saying that was becoming quieter and quieter because the rational part of me knew that I had *zero* experience with either women or men, therefore, how the hell did I know what I was?

With thoughts swirling inside my jumbled brain, I let myself into Chatham House and went straight for my suite. I changed into more comfortable clothes and headed over to Laurie's rooms to see if he was working. A flicker of butterfly wings tickled my stomach when I thought about him being in there, even though I kept trying to talk myself out of whatever feelings I couldn't seem to name, but the suite was unlocked and empty.

I backtracked down the hallway toward the kitchen, but I didn't find him there either. The Lotus had still been in the garage, but occasionally Laurie used a car service when he couldn't be bothered to drive, so that didn't necessarily mean he was home. I was about to go check the home gym when something on the fridge caught my eye. A note was stuck to the door with my Chewbacca magnet.

Mackenzie,

Some urgent business came up and I had to go out of town. Sorry to leave so abruptly but it couldn't be helped. I hope the interview went well.

—L

My heart sank. He was gone. I took the note and wandered into the communal living room, sinking down on into couch. The huge mansion felt empty and cold, even though it was only less one person. I wasn't sure why I felt so alone when I had friends I could call if I wanted. But I didn't want them right now, I wanted Laurie. I wanted to tell him how good I did in the interview and…

Opening my messenger bag, I stuffed the note inside and pulled out two embossed envelopes. Graduation invitations with the tickets inside—one for River and one for Laurie. Deep down, I didn't really think River would make it, but I was still holding out hope. And Laurie…coming to his housemate's college graduation probably wasn't high on his list of fun things to do, but something made me want to invite him anyway, just to see what he'd do. But with graduation less than a week away, I didn't even know if he'd be back from where-the-hell-ever in time for me to invite him.

With a heavy sigh, I went back to the kitchen, tossing the envelopes on the counter, and went to my room to study for my exams. If I screwed those up, there wouldn't be any graduation anyway, so I had work to do.

NINE

After checking in at the commencement registration table, I joined Taylor, Charles, Emily, and a few of our other friends. A robing area had been set up in one of the activity rooms connected to the auditorium, and we busied ourselves helping each other put on the regalia of our graduating class. Once I was dressed, I stared out the window, watching cars pull into the two student lots attached to the auditorium complex.

River wasn't coming. Even though I hadn't heard from him, I knew it deep down. I might have even known it from the beginning when I asked him. I didn't blame him at all—I loved my brother, and I felt that he'd given up enough of his life to take care of me, so I never complained other than to say that I missed him. But it did depress me a little bit to have no one in the audience cheering me on.

Luckily, there weren't assigned seats in the auditorium, but each different department had a section roped off for their guests, so we students would know where to look for our loved ones. At least there wouldn't be empty chairs glaring back at me, but it was still disheartening that there would be no one familiar to wave at from the stage.

All of a sudden, the depressed feeling welled up in my chest and tears prickled the insides of my eyelids. For fuck's sake, I was *not* going to cry before I even got my diploma—at least, not in front of anyone. "I'll be right back, going to hit the bathroom," I tossed over my shoulder before hurrying out of the room.

Finding the nearest bathroom, I hid myself away until the urge to cry had somewhat passed. I gripped the sink and stared at myself in the mirror. It was time to pull myself together and enjoy my graduation. I had worked hard for this, at the expense of everything else in my life, so I shouldn't let my lack of guests ruin it for me. Besides, River would make it up to me the next time he visited. He always did.

"He isn't coming."

I'd been spacing out and hadn't seen Taylor's reflection in the mirror, so his voice scared the ever-loving shit out of me. I jumped and whirled around to face him, my back pressed up against the sink. "What?" I squeaked, pretending not to know what he was talking about.

"Your *brother*. He can't be bothered to take a day off of work to come to your graduation."

Taylor was not River's biggest fan. At all. He'd been around before and after Dad passed, so he knew everything River had given up for me, but he seemed to think that River should drop everything whenever I requested his presence, and it always pissed Taylor off when he didn't. It also pissed Taylor off that I never got mad at River for it. As my best friend, he was protective of me, but he didn't really understand the dynamic between me and my brother.

"Taylor..."

"No! Mackenzie, he's a freelancer. He makes his own

schedule! So that means, if he doesn't come, it's because he doesn't want to."

I scowled at Taylor. I got that he was being protective of me, but River was family. "Yeah, and freelancers take contracts. If he's contracted for a job, he has to do it, regardless of what's going on in *my* life."

"Yeah, but he could—"

"Tay, could we just not do this right now?"

His eyes softened, and he patted me on the shoulder before taking a couple of steps back. "Of course, I'm sorry. That's a hot button issue for me but I shouldn't have gotten into it right now. You know it just drives me crazy when you don't expect more from people. You deserve better," he finished with a weary sigh.

"I appreciate you having my back," I said, squeezing his arm as I walked passed him.

"Always. And Beaudry said—" He clamped his mouth shut and shook his head.

"What? He said what? You've talked to him? Is he okay?"

"It's nothing. I was at the office, so it was just work stuff."

I didn't believe him at all, but I didn't know how to press him without acting like a teenager with a crush. In the end, I wasn't proud of what came out of my mouth. "Did he say anything about me?"

Taylor's eyes did the shifty thing that always happened when he was trying not to say something, making my curiosity skyrocket.

"Mackenzie, I don't think— Oh, hey, they're calling our sections. We've got to hurry up and get out there or we won't be able to get in line!"

All discussion of Laurie and River was tabled since we had a commencement to go to. We dashed out of the bathroom and joined up with our respective sections. And even though Emily and our friends Hiro and Shay were with me, I still felt a little pinch of loneliness deep in my gut.

"Anna Jade Nielsson…"

I blew my bangs out of my eyes and sighed. I'd been standing and waiting for an hour, and I still hadn't made it up to the stage where I could see the audience. I'd made sure to wear comfortable, broken-in shoes, but even so, my feet were starting to throb.

"Albert Hiroki Noriega…"

Hiro was my marker. I'd told myself to pay attention when they called his name because there were only a few names between us. I'd made it to the wings of the stage, but I was hemmed in by the heavy, blue velvet curtains so I still couldn't see anything. The line took another collective step.

"Wade Edward Pekus…"

At the edge of the wings, my stomach flip-flopped with nerves. I'd worked so hard for this. Given up everything. It was almost over…

"Anoop Aziz Pranjal…"

I took a step onto the stage and my worldview became the auditorium full of hundreds of faces looking up at me. Unfamiliar faces. Strangers. Okay, they weren't *all* strangers—I knew Taylor's moms and his sister, as well as Emily's parents, and I'd met Hiro's dad a couple of times—but they weren't *my* people. Still, to make myself feel a bit steadier, I scanned the audience for them.

I tripped over my feet when I noticed a lone figure seated between two empty chairs in the department of education section. A lone figure in a thousand-dollar suit. *Laurie.* My heart gave a painful thump and I felt hot all over from a mixture of embarrassment and happiness because he watched me with such intense, single-minded focus that he became the only thing I could see in the room. Then he smiled and winked, and I could feel the big, stupid grin that spread across my face. I was finally graduating, and I wasn't alone after all. He was here, my landlord, my friend, my...Laurie.

"Mackenzie Daniel Pratt."

Crossing the stage while barely taking my eyes off Laurie, I shook hands with the Dean—hopefully I was polite enough because I sure as hell didn't remember anything about my interaction with her—and collected my scroll. There was a smattering of applause for me and one long, loud wolf whistle. I didn't have to look to know where that had come from, and I smiled even harder as I walked off stage.

Pressed up against a wall in the living room of his suite, I stared at Laurie, who stood a few feet away, with a mixture of suspicion and gratitude. Taylor had invited me to come to dinner with his family, but I'd had to politely decline because I couldn't subvert the need to spend some time with Laurie after he'd been gone.

That was as far ahead as I'd thought. Once we were at home facing each other, I had no idea what I wanted to say. I was gulping air like a drowning victim, and sweat prickled my scalp, giving me goosebumps. "Why... Why did you come?"

His face registered genuine surprise. "You invited me, didn't you? There was an invitation with my name on it."

"Well, yeah, I mean I was *going* to invite you but I never saw you again! Where the hell did you go? I was worried."

He sighed, shifting his weight from foot to foot. "I was in Quebec. I had to take care of some business with my uncle. I was going to ignore it but...it wouldn't have gone away if I had."

"That phone call."

"Yes."

His hands were in the pockets of his suit jacket, and he stared down at his shiny shoes that were probably Ferragamo or Gucci or something similar. I was struck for the first time by just how incredibly handsome he was. I mean, I'd always obliquely noticed that he was a good looking guy, but this was the first time it had gut-punched me out of nowhere. His slim-cut steel gray suit fit his slender, broad-shouldered frame like a glove, though his skinny tie was loosened and his top few shirt buttons were undone. His dark, too-long hair was brushed away from his face with minimal product, and it boyishly curled about his ears. I had to keep my body plastered against the wall to stop from reaching for him.

"You didn't answer me. Why did you come?"

"Well, I had your graduation marked on my calendar at home, but I'd forgotten about it. When I called Morrison to see if you were okay—I wasn't sure if you wanted to talk to me after the way I skipped out of here so fast—he mentioned that you might be upset because your brother couldn't make it to the ceremony but that you'd pretend you weren't. I wanted you to have someone there for you, even if it was only me, so I came home early. That's when I found the invitation."

While he was speaking, my feet involuntarily carried me closer to him. His words had my blood thundering through my body, deafening my thoughts and drowning out all reason.

"I—I hope that was okay," he asked, sounding uncertain.

I took another two steps until we were nearly toe to toe. "Why did you care if I had anyone cheering me at commencement?"

He swallowed hard, but his expression was intense and sure. "I've told you already. I love you. I know you don't get it…but you will."

Later I would blame those words for what I did next because being the sole focus of that kind of fervent adulation was intoxicating. I was drunk on it, and on gratitude, and on pure, pent-up sexual tension. I'd been soaking in it for weeks, and I'd finally lost my mind. I raised my chin so I could stare up into his eyes, then reached out and ran his silk tie through my fingers, savoring the slide of the material.

Then I gripped it and pulled so he was forced to bend down to my level. I could tell I'd surprised him by the widening of his eyes and his momentary flailing for balance. When we were almost nose to nose, I swallowed down the nerves clawing at my throat and touched my forehead to his while still keeping my grip on his tie. "Thank you," I whispered. Rearing back for a fraction of a second, I then yanked him even closer and kissed him.

Jesus, fuck, it was like unleashing a caged lion the way he came at me. While my kiss had been tight-lipped and tentative due to nerves and inexperience, his was an all-out assault. The way he licked into my mouth, growling to himself, was erotic as hell. My dick rose to duel with the hardness behind his zipper. His arms threaded around my waist and pulled me tight against him, almost restricting my breathing, as he continued to fuck my mouth with his tongue.

My head was spinning. I felt delirious, drunk on the feeling of him touching me. When my knees buckled, his hands gripped my ass and lifted me up. Instinctively, I wrapped my legs around his waist and arms around his neck, and he grunted his approval. He sucked on the side of my neck below my ear as he stumbled backward into his bedroom.

No thinking, all feeling, I relaxed into his hold and let him do what he wanted because I was *done* ignoring the rest of my life for responsible things like school and jobs and whatever-the-fuck. So. Done. I wanted something for myself. I didn't know what this thing between he and I meant, but I was all fresh out of fucks to give when his nails were digging into my ass cheeks and his teeth were scraping along my neck.

When he ran into his bed, he briefly set me back on my wobbly legs, just long enough for him to undo my slacks and shove them down to my ankles, along with my briefs. I thought maybe he'd finish undressing me or go back to ravishing me or whatever, but instead, he removed his jacket and tossed it aside. He unbuttoned his cuffs, and then the front of his shirt, but then it was like he just couldn't be bothered with the rest.

Without a word, he crawled onto the bed and lay down on his back. He stared up at me with a flushed face and wide, dilated eyes. His shirt fell open, revealing a startlingly well-defined chest and chiseled abs, which made me consider my own slender form and question my life choices. As I stood there watching him and wondering what in the hell he wanted me—the virgin— to do, he licked his lips and cupped the sizeable lump in his slacks, and I nearly fainted.

"Mackenzie."

"Yeah?" I rasped.

"I want you to sit on my face."

I got a head rush as all the blood pooled in my face in a fiery blush. "What?" My voice cracked into a squeak on the tail end of the word.

"Get your ass up here," he growled. "Literally."

"Umm..." I waffled, but I had to admit I was curious and turned on and probably a lot horny. So I turned my brain off and crawled onto the bed until I was beside him, then I swung a leg over him so my knees were on either side of his ribcage. My cock jutted out from my body, obscenely straining toward him.

"Try again," he said, gripping my ass and pressing me forward, so I knee-walked until I was straddling his head instead.

My whole body was burning with embarrassment and, okay, other stuff, and I held my breath because I didn't know what to do. Turned out I didn't need to do anything because Laurie went right to work, giving my balls a thorough tonguing as I proceeded to grip the headboard and make all kinds of inhuman noises.

When he started jacking my cock while he laved my balls, I

tipped my head back and closed my eyes, lost to the world. His other hand had been caressing my ass gently, but his fingers began questing closer to my crease.

"L-Laurie," I stuttered, my voice barely a whisper.

He didn't answer. Instead, he dipped his finger into my crack, grazing my hole. My body jerked at the unfamiliar sensation, all my muscles tensing up. He slapped my ass lightly and grunted. "Move up and spread 'em."

"*Huh?*" I questioned, even though my body immediately obeyed. I widened my legs as much as I could without *literally* sitting on his face, but he pushed against my thighs until I lost my balance and did exactly that.

Before I could right myself, I felt something warm and wet flickering over my hole. "Laurie! Wait. What—?" But I just couldn't make any words because his tongue was rasping over my most sensitive spot and turning my whole body into a live wire.

Then he pointed his tongue and pushed it inside me, and I basically lost my mind, grabbing his hair and tugging hard, making him growl against my ass. My cock leaked a steady stream of liquid, and it flexed every time he tongue-fucked me. I heard the clink of his belt buckle and the rasp of his zipper, then rhythmic clinking as he jacked himself without even opening his pants all the way.

His tongue was heaven, but then he slid one finger in beside it, the stretch and burn making me yelp. His oral assault intensified until pain became pleasure, and I was once again groaning like a dying man. He said something, but it was muffled, of course because of, you know, face-sitting, so I raised myself back up. "What?" I panted.

He pushed me back, and being the graceful creature that I was, I tumbled onto the mattress beside him. He got up on his knees, his face tight and drawn, almost as if he were in pain. "Turn over. Hands and knees." His voice was clipped and full of tension.

I have no idea why I complied with such a request, but there I was rolling over and facing away from him. My head hung from my shoulders and all I could see was the rumpled duvet, so I flinched when I felt his tongue again. He fucked into me like I was his last meal, and I was embarrassed that it felt so good. My trembling arms gave out, and I face-planted onto the bed with my ass still in the air. Apparently, Laurie approved of the change in position because he groaned against my ass.

The tongue-fucking ended as abruptly as it had begun, and my body was left feeling bereft. That was, until I felt the scrape of his belt against the backs of my thighs, and the hot, hard column of his dick riding my crease. He ran his hand along my back, slowly, as if he was savoring the feel of my skin.

When he spoke, his voice was raw with need. "Let me have you, Mackenzie."

That just shorted my brain right out. I pretended not to know what he meant, but I really did know, and the thought of putting myself at his mercy made me shudder and moan. I couldn't form words, but he must've taken my reaction as agreement, because I could hear him fumbling around in a drawer, and then I felt a cool, slick finger probing at my hole.

I felt the same burn as before when he slid his finger inside before, but the lube eased the way and the discomfort didn't last long. With his other hand, he alternated between leisurely stroking my cock and pinching my nipples, until my body was just one giant raw nerve. Then he plunged in a second finger at the exact same time he gave one of my nipples a vicious tug. *"Laurie!"* I cried, overwhelmed by the unfamiliar pleasure/pain sensation. I'd never had any clue that those two opposites were so closely linked when it came to sex.

After a few minutes of his three-point assault, I was biting my hand to keep from screaming out in pleasure and frustration. My body was straining towards something, not just orgasm, but some kind of all-encompassing explosion, the likes of which I'd never felt before. If only I could…just…get there. Suddenly he changed the angle of his fingers and hit some spot inside me that had me babbling and cursing and crying because it felt so good. As much as the noises embarrassed me, I couldn't possibly hold them back. I was helpless and flying higher every second.

"Sorry, Mackenzie, I just can't wait any longer."

I heard sounds that I couldn't wholly identify, but the click of the lube bottle cap was pretty distinct, so it wasn't a total surprise when his gloved cock pressed against my entrance. It *felt* big. Like defying-laws-of-physics big. I knew it was an illusion, that things always seemed way bigger when you could only feel, but I was definitely nervous.

He caressed my ass before spreading me open and breaching my hole. He gave me a moment or two to adjust as the wide head of his cock breached the tight muscle, but I couldn't breathe because the burn stole all the air from my lungs. He didn't wait long, just continued to press in, stretching me slowly but steadily as I squirmed beneath him.

"Laurie… Jesus… Hurts," I cried, gasping.

Smoothing his hand down the small of my back, Laurie bottomed out, his hips flush with my cheeks. "I know, baby. It won't for long, I promise."

And fuck me, I believed him. Laurie didn't say things that weren't true and didn't make promises he didn't intend to keep. Everything rolling around in my head just stopped, zeroing in on what I'd just thought to myself. Didn't that just put a glaring new light on the whole confession of love thing?

My thoughts were shattered once again as he pulled out almost completely, leaving my body feeling strangely empty. "What—*ah!*"

He pushed back in with more force, obviously deciding I'd had enough time to adjust.

Apparently he was right because the burn began to fade into a delicious fullness and stretch that was like nothing I'd ever experienced. His dick sawed in and out of me, stretching the limits of my body and stringing me out until I was a howling mess. My face and chest were still plastered to the bed, and the sensation of my oversensitized cock dragging against the duvet was driving me batty with the need for...something.

"Laurie, I can't... I need..." Hell, I didn't even know.

But he seemed to. He sat back on his heels and pulled me with him so I was straddling his thighs and riding his lap. His cock was still buried deep inside me, only now it was hitting me at a different angle, making my cock twitch and my body shiver all over. He wrapped his long fingers around my shaft and stroked lazily while rocking his hips. His other hand went back to my nipples, pinching, pulling, tweaking until I was so dizzy that I arched my back so I could rest my head on his shoulder.

His big, lanky body shuddered. "Fuck, you're flexible," he breathed in my ear. "So sexy."

The hand he'd been using to torture my nipples slid across my waist until he was holding me tight. Then he lifted me slightly so he could fuck up into me while jacking my cock. I kept my back in that exaggerated arch because my body was strung tight as a bowstring and I couldn't handle all of the pressure building in my spine, my dick, and my balls. He fucking owned me right then, and he knew it. He turned his head so he could suck on the side of my Adam's apple, and he bucked his hips, pounding away while I rode him.

I could feel the electricity racing up and down my spine, the signal of my impending orgasm, but it was fifty times more intense than when I took care of things myself. It was so all-consuming that I thought I might burn alive and disintegrate into dust, floating away with the breeze. "L-Laurie... I can't... It's too much... I'm..."

And that was it. All she wrote. My back strained and my hips bucked as I erupted, coating his hand and probably a good portion of his bed with my release. I clawed at his shoulder and tugged his hair as I was racked with full-body, jolting aftershocks. He squeezed me tight as he pistoned his cock into me a few more times before letting loose a low groan, then whispering my name against my neck.

"Jesus Christ," I panted. When I tried to sit up, he slipped out of me and I winced, but it only hurt for a second. It was nothing compared to the way my body buzzed with leftover adrenaline and my muscles liquefied with satiation. I slumped over onto my side as Laurie got up to deal with the condom and wash his hands. He brought me back a towel so I could clean off and then tossed me my briefs. He didn't offer me any of my other clothes, but he'd somehow guessed that I'd be uncomfortable sitting around completely naked.

I laughed when he shucked the remains of his own clothing and pulled on his briefs. "You didn't even bother to take your clothes off," I teased, shaking my head.

He crossed his arms over his chest and raised a brow. "You kissed me," he said as if that was the answer to all the mysteries of the universe. "Despite it being all timid and virginal, you did it, and I wasn't going to give you a chance to think better of it. *Fuck* clothes."

He climbed onto the bed and sat with his back against the headboard. Then he grabbed me under my arms and dragged me against him. I secretly liked the way he manhandled me, but he was so *calm*. Even when we were in the middle of…that, he never let go and lost his shit. Not like I had. Next time, I wanted to figure out how to rile him up. How to get him to lose his mind like I had.

And then it dawned on me what I'd just said to myself. *Next time…* When had I gone from not…into men, and just getting swept away in the moment, to actually thinking about having sex with Laurie *again*? Like who was I right now?

He wrapped his arms around me, squeezing gently, and set

his chin on my shoulder. "You're going to freak out, yeah?"

I huffed out a breath. Might as well be honest...with him and with myself. "Yeah. Most likely."

"I understand. Can you maybe put a pin in that? Just for a little while. Stay with me?"

"All right," I sighed. "I think I can do that." It was the least I could do, really, when he'd shown up for me when nobody else had.

TEN

The next day, as I drove to the gym to meet Taylor for racquetball, I decided I was not going to freak out. I was not going to have some existential crisis about my sexual identity, nor would I flog myself out of self-hatred... I would just ignore the issue. So I had sex. I wasn't going to analyze it. I was going to pretend it wasn't some huge momentous thing that would probably change my life. Yeah, I checked out from that shit and just went about my daily life.

Racquetball with Taylor was basically the only reason I was in shape. I was most definitely not a gym-bunny because my attention span was too short to do things like weight-lifting or machines, and running was too boring. I wasn't athletic enough for team sports, but racquetball was perfect because it wore my ass out—lots of running but with a purpose.

I got held up a bit in traffic on the way to the gym, so I was glad I was already dressed to play in my mid-thigh compression shorts under loose basketball shorts and a yellow Morrell college

T-shirt. My Harrow sneakers skidded on the buffed linoleum as I ran to the racquetball courts. When I rounded the corner, Taylor was standing in front of the middle court making a big show of checking his watch and tapping his foot.

Rolling my eyes, I tossed my gym bag on a bench and started to gear up. Sweatbands, eyeguards, gloves, racquet, and I was ready to go.

"You're late," Taylor muttered as he followed me through the door in the tempered glass that made up the front wall of the court.

"Oh, calm your tits. You've been waiting five minutes."

He *hmmphf*ed as I tossed him a canister of balls. Then he narrowed his eyes and leaned closer to me. "Dude, again? Your new chick sure is a little bloodsucker."

"What?" *Shit, not again.* I walked close enough to the front wall so I could see my reflection through the scratches and scuffs. Sure enough, I had one dark mark just below my ear and another on the side of my Adam's apple. "Damn it."

Taylor walked up behind me and clapped a hand on my shoulder. "Hey, man, I'm happy you're finally getting some, but if you're gonna be a schoolteacher, you might want to tell her to keep it below the collar line," he snickered.

"Believe me, I will," I said through clenched teeth. I faced Taylor again and he handed me a ball.

"You can serve first. And by the way, I'm trying really hard not to be all butthurt that you won't give be any details about her."

My neck heated, and I couldn't meet his eyes. "There aren't really details..." *Liar.* "I'm not sure it's even a thing." At least that was the truth.

Taylor nodded like I'd given him something more than non-answers. "So a fuckbuddy thing. I get it," he said, chuckling. "Don't forget to tell her about the neck thing."

I felt shitty for not correcting him about the "she" part, but I wasn't ready for some big coming out party when I couldn't even say the G-word inside my own head.

"Let's just play," I said, taking position in the drive-service zone.

I tossed the ball in the air, swung my racquet, and delivered a perfect rollout shot. It ricocheted off the bottom of the front wall without a bounce and flew past Taylor. He made a valiant leap for it, hitting the ground hard, but he wasn't even close.

He stood up to collect the ball, dusting himself off. "Getting laid agrees with you, apparently," he muttered.

"Hey, now. Don't be a sore loser."

"Who's losing?" he griped as I set up another serve.

We volleyed for a solid half-hour, score remaining neck and neck, but ultimately Taylor was a stronger player. We'd both gotten a few welts from drive strikes, and he'd just pulled farther ahead with a killer wallpaper shot that I had no hope of returning.

Going in for the kill, Taylor hit an around-the-wall drive that was meant to force me out of center court, but it smashed into my eyeguards instead. Even though the streamlined safety glasses took the brunt of the hit, as they were meant to, pain exploded between my eyes as the hard plastic dug into my orbital bones and the bridge of my nose.

"Mother*fuck*—" I gasped as I fell to my knees, nearly blacking out from the pain. I could hear Taylor's feet pounding toward me, and then his hands were suddenly on my shoulders.

"Oh, *shit*, Mackenzie. Are you okay? Are you like dying? Should I call an ambulance?"

I flung my eyeguards off and clutched my face, then leaned back to lie flat on the lacquered hardwood. The hit had knocked the wind out of me, but I could tell my nose wasn't broken— thank fuck—and it likely felt worse than it was. "No, just get me some ice, will ya? I'll be fine once it stops feeling like my face got stepped on by an elephant."

Genuinely worried, Taylor scurried off to comply with my request. When he came back, he led me off the court, while I held the icepack to my face, and then gently pushed me down onto the bench. "I am so sorry," he said.

He sounded near tears, and I felt bad because ball strikes happened all the time in racquetball—it wasn't like he'd done it on purpose. "Don't even worry about it," I said, trying to keep the pain out of my voice. "It could've been worse."

"*How?*"

"Um, well... We could've been into baseball."

He huffed out a laugh and the tension dissipated. "I have some ibuprofen in my bag. If you take it now, it might cut the swelling some."

I tried to nod and realized too late just how much that would hurt. He rummaged for the pill bottle, shook out three, and handed them to me. I dry swallowed them, then took a big chug from my water bottle. "Thanks."

My phone started going apeshit in a side pocket of my duffel. "Damn it. Can you reach that for me?"

Taylor passed me the phone and I answered it without checking the caller ID. "This is Mackenzie."

"Hi, Mackenzie, this is Angela Fiori from Forest Hills."

I sat up straighter, dropping the icepack so I could grip the phone with both hands. "Ms. Fiori! Good morning, how are you?"

"I'm well and hope you are. I'm calling to tell you that we've decided to offer you a position here at Forest Hills. You'd start off in an assistant position for our summer terms, alternating between age groups so you can learn the ropes—sort of like a trial period, you could say—and assuming everything goes well, you'll get your own class in the fall. Does that sound like something you would be interested in?"

I'd frozen when she started talking, just sure it was going to be a "thanks but no thanks" conversation, so it took a moment for my brain to catch up. Taylor elbowed me and I jumped. "Yes! Yes, of course I'm interested. That sounds like a good plan to get me used to everything. When will I start?"

Her fairy-bell laughter tinkled in my ear. "I like your enthusiasm! First summer term starts in two weeks, and we have a planning week before that. Do you think you can start next Monday?"

My heart raced like I'd just chugged ten Red Bulls, and the grin I'd been wearing for the last few minutes was starting to hurt my cheeks. "Absolutely!" *Wait.* "Er... I should probably mention... I'm at the gym right now and just finished up a racquetball game. I sort of took a ball to the face, so for a couple of days of that planning week, I might look like I went a few rounds in the ring. I hope it won't be too disruptive—I'll wear makeup if I have to!"

"Oh, my goodness! I hope you're not seriously hurt. As long as it fades before the children start, I think you'll be fine. I'll brief everyone in the staff meeting tomorrow. I'm going to email you an information packet and tax forms for you to fill out, and you can just bring all that with you on Monday."

"Great! I'm looking forward to it."

"We are too. See you soon, Mackenzie."

After we said our goodbyes and hung up, I leaped from the bench and did a little end-zone dance in front of Taylor before the pain in my head reminded me that I might possibly be concussed. "Ouch."

"Idiot," Taylor said fondly. "That sounded like good news."

"I got the job! I'm going to be a teacher!"

The two of us grinned all the way to the locker room.

"Wanna get lunch?" I asked as I undressed to shower.

"Can't. Already got a date with my bio-dad."

Taylor's "bio-dad" was actually his mom Lane's brother. When he decided to donate for them, he'd insisted on being part of the child's life instead of just a sperm donor. It was actually kind of cool, especially to me, that he had three parents. "No problem. Raincheck."

I rushed through my shower, ready to get the hell out of the gym and back home. I told myself that I was excited to check my email and start studying up on the school information and that it absolutely did *not* have anything to do with being excited to tell Laurie the news and see his face light up with pride. Nothing at all.

Rubbing my hair dry with my towel, I walked back to Taylor from the showers, wearing nothing but briefs, having discarded my compression shorts beforehand. When Taylor's gaze landed on me, his eyes widened and his mouth dropped open.

"What the actual fuck, Mackenzie?"

"Huh? What now?"

He gestured vaguely at my lower half. "How about how you look like you dipped your dick in honey and got mauled by a hungry bear."

I looked down and saw tracks of hickeys and love-bites all up and down my inner thighs, disappearing underneath the fabric of my briefs. Dear lord, I was going to have to go home and have a conversation with Laurent fucking Hoover, because I did indeed look like some kind of animal had been gnawing on me. After I'd agreed to put off the inevitable freakout and share his bed, he'd spent a full hour worshipping my cock with his mouth, keeping me on the edge of orgasm for longer than I thought was physically possible. But fuck all these marks.

With a frustrated sigh, I yanked my spare shorts out of my locker and pulled them on, though I could still feel the weight of Taylor's stare.

"Dude, seriously, who *is* this girl?"

"Nobody," I grumbled.

Hurt flashed in his eyes for a brief second before his affable frat-boy mask slid back into place. I felt shitty for not telling him. Really shitty. But I wouldn't even know where to start.

"Sorry, man. I don't even really know what's happening. You'll be the first one I tell when I figure shit out. Promise."

"I'm gonna hold you to that." He tossed his sweaty gym towel in my face.

I slung the towel off, feigning a gag. "You're a monster."

I should've picked up on the aura of doom that permeated Laurie's suite the minute I entered.

Oblivious, I stormed into his dark bedroom and shoved at the lump under the covers. "Hey! What is with marking me up like that? Taylor saw! If you're trying to keep me from freaking out, you're not doing a great job."

I shook him again until he finally sat up, and I was face to face with a massively sleep-deprived Laurent Beaudry. His sharp cheekbones looked gaunt because of the shadows under his eyes. His thick brown hair stuck up in odd places, and he had pillow creases on one side of his face.

"Somebody better have died," he growled, glaring at me, which was kind of hard to do with droopy, exhausted eyes.

"Yeah, somebody died. *I* did. From embarrassment when Taylor saw what you did to me." I gestured vaguely at my thighs, though the marks were covered up by my shorts.

"Oh, so Morrison knows? Good. Secrets are tiresome."

My head nearly exploded. "That is not even what we're talking about. What is the matter with you? No, Taylor doesn't know! He thinks I'm hooking up with some kinky girl. That's not even the point! What were you thinking, making all these marks?"

He rose up on his knees and loomed over me. "Let me see." Before I could respond, he yanked down my shorts and underwear to take a good look.

"Hey! At least wait for consent, you jerk..." I didn't really

107

make any move to stop him, though. In fact, I was already starting to get hard. I didn't want to think about what it meant. Couldn't.

"Looks like they're fading. I'll have to make some new ones."

He dipped his head with the intention of latching onto my inner thigh again. Pushing his head back, I scrabbled away from him. "New ones? No, I said no more marks!"

He looked up at me, his eyes glittering. "I like people being able to tell I've been here." He lowered his head again and licked a path along my inseam.

My legs trembled and fell open because he seemed to know just what to do to get my heart racing. Even though my cock was straining towards him, I wasn't going to let him win this one. "Off me," I said, pushing him off again. "Whatever you do in the future, keep it below the collar line, jeez."

I froze as soon as I played back my words in my head. So wrong on so many levels. I regretted it even before I saw the predatory grin he gave me.

"So that's a definite green light for 'future' playtime. Copy that. Below the collar line? That I can do."

He swooped down and took my cock in his mouth, all the way to the hilt in one long swallow. My back arched up off the bed because all that warm, wet heat was almost too much. He took me hard and fast, sucking till his cheeks hollowed out and chasing his lips with his hand to intensify the friction.

"Laurie... I can't... What're you..." I babbled incoherently as he tugged my balls and tongued the head of my dick. When his fingers ventured lower and brushed my hole, I came with a ragged moan, surprising myself. If Laurie had been startled by the quickness of it, he didn't show it, swallowing every drop with a hungry growl.

I flung an arm over my eyes as my breaths sobbed out of my chest. What the hell was this man doing to me? It was fine when we were cocooned inside the mansion—it didn't seem real—but once I was outside in the real world, my brain just couldn't seem to deal with the question.

With a huff, I pulled up my shorts and backed up against the headboard, pulling my knees to my chest. He cocked his head at me, and his brow furrowed. "Something wrong?"

"No, I just... I don't know what I'm doing here. What we're doing."

He narrowed his eyes, then shrugged. "Don't worry about it."

"How can I not?"

"Just don't. It's a silly thing to worry about. We're doing what we're doing. Doesn't need an analysis."

Jesus, the man was completely in his own little headspace. Sometimes I found it oddly endearing, but when it involved *my* life, it was harder to swallow. "You're a child."

"Sometimes." He sat up and mirrored my position, only he sat cross-legged. "Aside from worrying about trivial shit, are you okay?"

"Yeah, I'm good!"

"Really? Mackenzie."

"Yeah?"

"The fuck happened to your face?" He gently probed the bridge of my nose.

"*Ow!*" I swatted his hand away. "Jesus. It was a freak racquetball accident. It's fine."

"And you wonder how *I've* survived this long?"

I rolled my eyes and waved it off because I was anxious to tell him the good news. "Forget the black eye. Forest Hills called. I got the job!"

That got a grin out of him. A real one, not the fake one he put on for the guys at the Mindstream outings. "That's fantastic! I knew you had it. How could they not love you?"

He said it so easily, yet so sincerely, my eyes watered just a bit. Allergies. Totally.

He leaned forward and placed a sweet kiss on my lips. "We should celebrate. Let me take you out, okay?"

"Out where? Like the King's Shield or something? I guess we could invite—"

"No. You and me. Like a date."

"A date?" My stomach clenched with nerves.

"Yes, a date. Like a real restaurant that doesn't have plastic menus. Maybe a movie or a museum, something. A hotel?"

"What? Why on earth would we need to go to a hotel when you have a fucking mansion?"

"It's not about the space, it's about the experience. Come on, let me plan something for you. I want to treat you to something...you've worked hard for this."

I didn't want to tell him that I'd never actually been on something that I'd classify as a "date." Same with all the other aspects of my love life, it was something I never made time for. Then again, I wasn't sure how I felt about a man—*Laurie*—being my first date. Still, somehow, without conscious choice...

"Okay."

ELEVEN

That Friday night, the weekend before I was supposed to start my new job, Laurie did indeed take me on a date.

After I made lunch for us, I went back to my suite to start the cleaning. I noticed a heavy gray garment bag on my bed with a note on top of it. I picked up the paper and read the surprisingly elegant script:

I would be honored if you would wear this tonight.
(No arguments, let people do nice things for you!!)
Meet me at the front door at 7.
Can't wait.
Love,
—L

I unzipped the bag slowly, with trepidation, as if snakes might come flying out. Nevertheless, it was just a suit. A beautiful, gunmetal gray suit with a subtle pinstripe and the faintest metallic sheen to the fabric. I took a covetous moment to caress the fine material before I searched out the label.

With a sigh of relief, I saw that it wasn't Gucci or Versace or any other designer of clothes worth more than my life. Perry Ellis was still damn nicer than what I would've bought, but at least it wasn't worth a small mortgage. Perhaps that was intentional. Maybe Laurie had known I wouldn't accept something extravagant and he really wanted me to wear it, so he'd gotten something reasonable. For that reason alone, I hung the suit in my closet for later.

Hours later, after I'd showered, shaved, brushed my teeth, and tamed my shaggy hair into...something, I put on the suit. Jesus, it really felt like I was getting ready for a date. Butterflies fluttered in my stomach, trying to tell me that's what I was doing, but I ignored them.

Laurie was waiting for me at the front door. He was wearing a trim black suit—which should've looked more *Men in Black* than it actually did—that was perfectly tailored to his tall, lanky body. He'd left his hair unstyled so it fell into his eyes and curled around his ears. I did not want to run my fingers through it. Did not. I shook myself when I realized I was staring, but his small smirk told me he'd noticed. He was a gentleman enough not to point it out.

"Are you ready to go?" he asked, opening the door for me.

I saw that he'd pulled the Lotus out into the driveway so it was just a short walk to get in. "Sure. Where are we going?"

"It's a secret," he said as he went around to the driver's side and got in.

"Ugh. Why?" I got in on the other side and settled into the comfortable seat.

"Because I want to." With a cheeky grin, he turned on the car and the engine rumbled to life.

As usual, when I got in that car, I melted into it, its purr and growl putting me into some kind of trance as we rolled toward the city. Laurie didn't say much either, but it wasn't an uncomfortable silence. We were both just enjoying driving around Baltimore in a sexy car. When I realized it was taking longer than it should to make it to the harbor, I looked up at my surroundings. We were in Canton, a trendy neighborhood that seemed mostly populated by young professionals. I didn't spend much time there, but I knew there were some great restaurants and nightlife.

"Gonna tell me yet?"

"Nope."

A couple of minutes later, we pulled down a street that had a ton of restaurants, so I assumed he was taking me to dinner. At that moment, my stomach let out a loud growl, making us both laugh. He found a parking spot and we got out, then he locked up the car. I cringed at the idea of leaving that beauty out where anyone could mess with it, but Laurie didn't seem concerned.

"Follow me," he said.

So I did. We walked for a couple of blocks and then he stopped in front of a building. The sign above the door read *Atomic–Fine Japanese Cuisine*. "We're going here?" I'd actually heard of this place. I'd heard it was super expensive and super exclusive—like you had to know someone to get a table unless you wanted to be on a six-month waiting list.

"Mm-hmm." Suddenly he looked over at me, his brow furrowed. "Oh, maybe you don't like Japanese food?"

"No, I do!" I patted his arm, feeling the supple material of his designer suit. I hadn't meant to make him feel insecure. "I just…didn't know we were going somewhere so fancy. Are you sure we can get in?"

He chuckled and opened the door for me, then ushered me through with a hand on the small of my back. Just that simple touch had my heart racing. Deep down I knew I was in so much trouble, but denial was my constant companion.

A beautiful woman with thick, black hair piled up in a messy bun smiled at us from behind the hostess stand. "Ah, good evening, Mr. Beaudry. If you want to follow me, we have your booth ready."

"Unbelievable," I said under my breath. Then louder, "Of *course* you can get into a place like this." I rolled my eyes, wondering if Laurie ever got by without falling back on his wealth.

As if reading my mind, Laurie spoke into my ear as we were led through the fancy dining room. "Money opens doors. But in this case, it's not what you think. The chef-owner is an old friend."

The dining room looked fancy, low lighting with everything done in the same gleaming dark hardwood. The main space had regular tables and chairs, but we walked past all those to another section with booths. Here the dividers for the booths were solid from the floor nearly to the ceiling, so they were almost like little one-table private dining rooms.

The hostess took us to one of the booths and gestured for us to sit, then filled our water glasses from the carafe on the table. As we slid into our seats, she asked, "Would you like anything else to drink?"

"We'll have a bottle of the Kenzo Murasaki and a carafe of the Born Gold Junmai Daiginjo."

"Of course. Atami-sensei will be with you shortly."

"I'm scared to even ask what you just ordered." I was not going to be rude and keep asking how much things cost, but I was still wondering in my head.

"Just a red wine that will pair nicely with dinner and some sake."

"Are you trying to get me drunk?" I asked, narrowing my eyes.

He shrugged, and even that simple gesture looked elegant on him. "You could stand to loosen up a little, Mackenzie."

I glared at him. "Pot, kettle."

"I'm not uptight, I'm just a workaholic. There's a difference," he said with a smirk.

"If you say so…" My voice trailed off as I caught sight of a man striding toward us. I didn't really make a habit of checking out guys—seriously!—but I could safely say he was probably the most beautiful person I'd ever seen in real life. He could've been straight out of Hollywood.

The man wore chef's whites, leaving little doubt as to who he was. He smiled as he approached us, pulling off his black bandana-style cap, a few strands of silky black hair escaping from the long rope of a braid that hung down his back. His almond-shaped eyes crinkled as he smiled brightly, his cheek dimpling charmingly.

"Oi, Beau!"

Ugh. Again with the nickname.

Laurie's head whipped around and he grinned at the man. "Ossu, Atami-san! Konbanwa," he said in what I could only assume was Japanese.

The way they smiled at each other caused an uncomfortable tightness in my chest. This guy knew Laurie. Like really *knew* him. Probably knew all about his family and his past—how Bruce Wayne became Batman and all that.

The beautiful man chuckled and put his hand on Laurie's shoulder. "I see you haven't forgotten what I taught you."

"Never."

I glared at that hand.

The way Laurie was acting…for some reason, I thought I was the only one who got to see that side of sullen, gruff Laurent Beaudry. That was stupid of me.

"Mackenzie, this is Toru Atami, the chef-owner. Tor, this is my friend, Mackenzie Pratt."

When I forced myself to smile, I realized I'd been grinding my teeth. I reached out to shake Toru's hand—which in turn removed it from Laurie's shoulder—and he gave me a kind smile

115

in return.

"Nice to meet you, Mackenzie. Welcome to Atomic." His voice was melodious, with just enough of a Japanese accent to be completely charming.

And then his fucking hand was back on Laurie's shoulder, rubbing and then giving it a slight squeeze. *Stop. Stop it.* Stop touching him! *Jesus, Laurie, don't let that guy put his hands all over you!* So that was what screaming internally felt like. I scowled at Toru's hand, hoping to make it burst into flames with some latent pyrokinesis, but alas... And then I realized the man was studying me, so I tried to wipe the hate out of my expression and make some conversation.

"How do you two know each other?" It came out roughly, sounding more like an accusation than an honest question.

Toru's mouth fell open, and Laurie's gaze snapped to my face. His brow furrowed like he was trying to puzzle out the answer to a math problem. If Toru picked up on my animosity, he didn't let on.

"I studied at Cambridge Culinary School, and after I graduated, I taught a few cooking classes at MIT," he said.

"Cooking at MIT?" I asked, confused.

Laurie interrupted. "There are a couple of chemistry-based cooking courses at MIT, but what Tor's talking about is the Independent Activities Period—a four-week session of how-to or human-interest classes available to everyone associated with the school—students, faculty, staff, and so on. I figured it would be a good idea to learn how to cook since I'd likely be living alone after I graduated. That's how we met."

"And we've barely seen each other since I moved to Baltimore," Toru said with another damn caress. "I can't believe you finally came out to the restaurant."

Smiling, Laurie tipped his head in my direction. "Mackenzie just landed a new job, so I wanted to take him somewhere special to celebrate."

"Oh yeah? Congratulations! What do you do?" Toru asked.

"As of Monday, I'll be a preschool teacher."

"That's fantastic!"

The man was making it very hard for me to continue hating him, but I was giving it the old college try. "Thanks."

"Well, boys, I'd better get back to the kitchen or no one will be eating tonight. I hope you enjoy your dinner. I'll try to pop out here again before you leave, but if I don't see you, don't be a stranger!" He directed that last bit to Laurie, then disappeared into the kitchen.

I scowled down at the white tablecloth, unable to come up with anything to say when all I could think about was that gorgeous man's hand all over Laurie. I kept quiet the whole time the waiter came to introduce himself and bring our drinks. I didn't say a word as Laurie poured us each a tiny cup of sake from the carafe.

"Okay, what's the matter?"

"Nothing," I grumbled. I took a sip of sake to keep from having to speak. The burn of the alcohol on my tongue felt refreshing and helped steady my mood. He nudged my leg with his foot, clearly not buying my answer.

"That guy… He was… You let… You guys just seem really close."

He narrowed his eyes. "Okay?"

"Is he an old boyfriend?"

Laurie's eyes widened. "Tor? Hell, no. We were just really good friends. That'd be like you going out with Taylor."

"Ew!" I shuddered.

"See? That's just wrong. Anyway, you should get to know him. He's a nice guy. Why are you so worked up about it?"

"N-no reason." I kept my eyes on the table as I fiddled with the heavy silverware that was probably actually real silver. It didn't matter, though, because I could still feel the weight of his stare. We were in a game of conversational chicken, and I was not going to lose. Too bad I could feel myself blushing hard.

"Oh my god."

My head snapped up. "What?" Oh, boy was that a mistake. His lips were pinched together like he was trying to keep from smiling, but his damn dimples were betraying him. "You're jealous. Of Toru. You think he wants me, and you're jealous!"

"I wasn't jealous!" I yelled, before casting a nervous glance through the open side of our booth. The next time I spoke, I whispered. "I wasn't jealous. It was just that he had his hands all over you, and you were *letting* him!"

Laurie finally let out the smile he'd been holding back. "Hate to break it to you but—"

"Shut up."

"Now you know how I felt when Taylor kept touching you the other night."

"That's different… You're… And I'm n—oh, for fuck's sake, can we just order? Where are the menus anyway?"

"There aren't any. It's not that kind of restaurant."

"I don't get it," I said, still feeling disgruntled and annoyed, wanting to get back to the sense of euphoria I felt about celebrating my new job.

"Atomic is a dining experience created by the chefs. We'll get one of several set menus for a thirteen-course meal."

"*Thirteen?*"

"Like I said, it's an experience. It's called Kaiseki."

"I'll probably die. Can you die of too much food? I think so." I was so totally out of my league.

"The courses are small, delicate, intricate. Designed to flow from one to the next to create a sort of transcendental experience. You'll be fine."

"Who decides what menu we get?"

"One of the chefs. Toru, in our case. He'll pick out which one he thinks we'll like best. He's never wrong."

That guy again. "Okay… If you say so."

"Trust me, you'll love it. It'll be the most delicious three hours of your life."

"*Three hours?*"

Laurie just chuckled and went back to sipping his sake, so I did the same. I wasn't very discerning when it came to Japanese liquor, but I could tell from the taste that it was the good stuff—I was *not* going to dwell on how good or how expensive. All I cared about was how it warmed my belly and calmed my nerves. And loosened my tongue, apparently.

"If you took a cooking class, how come you set the microwave on fire and can barely boil water?"

Laurie's eyes sparkled over his cup, but he simply shrugged. "It didn't take. Much to Tor's everlasting shame, I could not be taught."

"So you speak Japanese?" It was starting to get to me just how little I knew about Laurie, someone who'd ridiculously decided he was in love with me.

He nodded. "I do. When I was in school, there were several Japanese developers whom I admired, and I figured once I was working, it would benefit me to be able to converse with them. I've done a few collaborations with Japanese companies, so it's served me well. That was something Toru *was* able to teach me. When we became friends, after I took his class, I asked him if he would teach me his language. I did a lot of studying online too, but conversing with Tor was what really cemented the knowledge."

"Wow. I mean… Jesus, English is hard enough."

"Too true. There have been many times when I've actually thought Japanese was easier—speaking anyway. I still haven't mastered hiragana or kanji completely."

Talking with Laurie sometimes made me feel so young. Even though he was only thirty-five, he seemed to know so much, to have done so much. But he never bragged. In fact, he really never talked about himself much at all. Which brought me right back around to that niggling little thing that kept bothering me.

"Toru calls you Beau too."

"Mmhmm." Laurie seemed like he was trying to act distracted, or nonchalant, something, but I could tell it was fake.

"Can I?"

"No."

"Why *not?*" I whined, perfectly aware that I sounded like a toddler.

He sighed and rubbed his left temple with two fingers. "Why does this bother you? Why's it so important?"

"*Because.* You keep saying you," I lowered my voice to a whisper, "that you love me, but I don't really know much about you at all—like your past or whatever. And so, like, okay, you think it's okay to have sex with me but keep everything about your life *before* we met a total secret? So I can't call you the nickname that your friends do? So what am I, some rebound guy or like your little toy on the side? Because if that's the case, you can just go fuck off with Toru or Henry or who-the-fuck-ever and stop messing with my head." I was out of breath from my tirade, and I winced as my own words echoed around in my mind.

His eyes were wide as he blinked at me, his mouth forming a small *o*. Clearly, my situational Tourette's had surprised him. "Mackenzie, you've never asked me about my past. Not really, beyond the nickname thing."

Surely I had. Hadn't I? Or had I just taken the rumors I heard from Taylor as the truth. *Oh.* "I, uh… Well, I heard some things that sounded kind of…uncomfortable, so I thought asking you would seem nosy or bring up bad memories."

"Feel free to be as nosy as you want. I'm a big boy; I can handle a little nostalgia. All you have to do is ask."

"Well, I—"

"I'm not finished," he said, holding up a hand to stop me from talking. "You are not a rebound or a replacement or a *toy—*

although, I'll be glad to play if that's something you decide you want—so you need to get that through your head. I've told you I love you."

"Yeah, you keep saying so, but it hasn't been that long since you were going out with Henry. You can just move on that quickly?"

He shook his head, a soft smile playing at his lips. "That night when Henry came over...when you got so upset about the way he treated me? That's when I fell in love with you. It's for real, so you might as well get used to it."

"But we're both guys!"

"You're ridiculous." But his voice was fond.

"So why can't I call you Beau then?"

"Why would you want to call me the same thing all my old friends from college call me? A name from a long time ago before you knew me, when I was barely even the same person... Wouldn't you rather call me a name that I've never let anyone else call me besides my mother?"

My heartbeat thundered in my ears. "Of course," I breathed. "What is it?"

"*Laurie.*" He raised a brow and stared at me while draining the last of his sake.

I swallowed hard. Jesus. All along I'd been calling him by a nickname that was basically exclusive to me, and I'd never known. And I'd gone and made a jackass out of myself because, of *course* I did—it was what I was best at. "Oh. Well. Thanks, then." A furious blush heated my cheeks.

He just chuckled as he signaled for our waiter. "We're ready to begin the first course."

"Of course. I'll let Atami-sensei know."

He returned shortly with two plates of food, which he placed in front of us. I tried to contain my gasp when I saw what looked like the husk of sea urchin being used as a bowl for...something. The waiter bowed lightly and stepped back. "The sakizuke—first course—that Atami-sensei has chosen for you, an uni mousse, with kombu dashi foam, topped with ikura. Chef-sensei wishes you to enjoy." He uncorked our wine, poured two glasses, then disappeared.

"I didn't understand any of what he just said."

Laurie gave me an indulgent smile. "It's puréed urchin—uni is urchin. Ikura is salmon roe. Dashi is sort of a flavoring made with tuna stock, and kombu—kelp."

I watched Laurie spoon up a bite of his food, place it in his mouth, and close his eyes as if savoring the taste. A drop of sweat rolled down my back, tickling my skin. I mirrored his actions, and I couldn't help but close my eyes as well when the intense bouquet of flavors exploded on my tongue. It was...like nothing I'd ever tasted, so it was hard to even describe. Everything blended and married perfectly, a gustatory journey as each flavor passed different taste buds.

When I opened my eyes, he was watching me with an odd expression on his face. He took a deep breath, then a sip of his wine, before he continued eating.

Since it was a small appetizer course, it was gone in about three bites, and it left me hungry for more. The conversation had stalled with the strange tension that had gathered between us. I was just about to ask him what was wrong when our waiter, Suko, returned with more plates. A busboy whisked away our empty dishes as the new ones were set down.

Suko bowed again. "If it pleases you, our summer hassun course, unagi sashimi and imo."

He left swiftly, seeming to want to pick up the pace of the meal. I sent Laurie a questioning look.

"Raw eel with Japanese new potatoes."

I nodded. I'd never had sashimi before—I preferred my raw fish in little bits rolled up with rice and seaweed, usually fried. I was a little bit squicked out by the idea of just eating a raw slab of eel meat, but I picked up my chopsticks and tried it anyway. It was surprisingly flavorful if a bit on the slimy side.

"What do you think?" Laurie asked. His expression was earnest, like it really mattered to him whether I liked the food.

I swallowed quickly so I could speak. "It's good. Different from what I'm used to, but good. Thank you," I said quietly.

His lips tipped up in a half-smile as he refilled our wine glasses.

After that, the food kept coming. Laurie had not been exaggerating; it was *literally* thirteen courses. By the end of it, I was stuffed, but not unpleasantly so. The wine had also kept flowing, so my head was swimming a bit and my muscles were comfortably loose.

Once the last plates were cleared, Toru came back out to our table, all long, thick locks and dimpled fucking smiles. "How did you like it?" And his hand was back to Laurie's shoulder. Again.

"It was masterful, as always," Laurie answered. His voice was loose and velvety, so I thought the wine was just maybe affecting him a little bit too.

"Yeah, it was great!" I added, not wanting to seem ungrateful.

Toru's laughter rolled over us like a light breeze. "I'm glad you enjoyed it. And as promised, your meal is on the house."

Laurie was already shaking his head before Toru finished speaking. "You don't have to do that. You all work hard, you deserve to be paid."

"Your endowment to help me start this place was plenty. I told you I'd give you free meals for life after that," he said with a wink. And then his hand was sliding from Laurie's shoulder to the back of his neck, moving like maybe he was toying with the hair back there.

They'd known each other since college. Laurie had helped Toru start his business. Toru had tried to teach Laurie how to cook and taught him to speak Japanese. When they met, I was just a wet-behind-the-ears, barely-post-pubescent teenager who still had a whole family. How could I compete with that? Why was I thinking about competing? Why did I care that Toru was touching Laurie. Toru was…touching…Laurie.

A loud clattering bang made all three of us jump. Two pairs of eyes snapped to me, and it took me a moment to realize that I'd done it. I'd slammed my fist on the table hard enough to rattle the glasses and used silverware.

My breaths came out ragged, my shoulders rising and falling too fast with the force of it. My fist was still clenched, and I couldn't make myself look up from the table. The silence grew more uncomfortable as it lengthened until Laurie cleared his throat. I looked up automatically and saw that he was staring at me. His eyes were comically wide, his lips were slightly parted, and he looked like he was breathing almost as hard as me. He set his glass down slowly, deliberately, before turning to Toru.

"Tor, thank you for the meal, it was fantastic, but I'm afraid we have to go now. I'll call you."

"No you won't," he said good-naturedly. "I'll call *you*. Have a good night," he said as he backed away, throwing curious glances back and forth between Laurie and me.

Laurie stood up with graceful, measured movements, grabbed my wrist, and hauled me out of the booth. He didn't exactly drag me through the dining room, but he did keep a hold of my arm the entire time, and I was tripping over my feet trying to keep up. Once on the street, he strode to the car in long strides that ate up the pavement—it felt like I had to take two steps for every one of his.

Much to my confusion, he bypassed the Lotus and pulled me to a black Lincoln that was idling at the stop sign. When we got to it, a man in a chauffeur hat hopped out of the passenger side. Laurie tossed his keys to the man, and he jogged toward the Lotus.

Apparently Laurie'd had more to drink than I realized if he was unwilling to drive. He opened the rear passenger door and shoved me inside. The oiled leather of the seat swallowed me up like a catcher's mitt, and by the time I got my bearings, he was beside me and the driver was firing up the engine and peeling away from the curb.

I expected some sort of...something. Words, gestures, anything that would explain his strange behavior, but he was as chill as ever. And, shockingly, that started to make me angry. I felt like a scolded child being dragged out of the supermarket after a tantrum, and I wasn't even sure why. I had my guesses, but still, it was disorienting. But as always, he was the picture of self-contained, collected calm, and it made me want to strangle him. I wanted to see him get his feathers ruffled for once!

"*Well?*" I said, my voice dripping with irritation.

He glanced my way briefly, just a quick flick of his eyes before he focused on the view through the windshield. "Well, what?"

"Care to explain why you dragged me out of the restaurant?"

"In front of Adam?" He raised a brow and jerked his chin toward the chauffeur. "I think not."

I flushed and lowered my eyes because, yeah, he was right. I certainly didn't want anyone to hear us arguing like a married couple. So we sat in silence while the tension winched tighter with each mile we traveled.

I hadn't been paying attention to the scenery because I'd been concentrating so hard on *not* looking at Laurie that I'd been glaring at the back of the passenger seat. That was why, when the Lincoln ground to a halt, I looked up in surprise.

"We're here," Laurie said in a voice that was strangely detached.

"But we can't be," I protested. "We were driving less than ten minutes."

"And yet, here we are."

I looked out the window. "And we're still in Canton! Where is 'here,' exactly?"

"The Dunn-Warren Hotel." He got out of the car while the

chauffeur opened my door and came around to offer me his arm. "Come on."

"Hotel?" I squeaked, my voice breaking like a teenager's.

"Yes. I promised you one, remember?" He spoke through tightened lips, but other than that, he was as unflappable as ever.

He tipped the driver and took me by the hand, pulling me through the lobby of the opulent hotel. Bypassing the front desk entirely, he merely glanced at the concierge, who nodded in return while tapping a few keys on his computer. We boarded the elevator, and I knew which button he was going to push before it happened. Penthouse.

Instead of the usual keycard swiping mechanism, there was a combination keypad. Laurie punched in a few numbers and the lock disengaged. He opened the door for me and I went inside. The penthouse wasn't enormous, as this was more of an inn-style hotel, but what it lacked in size, it made up for in view.

The rectangular main room had vaulted ceilings, and three of the four walls were filled with huge picture windows, for a panoramic view of the Canton side of the harbor. The décor was trendy, geometric, and minimal, and I was actually pleasantly surprised with the lack of pretension. I was so busy admiring the suite that I'd forgotten the brooding man behind me. I jumped when he clicked the door shut and the lock slid back in place.

"Make yourself comfortable," he said while unknotting his tie and sliding it out from his collar.

The footprint of the suite was similar to our rooms at Chatham House—the main room was basically a living room, kitchenette, and wet bar. The wall without windows had several doors, which I assumed led to the bedrooms, bath, and maybe a closet. I took off my suit jacket and laid it carefully over the back of one of the dining chairs, then sank down onto the blocky gray couch. I leaned my head against the back of it and stared up at the ceiling.

"Are we going to talk now?"

Footsteps and the rustle of clothing filled the room, and the couch dipped beside me. I rolled my head to look at him sideways. "Hmm?"

"What is it you want to talk about?" he asked, feigning ignorance.

"You know damn well. I want to know why you dragged me out of there, but you're still acting like the same reserved, cagey bastard you always are. What happened?"

His stare bored into me, making my stomach shiver and twitch. "You were getting agitated because Toru was touching me, and *that* was turning me on. I wanted to get you out of there so I could get my hands on you."

"I wasn't—"

"You were."

I pinched my mouth shut and ground my teeth because it wasn't like I could really deny my little temper tantrum. I just hated that he caught on to the reason.

"I like it that you're jealous. Because up until now..." He shook his head as he let his voice trail off. "Up until now, you've been just letting me do what I want."

My brow furrowed. I wasn't getting his meaning.

"I don't know why you let me... It isn't as if you have feelings for me—maybe you just wanted the release and it was convenient. But all of our...encounters have been you just letting me do things to you or you putting up with it." He gave another rough shake of his head. "I'm not explaining this well. I guess the fact that you let me do things, but haven't really participated, is starting to make me feel a little rapey. Like I'm pushing myself on you. So you getting jealous sort of...helps with that." He finally finished, his head hanging down.

Shocked, I sat up straighter, and after a couple of tries at shoring up the courage, I placed a shaky hand on his shoulder. "Jesus, it's not like you *made* me do anything, so don't think that. I'm not really sure what's going on here, and to be honest,

I've been trying not to analyze it too much…because I guess I'm scared. But I know full well that if I told you to stop—for *real*—that you would. Immediately. I know."

He raised his head back up and gave me a small smile, but there was still a worry line between his brows. Without thinking, I reached out and smoothed it with my thumb. He sucked in a breath, and I froze when I realized what I'd done. He caught my wrist, brought it to his lips, and placed a kiss on my pulse point. I was sure he could feel the thundering of my blood through my skin.

"I love you, Mackenzie."

I sighed. I wasn't even close to believing it, but I was starting to like hearing it. And that was dangerous. "We've only known—"

"Only known each other for a few weeks. I *know*." His fingers flexed around my wrist. "I don't understand it either. Believe me, I've tried to talk myself out of it. But these feelings just won't go away."

"You have all these worries and feelings, but you never react. You always seem so composed."

He leaned toward me. "It's a defense mechanism. I've always been this way—it's one of the things Henry hated about me. But you pick up on the minutiae of my moods in a way he never did. You knew something had happened when I took you out of the restaurant, you just couldn't tell what. He just thought I was a cold-hearted bastard… Well, you heard it all."

"I don't think you're cold," I mumbled.

His lips twitched like he was trying not to smile, and then it grew into a mischievous, slightly scary smirk. "You really want to see me lose my composure?"

I nodded.

"Well, of course, if you ever told me you love me, I'd probably pass out. But if we're talking in the bedroom…I'd be putty in your hands if you ever initiated anything. Sex…

Foreplay... I don't think I'd be able to control myself if that happened. Hell, you saw how I was after you just *kissed* me on graduation day."

With every word, my face burned hotter, and my toes curled with embarrassment and probably a little latent desire. I wished I could be that man. Someone who was assertive with his lover, demanded what he wanted. Who admitted to himself what he was. But...

I grimaced. "I don't know... I can't..."

"I know, Mackenzie." He placed a quick kiss on my lips before drawing back. He began unbuttoning his shirt. "I'm not asking you to do anything you're not comfortable with. I'm just giving you an honest answer."

I stood up suddenly because his proximity was making it hard for me to breathe. I walked to the window and stared out at the lights on the harbor. Laurie walked up behind me, standing a few feet away. I knew because, thanks to the lamplight in the room, if I focused on the glass instead of the harbor beyond, I could see him just as if I was looking in a mirror. He was shirtless.

"Feel free to make yourself comfortable. I'm having Adam pick up some clothes for us from home so we don't have to do the 'walk of shame' in wrinkled suits tomorrow. The hotel was kind of a last-minute decision on my part, which is why I didn't think to have you pack a bag. They should be here first thing in the morning."

In the morning. Until then... Belt clinking, the swish of cloth, and Laurie's reflection was in nothing but black briefs. I swallowed the sudden lump in my throat and pretended to still be watching the harbor. God, he was something else to look at. As I tried and failed not to look at him, I thought maybe I should start admitting to myself that I probably was attracted to men. But it felt like once I did, everything would change, and I wasn't sure I was ready for that.

Still, when his hands slid up my back and I could feel their warmth even through my shirt, I closed my eyes and let my head fall back.

"Maybe I should help you," he rumbled in my ear. His hands went to my belt, and before I knew it, my pants and briefs were pooled around my ankles. Why was it that I was so weak for this man?

He unbuttoned my shirt but left it on, because he seemed to have some kind of kink about having sex while partially dressed. I wasn't going to pretend I didn't know that's where things were headed. My cock was already hard and straining upward, waiting for attention. Laurie didn't let me down, wrapping long fingers around my erection and giving it a few strong pulls.

My breath hitched, but I shifted my hips away from his hand, ineffectually, as it only served to push my ass against *his* erection. "Not here. Someone could see."

He licked along the back of my neck, then murmured into my hair, "Let them see. Let them look and be jealous that they're not having as good a night as we are." He punctuated the statement with more strokes.

My limbs turned to liquid and I slumped back against him. He kissed my neck where he'd licked, just a peck, then whispered in my ear.

"Don't move."

His heat against my back disappeared. I closed my eyes, not wanting to see what kind of expression I wore in the reflection of the window. My body was cooling, and I started to feel silly, but then he was back, hard-muscled warmth and slick fingers probing the divot between my cheeks. I gasped as one finger unceremoniously entered; I rose up on my tiptoes because it was too much too quickly. But he soothed the burn with more attention to my cock, and I settled enough for him to slide in another finger.

As his hands worked in tandem, he rested his chin on my shoulder. "Will you let me in again, Mackenzie?" His voice was strained, for once showing the effort it took to maintain his cool façade.

I stared at his image in the glass until he raised his eyes to meet mine. "I can't do any of those things you said, not yet. But what I can do is tell you that...I'm in this. This moment that's happening right now—I may seem nervous or embarrassed because that's just how I am, but I'm here of my own free will. Okay? So no need to go feeling like you're forcing me into anything."

I saw the moment he comprehended in the widening of his eyes and parting of his lips. It was my only warning before he gripped my chin, jerking my head to the side so he could claim my lips in a brutal kiss. He speared his tongue into my mouth while his fingers did the same below. When he broke the kiss, we were both panting and dazed.

"Put your hands on the glass."

"Why—?"

"Do it!" Then he added, "Please."

I complied, placing my palms on the window. His fingers disappeared, and then he was grasping my hipbones with both hands, jerking them back. Then he pressed down on the small of my back, forcing me to arch. Shortly after, the head of his cock slid along my crack until it nudged my entrance. He didn't take as much care entering as he had the first time, but then again, it wasn't *my* first time. My hands curled into fists, and I bit the inside of my cheek to keep from crying out from the burn as my muscles stretched and spread. I knew the payoff would be incredible and that I just had to bear with it until my body relaxed.

It didn't take as long as last time. Once he was all the way inside, my body gripped him like a perfectly fit glove. We both sighed in unison. He slid his hands along my arms until he could entwine his fingers with mine. And then he began to move.

This time the climb to arousal was swift and sharp, with

Laurie snapping his hips in earnest, driving deep inside me. The feeling of fullness was overwhelming, tightening my body until it felt like something would snap. He bent his knees so he could thrust even deeper, hitting my prostate with each stroke.

When he let go of one of my hands to stroke my cock, my breath became shaky and my muscles trembled and clenched. I came embarrassingly quickly. He let out a surprised grunt when my body clamped down on him, stuttering out a few more hard thrusts before coming himself, while biting down on the back of my neck. We both slid to the floor, me on Laurie's lap, still connected. He wrapped his arms around me and held me tight until our breathing slowed.

"I love you," he murmured.

My breath caught as it did every time he said it. I found myself wanting to believe him. Would it be so wrong to want something just for me? Taylor had Karla, and most of my friends had significant others. River had his work. My mother had whatever she'd been seeking when she left us. Was it so awful to think, why couldn't I be with Laurie? Sure, some people would look at us funny, call us names maybe, and I was still too shy and embarrassed to even admit what we were doing out loud, but my heart was starting to want things it shouldn't.

And I didn't have the willpower to shatter it.

TWELVE

My first week at my new job—also known as "planning week"—went faster than I could've imagined. I was the teaching assistant for the threes-and-fours class under Alison Grainger, a petite brunette whom I judged to be in her mid-thirties. She had a relaxed manner that didn't completely hide the air of a seasoned teacher, and I liked her instantly. She didn't treat me like I was an underling and she was the boss, like I'd experienced during my internships, and she made sure to include me in the curriculum planning.

The first day of school with students was always chaotic, but even more so with preschool, because a lot of these parents were dropping their kids off at school for the first time ever—and in some cases, dropping their kids off *anywhere* for the first time ever—so there was a bit of a learning curve. The parking lot was nearly gridlocked, and the halls were stuffed full of children, parents, and in some cases even grandparents.

The whole aura inside the school bristled with nervous

excitement. I sat in one of the miniature chairs at one of the miniature tables, checking off students on the attendance list as Alison greeted them. Since I was new, I had no idea who anyone was. Some of the children ran right to the toys that were carefully arranged in stations according to which type of sensory or cognitive development they stimulated, while others clung to their parents and cried. The names of this generation of children were...inventive, to say the least. And that was a big deal, coming from someone with a brother named River.

A boy named Arrow whined as his mother tried to peel his arms from their octopus-grip on her leg. I checked off Arrow Thompson from the list. Alison hugged a little girl named Coco and another called Sparrow. Check, check. There were some normal ones too—Ethan, Riley, Sam, Anna. I watched with interest as a little boy walked into the classroom, leading two women by the finger. They stopped just inside the door and hugged him, then straightened to say a few words to him that were too low for me to hear.

When I realized that one woman had a proprietary arm around the other, I looked up with interest to see how Alison would react to what was obviously a lesbian couple. It wasn't as if me living with Laurie was actually me *living with* Laurie, but I realized that it could be construed that way, especially the way the lines had been blurring in our somewhat undefined relationship. So it was important for me to know if it was something I needed to keep close to the vest.

Alison stood up and walked over to the couple. "This must be Zane?" she asked, stooping slightly. I wasn't sure how she could've possibly identified the child, unless she had been pre-warned that Zane had two mommies. I wasn't sure how I felt about the administration seeing the need to prep a teacher about that—on one hand, it was good they were taking steps toward sensitivity, but on the other, it was sad it was needed at all.

When Alison embraced the taller of the two women, I

realized I'd been making unfair assumptions. She knew the woman, and therefore, by association, knew who Zane was. Alison didn't seem at all phased by the unique family situation. I decided to take it as a good sign, so if any questions were ever raised about my relationship with Laurie, maybe she wouldn't look at me differently.

Once we got all of the children checked off and safely ensconced in the classroom, with their parents, grandparents, nannies, au pairs, et cetera, sent on their way, we lined them all up for a class trip to the bathroom. We lucked out that all of our threes were potty trained—Alison told me it was not always the case, especially with boys. After that, we had a morning of free play, gymnastics, and an early lunch—since the preschool let out at two.

We had decided during planning week that I would run the science section of class since I'd minored in chemistry—having done so on the off chance that I would ever get sick of early childhood education and want to move to a high school position. It would take just a few courses to upgrade my certification.

Jittery nerves washed through me as science time came upon us. This was different from my internship. Even though I was only the assistant teacher, this was responsibility. I took a deep, shaky breath and stood between our two hexagonal science tables. "Okay, friends. Gather!" I said, hoping the quote from *Finding Nemo* might break the ice. It kinda did.

The kids slowly trundled over from their centers and congregated around the science tables. "Okay, you guys, today we are going to explore chemical change. There are two types of changes, physical and chemical. A physical change is a forced change, like if you crushed a soda can or melted a piece of ice. You've changed what it looks like but not what it's made of. Got it?"

There were a few nods and several blank stares, plus one nose-picker. That was pretty much what I'd expected. Preschool science lessons had to be light on explanation and heavy on demonstration. "A chemical change is when you add a substance that changes the molecules of your original object. Meaning, you change what it's made of.

Before I lost them completely, I started the experiment, placing a beaker in the center of each table, then filling them halfway with white vinegar. "On the table, you'll see some fun stuff...you've got droppers of food coloring—that we're gonna be real careful with—glitter, and confetti. Take whatever you'd like to use and carefully put it into the cup. If you get the vinegar on your hands, it'll stink all day, so be careful."

There were giggles and squeals as the kids went about lacing the vinegar with colorful additives. Once the mixtures were sufficiently bedazzled, I added a teaspoon of baking soda to each beaker and listened to the shrieks of delight as the mixture began to foam, rise, and overflow. I let each child take a turn stirring, to make the reaction bubble over even more. Using the food coloring, I changed the color a couple of times, and the kids remained enthralled until the reaction slowed and finally stilled.

"Mr. Pratt?" Zane spoke up. Normally, the teachers were called by their first names with Mr. or Miss, but since Mr. Mackenzie was a whole lot of syllables, we'd decided to go with my last name.

"Yes, Zane?"

"What made it do that?"

"Good question. That was an example of a chemical reaction. The baking soda changed the molecules of the vinegar, causing a reaction. Can anyone tell me what the reaction was?"

Anna raised her hand first, so I called on her. "Suds!"

I chuckled. "It did sort of look like suds from soap, right? You're very close. By adding the baking soda to the vinegar, we created foam. Can everyone say foam?"

There was a chorus of little high-pitched voices saying the word—most correctly—and my heart soared. This was what I loved. The way kids' faces lit up when they learned something new…there wasn't anything like it. That feeling carried me through the rest of the school day, and my feet barely touched the ground all the way home.

After an exhausting but rewarding first week at school, I was happy it was finally Friday. I was lucky to have gotten a job I loved, but I definitely needed some rest. I headed into the communal living room with a book and a glass of wine, intending to spend the time until I had to cook dinner relaxing and recharging. But there was a stranger in the house.

I didn't recognize the man who lounged on the couch as if he owned it, but there was something strangely familiar about him, something I couldn't quite put my finger on. When he noticed me, his face registered surprise briefly, before a carefully cultivated pleasant expression overtook it. He was handsome for his age, I noticed as he stood to greet me—he was at least a decade older than Laurie, maybe more. He was immaculately dressed, and his salt-and-pepper hair was trimmed into submission and slicked back. He made the perfect picture of an attractive elder statesman, and yet, when I came within a couple of feet of him, something about the presence he exuded set my teeth on edge.

"How'd you get in here?"

"Laurent told me to wait inside. He'll be back soon."

It was weird. I didn't think I'd met anyone who called Laurie simply "Laurent." I wasn't sure if it spoke to familiarity or formality, but I didn't ask.

"Might I ask who you are?" the man continued.

I lifted my chin a fraction. "Mackenzie. I live here."

His brows raised slightly, the only outward reaction to my words. His gaze lowered to my book and my wine. "I'm sorry, it looks as though I've interrupted your peaceful evening. I'm Theo."

He stuck out his hand, so I had to set my things down on the coffee table to shake it. He didn't offer a last name, but then again, neither had I.

"It's not a problem," I heard myself saying, even though it kind of *was* an unwelcome intrusion. "I just got off work, so I was going to relax for a bit before I made dinner."

"You work?"

I wasn't sure why that fact seemed to surprise him. "Of course. I just started a new job, actually. Would you like something to drink while you wait?"

"That would be most welcome. I'll have whatever you're having."

Keeping one eye on Theo, I walked over to the wet bar, opened a new bottle of the Malbec I was drinking, and poured him a glass. After I handed it to him, I sank down on the couch with a sigh and watched as he did the same.

He put his nose to the glass, assessing the bouquet, then took a slow sip, presumably swirling it on his tongue before swallowing, his eyes sliding closed. "Ah, Laurent. His tastes are as predictable as the tide."

"Oh, I don't know about that," I muttered, sotto voce.

Theo's eyes crinkled at the corners, and his sunbaked skin creased around his wide mouth as he smiled at me. "You said you just got a new job. What is it that you do, Mackenzie?"

"I'm a teacher. Preschool."

His smile grew, feeling more genuine than it had initially. "That's wonderful. My mother was a teacher, God rest her."

"I find it very rewarding," I said, somewhat cautiously. Theo gave me the feeling of approaching a tamed jungle cat. It was likely to be on its best behavior, but it was still a wild animal—teeth, claws, and all.

Despite my trepidations, he drew me into a conversation that was both agile and interesting. I could tell that he had a sharp mind and he'd experienced a lot in his life. In that way, he reminded me of River. Just a little.

As we talked, we drank, and before I knew it, Theo had slid closer to me on the couch, so close that our thighs were touching. My brows pulled low over my eyes as he took my almost-empty glass and placed it on the coffee table beside his. Then he twisted so his upper body was facing me, with his arm propped on the back of the couch.

"Tell me, how did you come to live here with Laurent."

He was uncomfortably close. Too close for such a casual conversation. Not knowing how this man was involved with Laurie, I didn't want to piss him off, so I curtailed my flight response. I'd begun to feel a bit like prey.

"Um… Well, my apartment building got sold to be demolished, and I couldn't find another place that I could afford. Laurie offered me a room in his house."

His eyes widened. This time, he was unable to conceal his surprise. "*Laurie*. Hmm."

I tamped down the swell of warmth that washed over me when the exclusivity of the nickname was confirmed. The warmth turned to ice as Theo brought his right hand up to caress my jaw.

"My first assumption was correct, then."

My eyes narrowed. "Which was?"

"That you're my nephew's new toy."

Before I even had a chance to recoil, he moved his hand from my face to my thigh, slithering up my inseam. His hot, acrid breath wafted in my face as he whispered, "I'll tell you a little secret. I have more money than him—I can pay you better."

I gasped and tried to scrabble away, but his other arm that had been oh-so-casually draped over the back of the sofa suddenly curled around my shoulders and held me still while he leaned in for what I could only assume was a kiss.

Gathering all of my strength, do or die, I shoved his barrel chest with both hands. I'd thought it would've been sufficient to dislodge him enough for me to squirm away. What I hadn't expected was for him to go flying halfway across the room. Another surprise was seeing Laurie standing between me and Theo, breathing hard and fists clenched, looking like some avenging angel of doom.

His gaze searched me, as if he were looking for injuries. When he found none, he rounded on Theo, who was ineffectually struggling to right himself, like an overturned crab. "How did you get in here?" Laurie's voice was low and dangerous, full of the promise of barely contained violence.

"The front door," he said as he finally gained his feet. I took a small amount of pleasure at the pained sounds he made while doing it.

"You need a passkey to get in."

"As I was telling your young pet here, you are, as always, delightfully predictable. The password is Josephine. It's always *Josephine*," he answered, his lip curled in derision.

Laurie's back was rigid, his body fraught with tension. He pinched the bridge of his nose before addressing his uncle again. "If you've hurt him, I'll kill you." His tone left no doubt that he would follow through. "Mackenzie?"

"I'm fine. Just, you know, a little creeped out."

Stiffly, Laurie rounded the coffee table and sat down beside me. He didn't touch me, but his body language made it clear that his uncle was not to come near me again. He didn't invite Theo to sit; he just fixed the man with his patented Laurie glare. "What are you doing here?"

"You left home before we concluded our business."

"This is home."

"You know what I mean!" Theo roared. Then he collected himself, taking a breath in an obvious effort to calm down. I had a brief moment of commiseration because Laurie could indeed be infuriating a lot of the time.

"Which 'business' are you referring to? The genome lab you want B & E to invest in, or the absurd idea that you're going to force me to sell you my controlling interest."

Theo turned red to the roots of his hair. "You don't even *care* about the company! You just sit here in your mansion with your *pets...*" He cut a glance to me. "And design your little video games, flitting about through life like the spoiled little brat that you are, so why do you even care who runs the company?"

"*You* run the company, Theo. I promised you that when I turned down the job. However, you'll have to pry my shares out of my cold, dead hands. My parents built that company up from nothing, and I'm not going to let you run it into the ground."

Theo scowled at Laurie, then at me, as if I'd had anything to do with whatever they were talking about.

"If you want to discuss the genome research further, I'll be glad to sit down with you some other time. Somewhere else." Laurie made a little flicking motion with his hand. "Now get out of my house."

Knowing he was beaten and obviously hating it, Theo turned on his heel and stalked out of the house. As soon as the front door slammed shut and we heard the automatic lock engage, Laurie slumped back against the couch, as if all of the energy drained from his body in one quick rush. His head lolled in my direction.

"I'm sorry you had to hear that. And that you...had to be alone with him. I never thought he'd come into my house like that."

I turned in my seat to face him. "What's the deal with you two?" I backpedaled when Laurie winced like it hurt to even think about. "Never mind. It's not my business, you don't have to tell me."

The look he turned on me was unreadable. "It is, and I should. It's just...not a pleasant story."

"Yeah, I kind of got that impression."

I thought he was just going to let it drop, so I was taken off guard when he spoke again. "My parents started their venture capitalist firm before I was born. B & E Investments—stands for Beaudry and Étienne, my parents' last names. My mother was an economist who came from money, and my dad had a nose for investing like a shark does for blood in the water, so they pooled their considerable talents. They hit it big financing a fledgling production company and had a string of successful products that cemented their reputation.

"After I was born, my mom wanted to spend more time at home with me, so my uncle was brought in to help fill the gaps. She just wanted to be a good mom." His voice broke ever so slightly, and it tore me up.

"Josephine…"

"Yeah. We were really close. For a while."

"What happened to them?" I asked, my gut twisting because I knew it couldn't be good.

"Plane crash." His head was down, his hair falling over his eyes. He shrugged. "At least they were together. That's something, I guess."

"And what…what happened to you after that?"

Laurie tipped his head back, staring up at the ceiling but not really seeing. "My uncle took me in. We moved to the States so he could set up a US branch of B & E. At first, I was just grateful not to be alone. But as I got older, I began to see that I was his meal ticket. My parents had left the money, the company…everything, to me. If Theo had shown his true colors back then, I could've tossed him out without a penny."

"What did he do?"

"He certainly wasn't interested in parenting, although he did occasionally have a sentimental moment where he'd want to play catch or whatever-the-hell, but mostly I was raised by the staff.

The money was in trust, and I didn't want to run B & E. I had my own dreams. I appointed Theo as the CFO and Head of Acquisitions, back when I still trusted him—though I still maintain controlling interest."

"I'm afraid to even ask what he did to lose your trust."

He huffed out a humorless laugh. "Once his position was secure, he started treating me like shit. Any guys I brought home, he tried to fuck them. He succeeded many times. He had a thing for young guys and had a hard-on for taking things from me, since he felt that he'd somehow been cheated out of owning the company. It's just a bunch of ridiculous family drama," he said with a dismissive wave of his hand.

"Young guys... He didn't ever...with you...?"

"God, no. I mean, not that his character didn't suggest he was capable of it...but by the time his position was secure, I was a little old for his taste. And I think it always shook him up how much I look like my father."

I closed my eyes, wishing like hell I could erase the feeling of that man's hands on me.

"So that's why he was messing with you. He assumed that you were my...well, you get it. Ugh, anyway. That's my sad little orphan story for you."

"I guess we both have one of those, huh?" I said, realizing it was true. "Thank you. For telling me. All I really knew about your past was what Taylor learned second-hand in the office. Sadly, most of it was pretty accurate." I cocked my head at him. "You know, when he told me that stuff, I told Taylor that I was living with Bruce Wayne."

"That is...uncomfortably close to the truth." A half-hearted chuckle rumbled up from his chest. "Only I didn't have a Batmobile *or* an Alfred."

Hearing that, being faced with the knowledge of just how lonely he'd been, splintered my heart into tiny shards. And then he gave me a rueful smile that did its best to try and glue it back together. I couldn't take it anymore. Everything inside me was reaching out to the sad, scared little boy inside the calm, reserved, brilliant man beside me. Christ, I was so done for.

Without conscious thought, only instinct, I leaned over and ran my fingers along his jaw, just a whisper of a touch. His gaze bore into me, searching. He was holding his breath. That was probably the tipping point, knowing he was watching and waiting, wanting and needing something from me that, inexplicably, only I could provide in that moment.

So I kissed him. A soft brushing of lips, sharing of breath. And then I did it again. And again. His cheekbones, his stubbled jaw, his eyelids as they slid closed, his furrowed brow, and eventually his lips again. Somehow, without realizing it, I'd crawled into his lap, my knees bracketing his thighs. Still I kept on, pressing my lips to his like I needed that contact to breathe. Maybe in that moment, I did.

His chest was rising and falling under my hands, rapidly and erratically, like he was just a half-step from losing control. Even as my face burned from embarrassment, I wanted it. I wanted that last thread to snap more than I wanted my next breath. I needed to see him come apart and know that I'd done it. That shy, virginal Mackenzie had coaxed out the trapped beast and tamed it.

I slid off of his lap, onto my knees on the floor. I couldn't think about it, couldn't look at him, or I'd freak out or chicken out. I wanted this. So much. I just needed the courage to do it. My fingers went to the waistband of his slacks, but when I started to unfasten them, his cool hands covered mine.

"Mackenzie." His voice was rough-edged, like being dragged over broken glass. "I don't want pity."

"This—" I swallowed hard, dislodged his hands, and grabbed his hipbones. "—is not that." I yanked his hips to the edge of the couch.

He let out a shocked gasp as he flopped back on the cushions.

I unzipped his pants fast, not wanting to give him time to stop me. He was hard enough to drive nails; I could feel it against the backs of my fingers as I worked. I parted the material, slacks and briefs, then dragged it down to mid-thigh, barely conscious of him lifting up to allow it. His cock had sprung free, smacking against his stomach. It was then that I realized this was more than just me wanting to do something for him. It came as a shock to me just how badly I wanted to taste him.

His flesh was hot and rigid when I wrapped my fingers around it. I experimented with a few worshipful caresses and strokes, enjoying the way his hips jerked, as if he was barely containing his urge to move. His hands were on his thighs, gripping the fabric of his pants as if he were hanging over the edge of the cliff. Maybe he kind of was. And me? I wanted to see him let go.

I bent forward, stretched my tongue out, and swiped at the head of his cock, just enough to gather his taste, to acclimate myself. I liked it. In fact, much to my embarrassment, I loved it. I took him further into my mouth, swirling my tongue before applying some gentle suction. The broken whimper that escaped him made my heart soar and my dick swell.

And then things sort of ground to a halt because I didn't *really* know what I was doing. I kept tonguing the head while I searched my mind through the haze of lust, trying to remember what he'd done for me. I felt him straining against himself, knowing he wanted to take over, to guide me. I felt him lose the battle and reach for me. Without taking my mouth off him, I clasped his wrists and pinned them to the couch cushion on either side of him. Because *no*. I wasn't going to lose this. This chance to be his undoing. I wanted it, and I wasn't sure if I'd ever have the cajones to try again if I didn't make it happen.

I pulled off his dick, letting my lips hover a hair's breadth away from where he wanted them, and I finally looked at him. His eyes were wide and dark, dilated so much that they were almost all pupil. His mouth hung open as his rapid breaths tumbled passed his lips. He looked like he didn't know what to do with me, and I liked that look on him. I squeezed his wrists where I still held them.

"Leave them there or I'll stop."

His head bobbed with rapid-fire nods that made me smile. I released his hands, turning my attention back to his cock. I gripped his shaft again, holding it steady while I licked from root to tip, tonguing the slit and enjoying the way his thighs trembled. *What's it gonna take? What will make you lose it?*

I was pretty sure my untested gag reflex would be an obstacle, but I closed my lips over his head and slid down as far as I could go. He bucked hard, making me cough just a little, but I gripped his hips when he tried to back away. Using my hand to make up the difference, I bobbed up and down on his cock until I got a good rhythm going. My other hand found its way to his balls, and I rolled them inside their lightly furred sack.

This seemed to drive him a little bit crazy, as he was unable to keep from thrusting gently into my mouth. He fisted the cushions, and he was showing remarkable restraint. But I didn't *want* his restraint anymore. I wanted his abandon. Sucking harder, faster, I took one of his hands and placed it on my head. His fingers immediately gripped my hair, but not enough to hurt.

He threw his head back and groaned. "Fuck. *Mackenzie.*" The way he said my name was full of awe.

But it wasn't enough. I engulfed as much of his cock as I could, pushing on when my throat tried to reject the intrusion. Feeling the buzz of arousal ricochet through my body, I liberated my own cock and started stroking hard and fast, impossibly turned on by the taste of him on my tongue.

I swallowed convulsively around his tip when it bumped the back of my throat. His back bowed off the couch and he clenched my hair. His breath became ragged, pushed out through clenched teeth, as I drove him closer to the edge. My questing fingers, which had been playing with his sac, drifted to massage just behind his balls, while I kept bobbing on his cock.

"Christ, Mackenzie—" He cut himself off as I tongued the slit.

That was apparently the magic spot, because he came with a shout, without any warning, flooding my mouth with an unfamiliar sharp, tangy taste. I did my best to swallow, but I couldn't keep up. I pulled off and what was left over dribbled down my chin. I looked up at him where he was sprawled on the couch, flushed and panting, eyes wild. He looked so wrecked that I couldn't help the smug smile that spread across my face.

Apparently that sparked something in him—or maybe it was seeing his cum dripping down my chin—because he tackled me flat on my back, my shoulder blades hitting the floor in a way that I was definitely going to feel later, but I didn't give a damn because I'd made Laurie lose control. I was still riding high on endorphins and self-satisfaction. His heavy body came down over me as he wedged a knee in between my legs, snug against my balls, the pressure making my vision swim.

His hand found my cock, in all its exposed, unsated glory, and he began stroking it with an almost violent rhythm. My toes curled and I lifted my hips off the floor, rising up to meet his pulls. He traced my jaw with his tongue, cleaning my skin, tasting himself, before he took my mouth in a kiss that matched the brutality of what he was doing to my cock. When I tasted him again, through his kiss, I lost it, pumping my hips erratically as I spilled over his hand.

He gave me one last lingering kiss as he stroked me through the aftershocks, before rolling off of me and flopping onto his back. His chest was still heaving, but then I supposed mine was too, at that point. He silently stared at the ceiling for so long, I almost thought he'd fallen asleep. But then he spoke.

"Holy shit. You have a mouth on you, Mackenzie."

The sexual haze was lifting, my body was cooling, and I

started to come back to myself. In doing so, the full force of how I'd acted hit me like a blow to the gut. I went from cold to blazing hot with a full-body blush. "Oh my god. I'm so embarrassed!" I rolled away from him, curling into a fetal position after discreetly stuffing myself back into my pants. God, I couldn't even think about what I'd looked like doing that. On my knees. In front of a man. Handsome, rich, aloof Laurent Beaudry, who's feathers never ruffled.

He grabbed my arm and rolled me back over. All the way, so I was curled into his body instead. I buried my face against his chest so I wouldn't have to look at him. I was literally shaking with mortification, desperate with the need to hide. But with my ear against his sternum, I could hear his heart beating fast and turbulent, like he was still stirred up over something. I allowed myself a tiny smile because I *had* ruffled his feathers, even if only for a moment.

Pressing a kiss to the top of my head, he whispered to me. He probably thought I hadn't heard, but I did.

"Stay close to me."

I didn't know if he meant there on the floor in his arms. Or always.

THIRTEEN

The summer was in full swing, oppressive humidity and all. Work was going great—the kids were eating up my science lessons—so I wanted to go out and enjoy the season. Something Taylor and I always did when we wanted to celebrate was to play tourists in our own city, finding some cheesy attraction that locals always overlooked. Last time, we'd gone to the Baltimore and Ohio Railroad Museum and nerded out over trains like we were five years old again. This time, we'd decided to go to Daredevil Park, an amusement park in the neighboring town of Bayview.

Taylor and Karla were picking me up at Chatham House, so I was practically twitching with nervous excitement as I cleared up our breakfast dishes. Laurie sat on one of the barstools at the kitchen island, reading a newspaper—did people even read newspapers anymore?—and I thought about how sexy he looked with his slim reading glasses perched on the bridge of his nose, inexplicably dressed in a dress shirt and slacks with a tie, even though he worked from home. I was admiring his strong profile, my hand having paused halfway to the sink as I zoned out. Then I caught myself, blushed furiously, and clattered dishes into the sink.

Laurie looked up at me over his paper and smiled. My heart gave a painful thump inside my chest. What was wrong with me? Even though we were sort of...sex-friends now, it surprised me that I could get so distracted just from looking at him.

"What are you up to today?" he asked.

I cleared my throat—to buy myself a moment to clear my head. "Um, I'm going to Daredevil Park with Taylor and his girlfriend. Don't worry, though, I put a pork roast in the slow cooker, so that should be ready for you to have for lunch, if you want."

He took a deep breath, and the exhale came out as an "oh."

I focused on his face, but his expression was the same as it usually was when he was forced out of bed "at an ungodly hour" because of work.

"I'm sure that'll be fun."

I frowned as he turned his attention back to his paper. I opened my mouth to ask him if anything was wrong, but I was interrupted by the obnoxious chiming of the fancy doorbell. Did it really need to play a full two-minute song?

"That's them. I'll be right back."

Making my way to the foyer, I opened the front door for Taylor, who stepped right in. Karla, on the other hand, was goggling at the size of the house and the intricacy of the architecture, as people often did upon visiting the mansion for the first time.

"Come on in, guys. Follow me to the kitchen. I was going to pack some snacks and stuff for the drive." Daredevil Park was about forty-five minutes away, but traffic would make it an hour.

Karla was dressed for the summer heat in tiny cutoffs, a bikini top with a breezy white cover-up over it. It showed off her petite but curvy figure to perfection. Karla's perpetually tanned and glowing skin was a gift of her Filipina heritage, as was her long, thick hair, a wavy fall of dark brown down her back. She was by far the most beautiful woman I'd ever met in real life, and yet it occurred to me now, for the first time, that I wasn't the slightest bit sexually attracted to her—and probably not just because she was my best friend's girl. I was a bit taken aback by it, to be honest.

Taylor was the perfect foil for his girlfriend, tall and muscular, with his blond-haired, blue-eyed, Captain-fucking-America good looks. He was dressed in board shorts and a black-and-gold Morrell Tigers T-shirt. Daredevil Park had water rides too, so I was wearing swim trunks and a dark blue rash guard.

The two of them followed me into the kitchen, and I felt Taylor's surprise when he saw that Laurie was actually in there, presumably being social with me. He looked over his shoulder when he heard us come in.

"Hi, Mr. Beaudry," Taylor said awkwardly. "You remember my girlfriend, Karla? She came with me to The King's Shield a couple of times."

Laurie nodded. "Of course. It's nice to see you again."

"You too!" Karla said brightly.

"You ready to go?" Taylor asked after I'd stuffed a backpack with towels, snacks, and water bottles.

"Y-yeah…" I took a couple of steps to head out, then stopped in my tracks.

I looked at Laurie, still reading, his back to us. On first glance, he appeared to be engrossed in an article, but I knew him well enough to pick up on the tension in his back, in the way he held himself, in how his fingers gripped the edges of the newspaper. I recalled every word he'd said to me about his childhood, and I realized I was disregarding him the same way everyone else had.

"Laurie, do you own anything besides suits and superhero

pajamas?" Out of the corner of my eye, I saw Taylor's head whip around, but I ignored him. Laurie was so serious, so austere most of the time, and it had only just occurred to me that it was at least in part because he'd had very little fun in his life.

Laurie looked over at me in surprise. "Um… yes?" he said to answer my question.

I stared him down for a few tense moments before I spoke. "Go change."

I expected him to say no or at least to ask why, but he wordlessly set down his paper, stood up, and disappeared down the hall to his suite.

As soon as he was out of range, Taylor whispered, "What are you doing, man?"

"Taking him with us, what do you think?"

"You want to take scary, broody millionaire dude to the amusement park? Won't that be kind of a buzzkill?" he asked, then let out an *oof* when Karla elbowed him in the ribs.

I sighed. I realized that Taylor could possibly be right, but there was also the possibility that Laurie could have a good time. To me, it was worth the risk. "Look, you guys are my friends, and so is he now. You know how he is, Tay. He doesn't have a lot of opportunities to hang out with friends. In fact, I think Thursday night drinks are the *only* times he does."

"Probably because of the whole scary, broody thing," Taylor muttered under his breath.

Karla glared at him. "Don't be such an asshole. It would be rude not to invite him anyway, and Mackenzie wants him to come. If you don't like it, maybe the three of us will go and leave *you* behind."

Knowing he was beaten, Taylor shut his mouth. A couple of minutes later, Laurie reemerged, wearing a pair of well-worn, ripped jeans that were tight enough to be distracting, and a simple black T-shirt with a yellow Batman symbol emblazoned on the chest. I pinched my lips together to keep from laughing, but I couldn't fool him.

"What? You didn't say superhero shirts were out."

"You're right." I cleared my throat, the urge to laugh suddenly gone, as the Batman reference reminded me of the night we talked about his childhood. Then I just wanted to hug the guy, standing there looking ten years younger in his *normal* clothes.

"So?" He spread his arms out as if to say, "Okay, I'm dressed, now what?"

"So, you're coming with us. Let's go."

"Coming with…to the amusement park?" His voice cracked endearingly. "You don't have to do that. You go have fun with your friends. I'll just get some work done."

"Mmm, nope." I grabbed his arm and started pulling him out of the kitchen. He resisted, but not as much as he could have. "No more. You work too damn much. Come have fun with us."

"Fun?" he asked, as if it was a foreign concept. He looked over his shoulder at Taylor and Karla, who were following behind as I dragged him.

"Yeah man, otherwise ol' Mack here will be a third wheel. You wanna be responsible for that?"

"Really, you should come," Karla agreed.

"O-okay…"

It was a pointless discussion because I'd already pulled him through the front door, and we were all heading to Taylor's SUV. Karla climbed into the passenger seat beside Taylor, while Laurie and I buckled into the second-row bench seat. He flicked his gaze to me, gave me a small smile, then settled in to look out the window. I grinned to myself as Taylor pulled out of the driveway and set out for Bayview.

We'd just managed to miss the morning ticket rush. The line

stretched about a quarter mile down the sidewalk as we were buying ours. I was thankful Laurie hadn't insisted on paying for everyone—instead he just bought his own ticket like the rest of us.

Past the ticketing booths was an open courtyard, from which the paths to all the attractions began. There was an elaborate circular fountain in the center. We sat on the concrete lip—Laurie to my right, Karla to my left, and Taylor on the other side of her. Kayla spread the park map out across her knees and we all leaned in to see.

"I want to do the Base-Jumper," said Taylor.

My stomach wobbled just thinking about it. Rollercoasters I could handle—mostly—but the Base-Jumper was a different beast. Riders got strapped into a row of seats that traveled up the length of a straight tower, equivalent to about two stories in height. Then they were dropped into a dead plunge that stopped just a few feet from the ground. Like...why was that even fun?

"Waterpark?" I suggested hopefully.

"I want to ride the Widowmaker," Karla said. It was a rollercoaster...the biggest one in the park—possibly in the state.

Our three pairs of eyes trained on Laurie. He jolted like he was surprised we were consulting him. Then he just shrugged. "I have no idea. Never done this before."

I rubbed at the sudden pain in my chest as I looked back over the map. "How about we compromise by making a pass through Daredevil Alley from this direction, on our way to the waterpark? You guys can get your thrill-seeking fix and I can cool the hell down because it's fucking hot out here. After that, we'll probably be ready to hit the food court."

"Sounds good," Taylor said, standing and pulling Karla up beside him.

The walkways were surprisingly narrow, so Laurie and I followed behind Karla and Taylor, who seemed to be off in their own little world. I stole surreptitious glances at Laurie as we strolled.

"You've really never been to an amusement park before?" I couldn't resist asking.

His returning look was bland. "You can name pretty much any normal childhood experience, and chances are I haven't done it."

I was rendered speechless, overcome with the need to hug him, hold his hand, *something,* but being unable to. I wasn't used to feeling this conflicted, to caring this much. "Well, then we're going to stuff as many of those experiences as we can into today."

"I told you I didn't want pity," he said, just loud enough for only me to hear.

I gave him my best side-eye. "This isn't pity, it's friendship. So suck it up, buttercup. Time to have some fun, even if it kills us."

He blinked at me, wide-eyed, for several seconds before offering a small smile. It felt like a gift.

The Widowmaker was a candy-apple red monstrosity with a seemingly endless number of loops, corkscrews, and death-drops. It was one of those deals where the riders are dangling from harnessed seats instead of sitting down inside a car. I remember living for those kinds of rides when I was a kid, but the older I got, the more I preferred to have my feet firmly planted on solid ground. *There's surely a metaphor in there somewhere,* I thought, as we took our spot in the zigzagging queue.

The line became stairs, climbing a sort of permanent scaffolding to the loading station, where it split into several lanes for boarding. The cars had four seats per row, so the four of us all got in the same lane. The coaster's train held a lot of people, so the line moved quickly. Before I knew it, I was trailing behind Taylor, Karla, and Laurie respectively. With my stomach somewhere in the vicinity of my throat, I forced myself to sit still

J.K. HOGAN

while an attendant lowered the heavy shoulder harness over me and locked it in place.

There were little mounds of plastic between the seats that seemed to serve as armrests for the apparatus. I set my elbows on them and clenched my fists. I tried to focus on the pain of my nails digging into my palms instead of my rising nerves. The train jerked and shuddered as it left the dock and started rattling up the first hill. I clamped my jaw and squeezed my fist even tighter.

A warm hand covered my own, blocked from view of the others by the harnesses.

"You okay?" Laurie said in a quiet voice. "You're a little...tense."

"I'm not exactly a huge fan of heights. It was okay when I was little, but now I weigh more, so more g-force...or something."

Laurie gave a breathless chuckle. "Then why did you want to come to an amusement park?"

"There's other stuff to do! I could live at the water park. And I love the arcade games and food," I said rather defensively. "And besides...Taylor and Karla love rollercoasters."

He squeezed my hand, and I gulped down the sudden lump in my throat.

"You're always trying to keep everyone else happy, huh?"

"I guess."

"One of these days I'm going to teach you how to be a little bit selfish."

While I was trying to think of something to say to that, the coaster reached the pinnacle of the first hill. I could just barely see around the thick harness to Laurie's smiling face. I knew how I probably looked, white-faced and bug-eyed, because there was definitely pity in his eyes. I closed mine and took a death-grip on his hand as the ride plunged back toward the ground at impossible speeds.

I kept my eyes closed and my knuckles whitened throughout half the ride, just concentrating on not puking. I finally opened them when I heard a whoop from my left. Laurie was grinning like an idiot, kicking his legs like a three-year-old, and him having fun was probably the most beautiful thing I'd ever seen in my life. It helped to loosen the knots in my muscles and dial back the vertigo I was experiencing. I watched Laurie through the last corkscrew-loop combo, enjoying seeing him let loose, but I was still totally relieved when the ride pulled back into the dock station.

Once the employees released us, we filed out to the other side of the platform. I wobbled on shaky legs, so Laurie slid his arm around my shoulders to keep me upright. Taylor flicked a glance between the two of us and I held my breath, waiting for him to ask what the deal was, but Laurie beat him to the punch.

"Why didn't you tell me this guy was such a lightweight at rides? He can barely stand."

I gave a weak laugh, perfectly willing to be made fun of if it got the attention off of me. It seemed to work for the moment, mainly because Taylor noticed the Base-Jumper, and was dragging Karla towards it. He knew I wouldn't ride it, so he tossed a look at Laurie over his shoulder.

"This one's too much gravity for Mack. You coming?"

"I'll just keep Mackenzie company, if that's okay."

Taylor shrugged and kept walking backwards. "Suit yourself!" He waved as they joined the line.

"You could ride it if you want. I'll just go play some games over there," I said, pointing to the little cluster of carnival games that were likely rigged.

"Are you kidding?" He tipped his head back to gaze up to the top of the Base-Jumper. "That thing looks awful. Pick out a game. I can beat you at anything."

"Asshole," I said, secretly pleased that he didn't ditch me for the horrifying ride. "How about this one?" I stopped in front of a stand that had a line of water guns. Patrons were supposed to spray at a target to make little boats race from one end to the other.

"I'm an excellent water gun marksman," Laurie said, his eyes twinkling. "You probably shouldn't take me on."

"Fine, beat all of those people then," I said, pointing at the big group of mixed ages that were approaching the booth.

"Huh? Just me?" His confused face was adorable.

"Yeah. Win me a stuffed animal, hot stuff. Isn't that what you're supposed to do for your date?"

He froze for a moment before blushing deeply. I gave myself a mental high five because surprising Laurie was turning out to be quite addictive. He seemed to accept my challenge, as he paid the employee and sat down on the stool at his chosen water gun. There were a couple of other adults, but he was mostly competing against several kids seemingly between the ages of about seven and fifteen.

A buzzer went off and the guns started to spray. I suppressed the urge to snicker at the serious expression he wore, jaw clenched, one eye closed as he stared at the target with the other. It paid off, though, because his boat reached the finish line at least a full two seconds before any of the others. He was grinning from ear to ear as he picked out a stuffed animal for me—a Pikachu about the size of a Thanksgiving turkey. I couldn't help but return his smile.

We made our way back over to the Base-Jumper just as Taylor and Karla were exiting the fenced-in area that surrounded it, both looking slightly green.

"Jesus Christ, it's hot out here," Taylor complained.

"You know what I have to say to that," I said.

"Waterpark!" said my three friends in unison.

In unspoken agreement, we headed down the path to the cool refreshment of the water rides. We walked in silence for about a minute before Taylor destroyed the peacefulness.

"What's with the Pikachu, man?"

The waterpark was a completely separate, fenced-in branch of the park that had its own locker rooms, bathrooms, concessions, rides, and even a few games. A group could come spend the whole day in it without having to go into the rest of the park for anything. We rented a couple of lockers to throw in our towels, shoes, phones, keys, and Pikachu. Laurie hadn't brought a bathing suit, so he ran over to the gift shop to buy some trunks while we were loading up the lockers. Taylor, Karla, and I found seats at an umbrella-covered table that overlooked the wave pool and sat back to wait for him.

"So the job's going well?" Taylor asked.

I'd been keeping him updated regularly, so I assumed he was just making conversation. It didn't matter because I loved talking about work. "It's going great. The kids love the experiments I come up with, and they're all so bright and eager. I like getting them before they lose that love of school."

"Yeah, I wonder when the whole I-don't-wanna-go-to-school, five-more-minutes phase starts," Karla said with a smile. She was a pediatric nurse, so she dealt with small children almost as much as I did.

"I think it's probably somewhere around when the homework starts."

"Hey, so any luck finding a place?" Taylor asked.

I blinked at him, confused. "Huh?"

"Well, you're just staying with Beaudry until you can afford something decent, right? So have you found anything?"

The question completely took me by surprise—even though it probably shouldn't have—and I struggled to come up with anything to say. I'd gotten so used to being with Laurie, settling into our odd little routine, that I hadn't given much thought to looking for apartments. I'd been operating under the idea that I'd work over the summer to build up some savings so that I could move somewhere that wasn't a hovel.

Still, the idea of leaving Laurie's caused this slick, quivery feeling in the bottom of my gut, like my body was rebelling. Of course I wasn't going to share that with Taylor, so I gave him the best canned answer I could come up with, which was pretty close to the truth. "Nothing so far. I'm hoping to save up a little so I can get something a little better than I had before."

Taylor considered me for a moment, then nodded. "So what do you guys want to do first?"

His voice faded into the background as Laurie appeared on the path, walking towards us. I didn't know if maybe he couldn't find a suit in his size or he just couldn't get pants to stay on his narrow hips, but the dark gray swim trunks with turquoise cabling rode so low that they were about a millimeter from being R-rated. His chest was bare, his rangy, corded muscle on display, already finely slicked with sweat from the humidity. I finally tore my eyes away from his body to meet his gaze, and there was unabashed heat there. He'd caught me checking him out, and he liked it.

A throat cleared beside me, interrupting my thoughts, and I jolted. Laurie smirked. I whipped my head around to glare at Taylor, who was eyeing me suspiciously. "You gonna answer me or what?" he said.

"Um... What did you say?"

"I *said*, what do you guys want to do first? I vote for the Typhoon Plunge."

Of course he did. I glanced over my shoulder at the horrific ride. I was okay with the swirling pipe slides, but the Typhoon Plunge was just an open slide, a death-drop from a dizzying height, with nothing but your skin and the water. I was so not into it. I could feel the color drain from my face just imagining the vertigo of being on top of that platform as it swayed slightly in the wind.

Laurie didn't miss a beat. "You know, guys, last night was pretty rough, so I think I want to do something relaxing. Like maybe the lazy river or a couple of laps in the pool. If Mackenzie doesn't mind staying with me, you two should go on ahead."

I was almost dizzied by the wave of gratitude that swept through me. I smiled at him. "I don't mind. You don't wanna go in the wave pool, but the lazy river sounds great right about now."

"Yeah, seriously, stay out of the wave pool," Karla agreed, and Taylor nodded.

"Why?" Laurie asked.

"Kids pee in it," the three of us said in unison.

"Okay, we're gonna hit the Typhoon. Let's meet back over here in about an hour?"

"Sounds good." I waved them off and started walking in the opposite direction. Laurie had fallen into step beside me, a silent wall of support. I was a bit self-conscious of my slender frame walking bare-chested next to Laurie, who might as well have been chiseled from granite.

The quickest way to the lazy river was to take a detour through the kid's area—it was labeled as such for the kid-safe attractions like fountains and splashpads and things to climb on, but a lot of adults went in there too because it was refreshing to get sprayed with water from every direction on a hot day. As we stepped onto the colored pavers that delineated the perimeter of the section, I cast Laurie a sidelong glance and muttered, "Thanks."

"You're welcome." He gave me a small smile, then looked over his shoulder at the Typhoon. "That thing didn't look appealing at all, to be honest. I just used you as an excuse. Plus, we get some more alone time. Bonus!"

I shook my head, then ducked a stray stream from one of the stationary water cannons. It struck Laurie in the chest. He glared at the kid responsible, who gasped and ran away to a chorus of his parents screaming, "Don't run," and I had to bite my lip to keep from cracking up. I wasn't fooling Laurie. He scowled at me and pushed me under a waterfall that was supposed to look like it was coming out of SpongeBob's mouth.

The water was *cold*, and I lunged out of it, coughing and sputtering—and ran smack into Laurie's chest. He steadied me with hands on my biceps, then lingered longer than he should have. I planted my hand on his chest, intending to make him back off, but then I had a better idea. I walked forward, pushing with my palm so that he had to back up. When I had him where I wanted him, I stepped back and faced him.

He gave me a smirk. "Be careful, Mackenzie, this is a family area."

What I knew but he didn't was that there was a big bucket above his head, about nine feet off the ground, that was slowly filling with water. It was hinged, so once it passed the tipping point, all the water would pour out.

I just grinned at his usual cockiness. "Oh yeah? You think I'm hot for your bod? Right here in the amusement park?"

I expected him to laugh, but instead his gaze went all dark and hot, which had me shifting my stance at the uncomfortable attention.

"I don't know what you think, but I know I like what *I* see. You want to know what else I think?"

I swallowed hard because my throat was suddenly dry. "What?" I croaked.

"I think we need to find somewhere private and—"

Splash! Saved by the gallons of water being dumped on Laurie's head. He gasped and stiffened, because no doubt that water was as cold as the waterfall had been, and he *had* been getting all hot and bothered.

"You little…," he growled.

"Shit!" I yelped in faux alarm as he reached for me and

missed. Cackling, I took off running through the obstacles. Laurie chased behind me, probably only pretending he couldn't catch me, until a lifeguard from the wave pool whistled at us. We were both panting and giggling by the time we reached the lazy river.

When I looked at Laurie with his eyes crinkling and his cheeks flushed from running, it sent my heart racing and made me feel things I knew I shouldn't be feeling. He was my landlord—my friend, if I was feeling indulgent—and we were both men. I knew it was okay for people to be g— For people to be gay, it just wasn't on my radar in regards to myself. But as I noticed the water beading on Laurie's bare skin, the sun turning the droplets into tiny sparkles, I thought to myself that maybe it should be.

"What?" Laurie asked, his brow furrowing.

I gave myself a mental shake to bring me back to reality. "S-sorry, what?"

"You're looking at me funny. Something wrong?"

Still feeling rather dazed, I shook my head. "No, everything's fine. Let's go."

The lazy river was cool and refreshing, a nice rest after the stress of the Widowmaker. But it was also boring. By the time we floated into the little eddy built in for people to disembark and return their inner tubes, Laurie and I were ready for something a little more exciting.

"How about that tube slide?" Laurie asked, pointing out a swirl of aquamarine fiberglass. "The platform isn't that high, and it's not too loopy.

I grinned at how careful he was being about my weird vertigo problem. "That looks fun."

Once we were standing on the platform, it was a *little* higher than I'd originally thought, but it wasn't so bad with Laurie's warmth leaching into me from where he stood behind me—too close, but we were standing in line, so I let it go.

On the Sea Serpent—that was what they called it—riders went down in two-person inflatable rafts. This meant that when it was our turn, Laurie and I had to smoosh into a little raft together. We could've gone separately, of course, but neither of us mentioned the idea out loud. Since Laurie was the larger of the two of us, he had to sit in the back to anchor the boat. Which put me sitting in the front, bracketed on either side by Laurie's long legs.

Laurie was holding the boat in place as the water rushed by us, until the attendant gave us the go ahead to slide. I had been careful to leave appropriate space between us, but as soon as Laurie let go and we were inside the tube, he wrapped his arm around my waist and yanked me back flush against him.

The Sea Serpent wasn't quite as slow as the lazy river, but the pitch was shallow, so it was a laid-back, meandering sort of ride, with the exception of a few loops where it picked up speed. That meant there was plenty of time to feel his hard body pressing against mine and to will myself not to respond. Plenty of time to feel his arms wrapped around me instead of grasping the handles on the sides of the raft, his thumb lazily brushing over my nipple. Plenty of time to feel his breath fanning my ear. And then it was over, and we were splashing into the pool at the bottom, our boat capsizing and tossing us headfirst into the water.

Laurie popped up, laughing, water sluicing off of him as he shook his hair like a dog. I didn't dare look lower. As it was, I had to clasp my hands in front of my lap as I sloshed out of the pool. I also didn't look him in the eyes, because I didn't want to see the stupid smirk he probably had on his face if he'd noticed my discomfort.

We rode the Sea Serpent three more times. On the last run, when our raft unceremoniously dumped us, I tumbled into the water and my head bounced against the concrete bottom of the pool. I knew I wasn't seriously hurt, but I was dazed from the blow, and having gone in headfirst, I'd lost my bearings. I knew

I had to swim hard to the surface, but I didn't know which direction to go, so I ended up just flailing around. It took a moment to orient myself in the water and find which way was up, while realizing that the burning in my chest meant I needed to breathe *soon*.

I was in the process of clawing my way to the surface when hands gripped me under my arms and dragged me out of the water. I wobbled a little after gaining my footing, and found myself staring into Laurie's face. He'd gone very pale. His eyes were wide, and he was breathing like he'd just run a marathon, open-mouthed, gasping breaths. His fingers dug into my biceps like he was afraid I'd disappear if he didn't hold on tight.

"What. Happened?" he croaked.

"Sorry, I…" The way he was looking at me, all worried and possessive, was sending shivers skittering over my skin. "I just landed wrong, got disoriented, bumped my head a little. I'm fine, it's nothing—*ow!*" He'd gingerly prodded my aching temple, making me wince.

If possible, he paled even more and let out a soft curse. "Jesus, I'm going to have to roll you up in bubble wrap. How'd you even survive to twenty-three?"

"Hey! I'm not that b—"

"Come on, let's go," he interrupted, grabbing me by the wrist and pulling me out of the pool.

I tripped up the concrete steps, basically proving his point. He turned narrowed eyes on me, then tugged me harder. I'd never get the chance to find out where he intended to take me because we crossed paths with Karla and Taylor halfway between the lazy river and the wave pool. Sneaking a glance at Laurie, I could tell he was annoyed by the interruption.

"Did you guys have fun typhooning?" I asked.

"It was awesome!" Karla said. "We went down six times."

"Did you guys have fun being *boring?*" Taylor chimed in with a smile to let us know he was kidding.

"It was sooo relaxing, right Laurie?" I elbowed him in the ribs because he was looking decidedly *not* relaxed. When he didn't agree, I scowled at him.

"What? You almost cracked your skull open."

Taylor snorted out a laugh. "Yeah, that sounds about right. Welcome to life with Mackenzie."

Laurie made a choking sound in the back of his throat, but I didn't think anyone heard but me. I took a swipe at Taylor in retaliation, which he easily sidestepped.

"Fuck, it's hot," Taylor said, fanning his torso with his T-shirt. "I'm already almost dry after the Plunge."

"You know what we could do?" Karla raised a brow at us. "Daredevil Falls."

"My girl is brilliant. Let's go, guys!"

Too tense to argue, Laurie and I followed Taylor by rote.

Daredevil Falls was supposedly the attraction that would leave its riders the wettest. It wasn't scary; it was just a big, flat-bottomed boat full of people that was pulled up a medium-sized hill via conveyor belt, released into a deep, artificial river, where it made one turn and splashed back down the hill. In fact, it was pretty boring. The only draw was the gigantic wave that was kicked up from the boat's descent down the falls. It sprayed out in all directions, leaving the riders and anyone near the landing zone totally drenched.

Situated at the eastern edge of the waterpark, between the food court and the entrance to the children's park, Daredevil Falls was where *everyone* went when it was too hot to breathe. And everyone had. The line filled up the canopied, fenced waiting area, and spilled out around the corner and down the blacktop path, and it wasn't moving fast since the ride only had two boats. If we waited in that, the sun would probably be down by the time we actually got to ride.

Taylor, who'd gotten to the end of the line first, turned back toward us, disappointment—and possibly a little heat stroke—

evident on his face. With a sigh, I wiped sweat off my face with the edge of my shirt. When I looked over at Laurie, he quickly averted his eyes.

"Why don't we just go to the lookout?" I asked. The lookout was what frequent visitors called the observation deck that spanned the artificial river right over the impact zone. Even though the railing was like eight feet tall to prevent people from falling in, anyone standing on the deck when a boat came down got even more soaked than if they'd been on the ride. Since it wasn't an official attraction, people only knew about it from word-of-mouth, so it wasn't usually too crowded.

Taylor pointed at me. "Awesome idea." He grabbed Karla's hand and pulled her down the path. "Let's go, losers, keep up!" he tossed back over his shoulder.

"Tell me again why you hang out with that guy," Laurie asked in a low growl.

I scrunched my nose, trying to think of a time Taylor hadn't been in my life. I'd known Taylor since kindergarten, for better or worse, and we'd always been friends. "Eh, he acts kind of dumb sometimes, but he's a good friend."

Laurie shrugged and followed me up the ramp to the lookout. The C-shaped deck had one long side that faced the falls and two short sides that curled around a couple of locked rooms—probably for storage. The short sides were like little annexes, halfway private, only receiving a fraction of the spray. Most of the people hoping to get wet jostled for prime position in the splash zone at the front. The four of us took up residence right up front in the middle. Taylor and Karla tracked the position of the next boat, while Laurie was sending me confused glances.

"What are we doing?" he asked.

"Just wait," I whispered, pointing at the boat that was on the verge of plunging down the hill.

"Wait for *what?* Why are we just standing here?"

I suppressed a chuckle. "Oh my god, you are the most

impatient person I know! Wait for…that," I said, as the boat hit the deep water at the bottom and the huge wave started to form.

The wave hit the deck with what would've been brutal force if it hadn't been tempered by the thick wooden railing. But instead of hitting us hard, it just drenched us from head to toe, the coldness of the water knocking the wind out of us. I dissolved into laughter as Laurie gasped at the cold, then sputtered as water ran into his eyes and mouth.

"Asshole," he laughed, hooking his arm around my neck and giving me a vicious noogie. It probably should've seemed like a brotherly move, but I was hyperaware of the sensation of his hands on me. My breath caught, I shivered slightly, and Laurie gently shoved me away, his eyes going a little wild.

When I glanced back at Taylor and Karla, they were watching us with interest. Taylor opened his mouth to speak, but then we were blindsided by the wave from the second boat. After being drenched again, we were all laughing hysterically, all awkward, tension-filled moments forgotten.

Then Karla tugged Taylor toward one of the side annexes— one of the places couples sometimes went to find a little privacy—and he allowed himself to be led away, with a little eyebrow wiggle at me. I rolled my eyes and turned to Laurie, expecting to find him laughing. Instead, he stared at me, eyes wide and hot. Before I knew it, he'd grabbed my arm and dragged me toward the other side.

As soon as we rounded the corner, I stopped and glared at him. "What the hell are you—?"

I found myself slammed against the wall, and my words were cut off by Laurie crushing his lips to mine. There was desperation in the way he gripped my shirt with his fists, the way he wedged his thigh between my legs, the way he swept his tongue inside my mouth like he needed my taste more than air. My hands curled around his biceps, clenching convulsively. My thoughts splintered into errant fragments, floating by on silent wings, just outside my grasp.

As I parted my lips wider and angled my head, my tongue joined his in an erotic dance that seemed out of place in a semi-private alcove at a very public amusement park. That thought slammed into me, scattering all of the others like fireflies from the grass. Remembering where we were with a sudden, dizzying clarity, I used my grip on his arms to gently push him back.

He allowed me to break the kiss, but he didn't move away, didn't disconnect our bodies. Instead, he buried his head in the crook of my neck and huffed out a breath. When I wrapped my arms around his waist, I could feel him trembling. I pet his flank like one might a skittish colt. "Hey, hey, what's wrong?"

He lifted his head with a shudder, then pressed his forehead against mine. "You scared me, okay?" The words seemed almost forced out against his will.

I cocked my head, raised a questioning brow.

"Look, I get that you don't feel the same, but... I-I love you, and for a second there, I thought you'd drowned. Brought back bad memories," he mumbled.

My heart stuttered in my chest. My fingers twisted in the material of his shirt, and I pulled him closer. "I'm sorry," I whispered.

He nuzzled his nose behind my ear. "Being so close to you all day but not being able to show my feelings... A-and then that happened... I just need to touch you. Just for a minute."

And then he was kissing me again, as my pulse thundered too loud in my ears. Hands at the small of my back, he pushed up my shirt to get to skin. His leg pressed closer to me, and I unconsciously rubbed against it. He made a broken sound into my mouth, and suddenly he was unfastening my board shorts. I gasped as his big, warm hand wrapped around my length and started stroking. I broke the kiss, tipped my head back against the wooden wall to catch my breath.

"We're in public," I said in a harsh whisper.

"No one can see us," he murmured against my neck. Then he licked a trail up the line of my pulse and sucked just behind my ear, stroking me the whole time. My knees buckled but his thigh between my legs held me up. I didn't know if he'd figured it out yet—hell, I only had recently—but my neck was apparently a weak spot.

"I'll be quick. You've been just out of my reach all day, and I can't stand it anymore. I'll be quick."

It was wrong. It was illicit. It was exciting. I didn't stop him. Not when he freed himself from his own trunks. Not when he wrapped his hand around both of our shafts and stroked us together. After that, I was lost to the sensation of silky skin, searing heat, and steely arousal. "Laurie!" I choked out. My chest was tight, and my head felt like it would explode from the frenetic pounding of my pulse.

"Shh," he warned with a chuckle in his voice. He licked my neck again and whispered in my ear. "Later I'll take you home and fuck you all night. Then you can really let me hear your voice."

He sucked on my neck hard as he twisted his hand over the tips of our cocks, and I lost it. I bit my lip to keep from crying out as I came all over his hand. After a couple of slick strokes, he did the same, groaning quietly against my skin. He gave me a quick kiss before disentangling us. There was water everywhere, so it was easy for him to wash his hands off. He lovingly tucked me back into my shorts, righted himself, then brushed my hair out of my eyes.

"Sorry," he said with a rueful smile. "You were so close, but so far away. I missed you."

It should've freaked me out, his behavior should've felt clingy, but all it did was make me feel warm all over. I smiled at him, making a big show of looking around the little alcove. "Sorry for what? I have no idea what you're talking about."

I winked at him as I backed out of the space. When I turned

around, Karla and Taylor were back at the front of the lookout waiting for us. They didn't look suspicious…exactly, but their eyes were wide as they watched me approach. I focused all my energy on trying to control my body's desire to blush. "Hey guys, we were just checking out the view of the food court, deciding what to eat. Hungry?"

Things were a little awkward as we went through the motions of ordering food and eating, then making our way back toward the main gates. I knew they couldn't possibly have seen anything untoward, but it was clear that Taylor had something on his mind, and Karla was confused and worried about it as well.

Once we reached the courtyard at the main gate, the one with the big fountain, Laurie wanted to go buy something from the gift shop—something to add to his weird collection, I guessed—and Karla excused herself to go to the restroom. This left Taylor and me alone, sitting on the fountain wall, trying to ignore the weird, unspoken tension between us. After a few beats of awkward silence, Taylor spun around to face me, so quickly that I jumped.

"You okay?" I asked.

"You know you can tell me anything, right? I mean, we're best friends, so…"

"Um…yes?" My hands clenched Pikachu's soft yellow fur. *What does he know?*

"So?" He drew out the word, like I was supposed to fill in the blank.

I didn't understand what he was fishing for. "So, what?"

His expression dissolved into something like disappointment, then he narrowed his eyes at me, looking angry and…a little hurt. He hauled himself up off the fountain and gave a jerky shrug. "Welp, I tried. If there's nothing you want to talk about, I'm going to go find Karla. I'll see you guys at the car." He started to walk away.

Huh? "What?"

He froze in his tracks and looked over his shoulder. "By the way, you have something on your neck."

I touched a hand to the spot where I knew it would be, as he turned on his heel and stalked away.

FOURTEEN

There was barely anything there. I checked my neck in the vanity mirror of the Lotus for the fifteenth time as Laurie drove me to work the next day. I saw what Taylor had been talking about, but it was so faint, it could've been a bruise, a smudge— or a hickey—but it had obviously set Taylor off somehow. With a sigh, I slumped back in my seat, unable to even enjoy the supple leather.

"Stop obsessing," Laurie said without taking his eyes off the road.

"I can't help it! He thinks he knows something, and he's pissed off because I haven't told him whatever it is that he thinks he knows."

"That was barely coherent. Besides, he's not wrong. You are keeping a secret from him."

"There's nothing to tell!"

He glared at me sideways for a brief, poignant moment, before looking back at the road.

"Okay, not *nothing*, but it's not like I intended for it to be some big secret. I haven't figured anything out myself yet, so how can I go around telling people?" I mused as he pulled into a parking space at the school.

He leaned over and captured my lips in a kiss that, however brief, left my heart pounding. "It's okay. I understand that you're still figuring things out. You don't have to tell Taylor anything on my account. I don't really give a damn what he knows or doesn't know, I just don't want to see you fighting with your best friend."

I sighed again, giving him a grateful smile. "Thanks. I guess I'm going to have to say *something* to him, I've just got to figure out what."

"You will. In the meantime, have a good day at work." He brushed a stray lock of hair off my forehead. "I love you."

My breath caught, and my throat closed around the words I almost said. It couldn't be that...not yet...not a man... It was just my instinctive reaction to his words. *Yeah...that's it.* I almost convinced myself. I drummed up a bright smile for him and let myself out of the car. "Thanks for the ride," I said, tapping the hood before crossing the parking lot.

I turned and waved as he drove off. When I headed toward the front door again, I came face to face with Angela Fiori, who was on her way out to direct traffic for the parents who'd be showing up soon. Her eyes flicked to the flashy car disappearing into traffic, then back to me. I froze. What was she thinking? First Taylor and now her. It seemed like I was the object of everyone's scrutiny lately.

"Um, he's my—"

She held up a hand, cutting me off. "I don't need to know. Legally, I can't ask you, and I want to be perfectly clear that you do not have to explain."

"But it's just—"

That time she stopped me with a censuring look. "As long as

it doesn't interfere with your work, your personal life is none of my business." She smiled, probably to take the edge off of the words.

My shoulders, which had found their way up around my ears, drooped. I went inside with my figurative tail tucked between my legs, asking myself why I cared so much what other people thought anyway.

The early morning hours passed in a blur; the school was quiet, with a third of the kids out with some bug that had been going around. My science corner project for the day was teaching the kids how to make pinecone bird feeders. They all had a blast slathering the cones with peanut butter and rolling them around in birdseed to coat the sides. We tied fuzzy red yarn around them and hung them up in the small dogwood tree outside the classroom window so the kids would be able to see what kinds of birds they attracted.

As Alison and I finished cleaning up and the kids dispersed for free play, I noticed Zane sitting alone in the corner at one of the kid-size tables. I walked over and crouched down in front of him. "Hey, buddy, what's going on?"

He shrugged in that eloquent way tiny children had.

"Are you okay? You're not feeling sick, are you?"

"Not sick," he repeated.

"Are you sad?" I asked, taking a guess.

He took a deep breath and nodded.

I knelt down even further so I could put myself eye to eye with him. "Did something happen to make you sad?"

Another nod.

"Can you tell me about it?"

"Ethan and Sam were laughing at me. They said it's weird that I have two mommies."

My hands reflexively balled into fists, so I shoved them underneath the table. "There are all kinds of families in the world, Zane. Your family may be different from theirs, but different doesn't mean weird, okay?"

He looked at me with huge, limpid eyes and nodded again, but I wasn't sure if my words really sank in. "There's nothing weird about two mommies, Zane. I'll make sure the boys don't pick on you again."

He finally gave me a tiny, lopsided smile. "Can I go play now?" he asked in his husky, little-kid voice.

I chuckled. "Sure, kiddo, go for it."

After the kids had all been picked up, I told Alison about the incident.

"I'll email those kids parents so they'll be aware of what's going on."

"It seems like there should be more we can do, though," I said. "Can't we organize some kind of sensitivity lesson or something? Like maybe find a couple of books about diversity geared toward this age group."

"That's not a bad idea. I need to run it by Angela first, since there's always the possibility of parents resisting."

"Yeah, of course. Just... Just don't tell her it was my idea, okay?"

Alison gave me a suspicious look. "Really? Why?"

I shrugged, then smiled as I lied through my teeth. "In case she hates the idea. She'll blame you," I said with a wink and a grin. She threw a balled-up piece of paper at me as I walked out the door laughing.

Taylor and I stared at each other across a tiny table at Java Mike's, the coffee shop we used to go to between classes. I'd never experienced a more awkward silence in my life, but I wasn't about to ask him what he thought he knew. If he had something to say, he could damn well say it.

As I waited, I allowed myself to really look at him. I'd been so wrapped up in my own drama lately that I'd failed to notice the subtle changes in Taylor. His shoulders were slumped. He had dark circles around his eyes, a scraggly two-day-old beard, and lines of strain bracketing his mouth. He looked exhausted.

"Hey," I said to get his attention. When his gaze seemed slow to focus on my face, I gave him a concerned look. "Are you okay?"

His eyes widened as if he was surprised anyone had noticed. "Yes. No? Ugh…not really. I've got a lot going on, and things are starting to fall apart."

Taylor was supposed to start med school in the fall, but since school was out for the summer, I wasn't sure what he would be so stressed about. "Want to tell me?"

"You first," he said, raising a brow.

My hands clenched around my mug of coffee. "What do you want to know?" God, I was trash. I knew exactly what he was getting at, but I wasn't going to give up anything easily. It was too important. It was my life.

"This mystery person you've been hooking up with…"

It was not lost on me that he said "person" instead of "girl" like he had in the past.

"I told you, it's noth—"

"Let me rephrase because I know you're going to try talking your way around it. Mackenzie, are you gay?"

I flinched and darted my gaze around to see if anyone had heard him. "Jesus," I hissed. Then I seriously considered flinging my hot coffee in his face, when I saw Taylor's shoulders shaking with repressed laughter. "God, don't just say shit like that out of nowhere."

"Really? Out of nowhere? Maybe you need me to be even more direct. Are you fucking Laurent Beaudry?"

I'd just taken a sip of coffee, which had been a mistake because I gasped when he said that, and inhaled the scalding liquid into my lungs—what was with people always surprising me while I was drinking something? After my violent coughing fit had subsided, I glared at Taylor, who was absolutely unrepentant. Instead, he was staring me down, not intending to let me get out of answering his question.

I felt the hot blush creeping up the back of my neck and across my cheeks. I did not want to be having this conversation. I wouldn't be able to take it if my best friend looked at me like I was a freak.

"Taylor..."

"Look, I'm not judging you, okay? I hooked up with a guy or two in undergrad, so it's not like I'm gonna go all homophobic on you."

"What, *what?*" That was news to me. And he said it with such nonchalance, as if that was something everyone did once or twice in college.

"Aw, pumpkin, did I blow your mind?" He shrugged. "What can I say? I'm an equal opportunity horndog. I just happened to *date* mostly girls, but I'll hook up with anyone I find attractive."

"How am I just hearing about this now? I thought we told each other everything."

"Do we?"

Touché. "All right, fine. Laurie and I have...hooked up a couple of times, and I'm really conflicted about it. He seems to think he has feelings for me and I—well I don't know anything. You asked if I'm gay, and the truth is that I have no idea. You know I didn't really date while I was focused on school, and to be honest, I didn't miss it that much. Laurie is really the first *person* I've made any kind of connection with but...I'm not willing to label myself as 'gay' because of that. To be honest, the thought of that scares the hell out of me."

Taylor nodded as if that all had made perfect sense. I was glad somebody understood because I sure as hell didn't.

"It's fine, Mackenzie. You don't have to make any decisions or define anything or label yourself. I just don't want you to keep secrets from me."

"I'm sorry. I didn't intend for it to be a secret. It just happened, and I'm still trying to sort it out in my head."

"I forgive you," he said, giving me an irritating, brotherly pat on the head. "Do you like him?"

Did I? "Yes," I answered before I could stop myself.

"Just be careful, okay? That guy, he's... I don't know, he's just a big question mark. And an irritable one at that. I just don't want you to get hurt."

Suddenly I didn't want to talk about Laurie anymore. I didn't want to share the connection we had with someone who didn't *really* know him. I understood why people on the outside thought Laurie was eccentric, maybe even cold like Henry had said, but that wasn't the truth. However, for some reason, I wanted that truth to stay between me and Laurie.

"Duly noted. I'll be careful. Now what's going on with you? Spill it. You don't look well."

"Aw, you do know how to make a girl blush, don't you?"

"Shut up, you know what I mean. You look worn out. Stressed. What's up?"

"I'm kind of fighting with my moms right now."

That came as a surprise. Taylor, his moms, and his dad had the best parent-child relationship of any family I knew. "What about?"

"I... I decided I don't want to go to med school. They're really pissed about it." He tunneled a jerky hand through his short blond hair. "I don't want to be a doctor."

I took a deep breath, not wanting to say the wrong thing. That was the first I was hearing about Taylor wanting to change his future plans. I wondered how long he'd been stewing about it. "Okay. Setting your moms aside for the moment, what *do* you want to do?"

"Being a doctor was great, in theory, until I started thinking about spending my twenties in school, then spending half my life either moving up in the ranks at a hospital or building a practice, establishing a patient base, and it just seemed so…never ending. Like when would I ever just get to be secure in my job, instead of studying or working like a dog? I want to have a life, maybe even a family someday. I know there are doctors that are able to do that, but there are a hell of a lot more who aren't."

"Those sound like…reasonable concerns."

Taylor huffed out a laugh. "But I guess the main thing is, to put yourself through that kind of stress for the foreseeable future, you really have to be all in, you know? And I'm just…not. My heart's not in it, man."

"So where's your heart?" I asked.

"I don't have that all figured out yet. I know I still want to help people, just with less of a learning curve. Maybe I could be a paramedic or an ER nurse. I could do any of those with my bio degree. I could be a lab tech at the CDC, for chrissake. I just don't know." He gave a weak laugh. "Hell, maybe I'll be a teacher like you. But until I get it all figured out, I guess I'm going to keep working at Mindstream."

I nodded. I had a feeling Taylor didn't really need opinions— something told me he'd had plenty of those from his doctor mom and his lawyer mom—he just needed support. "What about your living situation? Are they going to let you keep living in their basement if you don't go to med school?"

He shook his head. "They won't kick me out or anything, they'd never do that. But I think if I keep living with them, we'll all start to resent the hell out of each other."

"What are you going to do then? Move in with Karla?"

A flash of hurt transformed his features before he smoothed out his expression. "She doesn't want to live together. She's 'not ready,'" he said, complete with air quotes. "But that's actually the other reason I wanted to meet with you. I might have the solution to both of our problems."

Huh? Problems? What problems? "What do you mean?"

"My dad just moved into a new house, and it has a detached garage with a small apartment above it. He said he'll rent it to us for dirt cheap if we want."

"Us?" It took me a moment to realize that everyone in my life still assumed I was only staying with Laurie until I found a place. And when had I decided that wasn't the case?

"Yeah, us. You and me. You're looking for a place, right? It would be cool to live together. What d'ya think?"

"I...um... W-well... Can I think about it?"

He narrowed his eyes at me. "What's to think about? Unless this 'nothing' with Laurie is actually something, and you're 'living with him' instead of crashing."

Taylor had a way of cutting to the heart of a matter. "I'm not 'living with him,' exactly, I just... We've kind of settled into a routine. And it's nice not having to pay rent so I can build some savings. I'm not freeloading!" I said when Taylor's eyes widened. "I work my ass off making sure he doesn't die of starvation underneath a pile of his own garbage. Like seriously, he might die if I left him."

"Yeah, okay, whatever you say, pal." His eyes had taken on a teasing light, and I knew he was just giving me shit. He wouldn't press me about the Laurie thing. Not today, anyway. "Well, just think about the place and let me know. I'll probably take my dad up on it regardless."

"Will do. Thanks for the offer. I'll talk it over with Laurie. Speaking of his highness, the high lord of helplessness, I need to head home to start dinner."

"All right, man, don't be a stranger."

I stood up and gave Taylor a long look. "Yeah, you too. No more secrets, okay?"

"You got it."

FIFTEEN

Chatham House was quiet when I let myself in through the garage. Lately, Laurie had been venturing out more, doing some of his work in the communal living room or in the kitchen, seeming to seek out my nearness even when we weren't talking. It was only during really intense projects with short deadlines that he retreated into his cave and shut out the world. This was why I was surprised to find no trace of him in the house.

The kitchen was dark; the halls were still and silent. I made my way to the door of his suite, telling myself that I just wanted to ask him what he'd like for dinner. First I knocked, but there was no answer. Then I buzzed him on the intercom, but there was nothing but static after. For some reason, my stomach fluttered with unease, and my mind spun with worry. He should've been home. Laurie stuck very closely to a schedule when it came to leaving the house and working. He should've been there.

I decided I'd risk facing his wrath and let myself into the

suite—he never locked it anymore, because he knew I wouldn't disturb him uninvited. Usually. "Laurie," I said quietly into the dim living room. I knew at once that he wasn't there either. I had no choice; I had to check the bedroom, even if he killed me for it.

When I opened the door and stepped in, I smacked into a solid wall of heat. It was oppressively hot, humid, almost tropical. Laurie didn't like to be cold at night, so he sometimes turned off the AC, but this was ridiculous. I stumbled around in the dark until I found the thermostat and turned on the air. A mechanical whir and a cool breeze immediately permeated the room. How the hell had he slept through that heat?

At this point, I was so used to navigating Laurie's room in the shuttered darkness, that muscle memory easily propelled me to his bedside. I could just make out the outline of the lump under the covers. "All right, time to get up," I said, poking the heap of bedding.

Normally he would groan and growl or pull me down on the bed and try to attack me. But he didn't move. Didn't make a sound. My pulse skittered. Something was wrong. I turned on the bedside lamp, then flung back the covers to reveal Laurie curled up in the fetal position. I had a brief moment of terror when I thought he might be dead, but I could see the slow rise and fall of his shoulder that told me he was breathing.

I shook him gently. "Laurie, wake up, okay? It's dinner time." He finally moaned a little, flopping over on his back and covering his eyes with his arm. Following a hunch, I touched the back of my hand to his forehead, then pulled it back with a yelp. He was burning up. I peeled his arm away from his face and placed my hands on his cheeks. He was pale and clammy, but his skin was blazing with fever.

I tapped his cheek lightly to get him to focus through the febrile daze. "Laurie. Hey, Laurie, I think you're sick. I need you to wake up now and look at me."

His lids fluttered, and his dark blue eyes made an appearance, glassy and unfocused though they were. His brow furrowed as he stared up at me. "What are you doing here?"

I let out a nervous laugh. "I live here. I came in your room to check on you, and you definitely have a fever."

"Really? You live here?" he asked in a croaky voice. He'd obviously focused on the first part of my statement and ignored the rest.

"Yes. I live here. It's me, Mackenzie."

"You live here... Holy shit, you're fuckin' hot. How'd I get you to live here?"

I could feel myself blushing, even as I worried about his words. I remembered watching a YouTube video once where a guy was waking up from anesthesia and had temporary amnesia, and he didn't recognize his fiancée. It was really funny, and everyone on the internet thought it was so cute, but I'd always thought it would be kind of freaky to be in the fiancée's shoes, being forgotten that way. Turned out I was right.

I gripped his face again. "Look at me. You know me. Mackenzie."

Sweat trickled down his temple, his eyes dilated then refocused. Finally, his lips curved up in a barely-there smile. "Mackenzie. There you are."

Relief flooded through me, and I switched over to crisis-control mode. "Yep. Here I am. And you have a fever. It feels like a really high one, too, so I think you need to go to the hospital."

"No, no. No hospitals. I'll be... I'm fine, I just... Sleep. I just need to sleep."

I drew the covers all the way off of him and tried to tug his legs to the edge of the bed. "No, you need more than sleep. You need fluids. Medicine."

He hissed through his teeth like he'd been stung. "Cold! Jesus." His teeth chattered.

Feeling contrite, I pulled the covers back over him.

"I've got a fully stocked med cabinet in the laundry room. Just get me some Tylenol or something," he said, hitting me with a pleading gaze.

We stared each other down, but as he gripped onto the covers and shivered, I realized that forcing him to travel to the hospital would probably make him feel worse. "Okay, fine. We'll try Tylenol and Gatorade, but if your fever doesn't come down in a couple of hours, off we go."

"Good, fine," he said, his eyes already drifting closed.

I hustled to the kitchen to get him a bottle of Gatorade and a glass of water, then grabbed some Tylenol and zinc tablets from the laundry room slash pharmacy. When I returned, Laurie was sleeping again, but he was thrashing fitfully in the bed. I shook him gently again and helped him sit up so he could take the meds. He choked a little on the water, but he kept it all down. God, he looked so pitiful, all ghostly-white and shiny with sweat. My heart clenched at the thought of how bad he must be feeling.

"Okay, now that you're medicated, you need food. I'm guessing you haven't eaten all day."

His grimace told me I was right, but he dismissed it with a wobbly wave of his hand. "No food. I'm just gonna sleep, I'll be fine."

I was so not up for arguing with the dog over the bone *again*. I just stared him down and thought murder until he huffed out a "Fine, do what you want."

"Damn right, I'll do what I want, you ungrateful bastard," I muttered under my breath as I stalked to the kitchen.

Laurie's grocery delivery service kept us completely stocked with quality food, so I had the ingredients to quickly whip up some chicken soup. I didn't have any noodles, but fuck it, he probably didn't want them anyway. Once the soup was finished, I filled a bowl with the steaming broth and brought it back into his room. This time he wasn't asleep. He was miserably squinting through his reading glasses, trying to see something on his phone.

I set the bowl of soup on the bedside table and plucked the phone out of his hand. He glared at me.

"Excuse me," he growled.

"You're excused. Forget work. Your job right now is to eat this soup, get some rest, and get better. Oh, and quit your bitching. Almost forgot that one."

His lips quirked, but he held in whatever retort he would've normally shot back with. I handed him the bowl of soup and stacked some pillows behind his back so he could sit up to eat it. He went a little green after a few bites, so I took that as his body's signal that it was enough for the time being. I helped him to lie back down, and pulled the covers over him—I froze when I realized I'd actually just tucked the guy into bed.

"So do you feel like the danger of imminent death has receded somewhat?"

He groaned and shivered. "I guess? I feel maybe slightly less like my insides are trying to crawl to my outsides."

"Vivid. All right, then, you should get some rest." I set his phone beside his pillow. "I'm only giving that back so you can call me if you need anything. If I catch you trying to work, I'll confiscate it."

"Yes, Mom," he said, then sucked in a breath when the weight of that statement sank in. Neither of us had had a mother for a very, very long time.

I couldn't help brushing his damp hair off of his forehead. If anyone deserved to have someone take care of him, it was Laurie. As soon as I had the thought, my face got hot and my heart started pounding, the way it always seemed to do around him. "Get some rest," I rasped, barely able to squeeze a sound past the tightness in my throat.

I stood up and turned to leave, but he grabbed my wrist before I could.

"Could you stay? Just until... Just, stay. Please?"

It was so uncharacteristic of him to show that kind of vulnerability, I was momentarily stunned. He looked so uncomfortable waiting for me to answer that I tried to make light of it. "Fine, but if I'm going to sit here and watch you sleep, I'm gonna read books on your iPad." I walked over to his desk and grabbed the gadget, then climbed over him to the far side of the bed so I could sit against the wall. "So I hope you hid your porn well."

His eyes were already closing. "Porn?" he mumbled. "Who the hell needs porn when I have you in my bed?"

I sat in silence for a few moments to allow my pulse to slow back down to a normal pace. I picked up the iPad and opened it to whatever Laurie had been reading. It appeared to be a gay shifter fantasy web serial that was so completely out of character for him that it was actually *in* character. He kept surprising me.

Realizing I wasn't interested in reading, I shut down the iPad, set it on the windowsill, and rolled to my side to face Laurie. Here, in the dark, as he slept, looking so much younger than he normally did, I felt the first stirring of something deep in my chest. And maybe not the *first*—just the first that I was willing to admit to myself. This was more than just hooking up with my hot landlord. This was not feeling indebted to him. It wasn't even a response to his constant confessions of love. I had feelings for Laurie. What exactly to call them, I wasn't sure, but they were no longer deniable. I just had to figure out how and *if* I would be able to tell Laurie, because I had a feeling if I didn't say something soon, he might get tired of waiting for me to catch up.

SIXTEEN

I was exhausted. Every bone in my body ached. I'd never realized teaching could be such a *physical* job, but running after little kids as we were coming to the end of the summer term was punishing. It was a good kind of tired, but it was pervasive. When I let myself into the house, I had one goal in mind: bed. I'd order some takeout for Laurie, and after that I planned to sleep the weekend away. In the entryway, I heard murmured voices echoing from further in the house. The voices weren't raised, exactly, but I could tell they were involved in a heated discussion.

I followed the sound down the hall, through the open kitchen, from where I could see Laurie sitting on the couch with a man who was facing away from me. The stranger had a mass of dark brown, shoulder-length dreadlocks tied into a ponytail at the nape of his neck. In his near-profile position, I could just barely make out a short but thick beard. Curious, I made my way to the living room. Laurie saw me first, and he started to stand.

"Mackenzie, welcome home," Laurie said. His voice sounded strained, maybe even a little desperate.

I started to ask him what was wrong, but I forgot all about it when the stranger turned.

"Hey, bro, long time no see!"

"River!" I dropped my messenger bag on the floor and ran to my brother, who engulfed me in a huge hug. Over his shoulder, my gaze clashed with Laurie's, his expression unreadable. "What are you doing here? No, wait—how did you know where I live?"

River pushed me back a little so he could look me over. "Yeah, I had to call Morrison since I couldn't get you on your cell. I'll never forgive you for that, you know."

"Don't know why you guys hate each other so much," I said without heat. Nothing could ruin my excitement of our reunion, even his mutual hatred with Taylor.

"How much time have you got?"

"Shut up!" I punched him lightly on the shoulder. Sobering, I flicked my eyes in Laurie's directions. "You two met, then?"

River's lips thinned as he followed my gaze. "Yes. We met."

Sweat gathered at the nape of my neck as excitement started to give way to nerves. "Okay, what did I miss?"

"Mr. Beaudry here was just explaining to me the conditions of your living arrangements. I have some concerns," River said in a dangerous voice.

"Should I call Morrison and tell him we can't make it?" Laurie interjected. It was the second Thursday of the month, when we would normally be meeting the Mindstream crew for drinks.

"No," I said firmly, turning back to River. "Can we table this discussion for now? Like, you *just* got here, and this is the first I've seen of you in almost a year—not to mention my *graduation*—so can you maybe take five minutes for us to be happy to see each other before you start 'dad-ing' me already?"

River hung his head, and a blush rode high on his tanned,

freckled cheeks. "Sorry, bro. You're right. It's great to see you," he said with a lopsided grin. "Even if you're still short."

"Hey!"

He ruffled my hair, while I growled and thrashed, and Laurie looked on with a fond smile.

"Uh…it sounded like you guys had somewhere to go?" River said once we'd stopped laughing.

I bounced on the balls of my feet. "Yeah, twice a month, Taylor and I drag Laurie out for drinks with their coworkers. It's just our small contribution to him not being a total hermit."

"Pretty sure hermits don't live in mansions," River said under his breath, but I heard him anyway.

I glared at him for a few seconds until he winced and rubbed the back of his neck. "If you can behave, you should totally come with us."

His face screwed up in obvious distaste. "I don't know, I'm not much of a drinker… Maybe I'll just go back to the hotel—"

"River!" I sent him a pleading look, into which I tried to infuse all of the love I had for him but also all of the loneliness of going brotherless most of the time. His shoulders slumped, and I saw the exact moment he gave in.

"Yeah, no, you're right. We should spend time together, even if…other people will be there too."

Recognizing it as the best I was going to get, I gestured for him to follow me out to the car. A gloomy Laurie trailed behind us. And while River took a moment to drool over the Lotus in the way everyone did, I fired off a heads-up text to Taylor: *Gird your loins, your arch-nemesis is coming with us.*

The King's Shield was busier than usual. Apparently the Orioles were playing a big game against their rivals, the Washington Nationals, so the bodies were packed in around the bar and the parts of the dining room that had televisions. It was an away game, which meant that most of the home-team fans couldn't be there in person, so they were at the pub to watch in shared camaraderie. Sportsball was definitely not my thing, so I only found this all out from our overly-talkative host as he showed us to our tables.

River had delayed us, so most of the Mindstream crew was already seated, including Taylor—sans Karla—and Henry—*ugh!*—and it looked as though they'd already started on the first round of drinks. There weren't as many people as there had been the last couple of times, and I sort of felt like that might be a good thing, with the way the three of us were tiptoeing around the elephant in the room.

I sat down across from Taylor, and Laurie pulled up a chair beside me. Taylor glared daggers at me when he realized that the only open seat left for River was the one right beside him. I shrugged. I wasn't in the mood for his drama with my brother. I had my own to deal with. "How's it going?" I asked him, my expression melting into fondness. "Any change in the situation with your moms?"

He gave a dejected shake of his head. "No... And now Karla's mad at me too."

"What? Why?"

"I don't really know. We're fighting about all this little stuff now...but I can't help but think that deep down she agrees with my moms, and she's just being passive-aggressive about it. I feel like she's mistaking my change in trajectory for a lack of ambition," he said. Then he mumbled something unintelligible into his beer mug.

"I didn't catch that," I said.

River scowled at Taylor. "He said he thinks she had her heart set on marrying a doctor."

"Thanks, asshole," Taylor growled.

"My pleasure," River said with a wink and a savage grin.

"Guys," I said in the tone of voice I usually reserved for squabbles between my students—my *preschool* students.

Taylor huffed, making a point to look away from River, who frowned at his beer like he could count the hops. It was obviously making Taylor uncomfortable to talk about his personal problems in front of River and Laurie, so I let the conversation fade.

I turned my attention back to my brother. "River, you never told me what you're doing back in Baltimore."

"Is it so hard to believe that I just wanted to check in on my baby brother?"

Giving him a bland look, I raised a brow and waited. I held no illusions about what motivated my brother, so the least he could do was be honest with me. I wasn't a kid anymore.

Eventually he sighed and set down his frosted mug. "I've been contracted for a long-term gig with *Wanderlust Magazine*. They're starting this Americana series, where in each issue they'll feature mostly undiscovered but awesome vacation areas and attractions. Calling it 'Roadtrip: Americana.' Anyway, so at least I'll be stateside for a few months, even though I'll be traveling around."

The excitement of seeing River deflated just a bit. I knew better. I knew not to get my hopes up that he'd ever settle down so we could be a real family again, but my disappointment told me I'd been subconsciously thinking it was possible. I was careful to keep my voice even, unemotional. "That's cool. Sounds like an interesting series. But...there's not a whole lot undiscovered about Baltimore."

River cracked a lazy grin. "Yeah, you're right about that. No, the first job is up in Maine."

I nodded. "When do you have to start?" Even though he wasn't back for me, maybe we could at least take advantage of it. Spend a little time together, like the real brothers we used to be.

He answered, but a cheer rose up from the baseball crowd, so his voice was carried away with the noise.

"What?" I shouted over the din.

A commercial came on and the crowd quieted right before River spoke, so his raised voice cut through the room like the crack of a whip. "Saturday."

Everyone around us stopped talking and blinked at us for a moment before going back to their conversations. My heart sank. Two days. He was staying for two whole days. Part of me wondered why he even bothered to pass through Baltimore at all. Then I felt ashamed of the thought. River came to see me, and I should be grateful for whatever time we had.

I glanced at Taylor, whose eyes narrowed as if he'd read my mind.

"So you're going where?" I asked.

"Little town called Rangeley, Maine. I wanted to talk to you about it, but—"

"No, it's okay, I get it. Work stuff. Sounds like it will be a fun project."

"No, I mean—"

"Excuse me for a moment, I need the restroom," Laurie said, turning to me. I nodded as he gave my shoulder a squeeze. "I'll be right back."

When I faced River again, he was glaring openly at Laurie's retreating back. "Could you maybe try not to be so rude to my friend?"

"That?" River said, pointing in the direction Laurie had gone. "That is not a friend. That is a *man*, who took advantage of a kid who was down on his luck."

I snagged a tortilla chip from the communal basket and munched on it casually while the battle to control my temper raged inside. "Not a kid."

River's expression softened as he regarded me. He let out a soft chuckle. "Yeah, when did that happen?"

"While you were out of town," Taylor muttered.

"Taylor!"

River held up a hand to stop me from scolding. "It's fine. That's not really what we were talking about anyway. What's up with this guy, Mackenzie? He told me all about your 'arrangement.' You lose your apartment so you just go live with a *stranger?*"

"He wasn't a total stranger. We had mutual friends, and I'd met him before."

"Okay, but… Can't you see he's targeting you? He took advantage of you, played the right cards so that you'd be indebted to him."

"God, if anything, I'm taking advantage of *him*. In exchange for a few chores, I live in his fucking mansion for free, and I get chauffeured around in his Lotus most of the time, for chrissake."

River's brow creased, a sure sign that he was getting annoyed. "Do you hear yourself right now? You sound like some gold-digger arm-candy, and you're so blinded by that, you don't see how *weird* this whole arrangement is."

"River, you're going to want to choose your next words very carefully." My own blood was boiling, rising up to match the vitriol spewing from my brother's mouth. I'd never seen this side of him before. "Like I said before, Laurie is my friend. Just like Taylor and Karla are my friends. So you're gonna have to back off."

Gritting his teeth, River growled at me. "Did you know he's gay?"

Conversation thinned out around us, enough that I could tell ears were perking up and people were catching on to the nature of my brother's tirade. Henry's head whipped around, his gaze darting back and forth between us.

I snorted out a mirthless laugh. "Yeah, I did. It's not a secret."

Talking resumed, attention from the group slid away from us once they figured out there wasn't some big outing scandal.

Everyone had already known Laurie was gay, and now they all knew I'd already known too. *Nothing to see here, folks; move along.*

"So how do you think this looks? An older gay man coerces a young guy in a bad spot to move in with him..."

"All right, listen," I snapped, my patience at a definitive end. "I am not some gangly teenager anymore. I am a working professional, a college graduate, not a wet-behind-the-ears kid that you need to protect. Just think about the things you're saying about a person you know nothing about. You're going off the deep end here, River."

"Mackenzie, you're still so *young*. You're a vulnerable guy who trusts people too easily. Has he—has he *tried* anything on you? Forced you into anything?"

I surged out of my seat. "That is *enough*. You are out of line. I suggest you not say another word."

Catching movement out of the corner of my eye, I turned to see Laurie standing behind us, wide-eyed and very still. I had no idea how much he'd heard of River's ridiculous accusations. My pulse was an angry rush in my temples as I tried to keep myself from telling my brother off. "We should go," I said through clenched teeth, addressing Laurie while glaring at River.

Laurie took a deep breath, his broad shoulders rising and falling, then he leveled an unreadable look at me. "Not at all. We should spend time with our friends. And...family." He cut his gaze away, not making eye contact with River. With cold, efficient movements, he made his way back to his chair and sat down. Before I'd even turned back toward the table, he'd engaged Shayna in a murmured conversation.

I couldn't have done it. After overhearing something like that, I would've stormed out crying or screaming. Or fucking punched someone. Not Laurent Beaudry, though. He was the picture of class and maturity. It looked like nothing could pierce that thick armor of his, but I knew that wasn't true. I also knew, by the end of the evening, even though he'd put on a good show as a sophisticated man-about-town, something was…off. None of his smiles reached his eyes, not even the ones directed at me. The tiny, subtle things he normally did to show that he was aware of me—a casual hand on my shoulder or knee, the brush of our legs under the table, a tap with the toe of his dress shoe—those were all gone.

At odds with everything I knew about myself, I found myself missing all those little things. Somehow, without me even being aware of it, those little signs had become crucial. I wanted Laurie back. *My* Laurie, back the way he was supposed to be.

After almost everyone had left, Laurie and I stood out in the parking lot, waiting for River to finish up a phone call in the pub's lobby. Taylor joined us on his way out. He stood shoulder to shoulder with me as we both watched cars go by on the street ahead. Laurie had discreetly stepped away to check something on his phone.

Taylor stood in silence for a minute or two before his voice cut through the void of sound. "River was being a dick. Even more so than usual."

"Taylor," I warned, suddenly overcome with weariness.

"No, no, hear me out. I have a point. Listen, I have my issues with River, right? But he's not a malicious guy—and I'm sure you know how much it costs me to admit that—and I don't even think he's homophobic, either. If River's being that much of a tool with such little provocation…maybe he's got his own stuff going on. Maybe it has nothing to do with Laurie at all, and he's just a convenient scapegoat. So just…keeping that in mind, take the shit River says with a grain of salt."

I gave a jerky nod as he patted me on the shoulder, then jogged to his car.

Once Taylor was gone, Laurie came back to stand beside me. I stared at my loafers, my hands stuffed deep in the pockets of my jeans. I could barely look at him.

"I'm sorry…"

"Hmm?" he said, looking up from his phone. "Oh, your brother? Don't worry about that. I've heard worse."

He was so insouciant about it, and he almost had me fooled. If it weren't for the stress lines around his mouth and the tense set of his jaw, I might've believed it. But if he wanted to ignore the issue, pretend it didn't happen, to save a little dignity in the face of my brother's hateful words, playing along was the least I could do.

River came through the door, stuffing his phone back in his pocket. He couldn't seem to look either of us in the eye. "Sorry to keep you waiting. And…for the other stuff," he mumbled.

I glared at him, trying to convey all of my anger and disappointment with a single look. "It's probably best if you just stop talking."

"Yeah, okay. You're right. If you guys could just drop me off at a hotel, I'll get out of your hair."

The lights blinked on Laurie's other car—the Jaguar sedan that he called the "practical one"—as he unlocked it. "Don't be silly. There's plenty of room for you at my house." He took off toward the car, his long-legged stride eating up the blacktop.

Something fluttered in my chest. Even after the shit my brother had been flinging, Laurie had still invited him into his home. Not a lot of people would do that, so I figured if he could be gracious and forgiving, so could I. "Yeah, you can have my bedroom."

"Nah, I don't want to put you out," River said as he followed me to the car.

"Are you kidding? You saw the living room couch. A whole soccer team could camp out on it, and it's more comfortable than my bed. Stop arguing, get in," I said, pointing at the back seat of the Jag.

River's head was down, his chin tucked against his chest, and I realized Taylor was right. Something was bothering him, and it was affecting his behavior.

Later that night, with River safely tucked away in my suite, I lay on the central living room couch, trying and failing to sleep. I hadn't been lying about that couch. I could've made up one of the other guest rooms, but the living room couch was so decadent, I didn't bother. I was plenty comfortable, I just couldn't get my brain to shut off. I tossed and turned, my body unable to keep still and my mind running on a hamster wheel, trying to sort out my feelings and my reactions to River's weirdness. I pulled the blanket up over my head to try to block out the world. It didn't work.

I jumped when my phone vibrated right next to my head. I unlocked it, wincing as the backlight cutting through the darkness seared my retinas. It was a message from Laurie.

Can't sleep

I smiled at the ridiculousness of texting each other from a few rooms away, but I still answered.

Me neither

I stared at my phone as the little flashing ellipsis appeared, then disappeared. When no message came, I frowned. Why had he texted me if he wasn't going to say anything? When I thought about it for a moment, I wondered if maybe he was insecure about talking to me after all that River had said. I could feel myself getting angry all over again. It was the first time I could ever remember wanting to hit my brother.

I was about to type something when another text bubble appeared.

I'm sorry

Huh?

What are you sorry for? River was the one being an idiot. I waited, breathless for some reason. The reply, when it came, had my eyes filling with unshed tears.

Sorry if

If I ever came off as forceful

If I coerced you into anything

I know I was pretty aggressive in the beginning...

"Jesus Christ," I whispered. "Goddamnit, River."

I climbed off the couch and crept through the kitchen and down the hall, holding my breath as I passed by the door to my suite. Once I let myself into Laurie's outer room, I had to navigate by memory, because all the shades were drawn and it was pitch black.

Inside his room was also dark, completely silent, as if he wasn't even there. I knew better though. There wasn't even a light from his phone, meaning he'd probably given up on me answering. I felt my way to the bed, pulled back the corner of the covers, and slipped in beside him. When I rolled onto my side to face him, I could just barely make out the outline of his silhouette.

I felt rather than saw him turn to face me. I reached above my head and pulled the shade up a couple of inches until I could see him in the pale glow of moonlight. I cupped his cheek, rasping my thumb over his bristled cheekbone. Inching closer, I pressed our foreheads together.

"You are not some...predator." My voice broke on the hateful word. "You are..." *Everything.*

I wasn't good with words. I hardly ever said the right thing. So I simply kissed him instead. He gasped into my mouth but held himself very still, as if he were afraid of scaring me off. Smiling against his lips, I pulled his arm around my waist and wedged my thigh between his legs. A shudder rippled through his body, and I realized what I was witnessing. The crack in the façade. This was Laurie flayed open, without the steely plates of armor he normally covered himself with.

I pulled back and kissed his nose, a silly endearment, but his eyes slid shut and his lips parted like I'd done something far more intimate.

"Is this what you've been worried about? You thought somehow you influenced me? Forced me?"

He didn't open his eyes, but he jerked his head in an almost imperceptible nod. I shook my head, remembering the first time he thought that he'd coerced me into one thing or another. I thought we'd settled that issue back at the hotel. Trying to get my point across, I jerked his hips forward until we were flush and there was nothing between us except underwear and misconceptions. "Can you feel me?"

Again he nodded.

"Can you feel how hard I am for you? I can't explain it in words... I don't know if I'm g-gay, or if it's just *you*..." I flexed my hips, skimming my hardness against his. "This...is not forced. I grabbed his face in my hands and waited until he opened his eyes. "I am not a child, and you are not some lecher. All right? Now put your fucking hands on me," I whispered.

With a growl, he shoved me onto my back and rolled on top of me. Desperate, frantic, his hands were everywhere. One second his hands were plunging into my hair as he ravaged my mouth, and the next, they were gripping my ass as we rutted against each other. His complete focus was dizzying, my feverish mind even missed the moment he removed both of our briefs, not even realizing it until he took both of our shafts in his big hand and stroked spasmodically.

I could already feel my balls drawing up, so I reached down to still his hand. "No-no-no, too *fast*, I'm gonna..."

His strokes slowed down to lazy pulls as he sucked on my tongue and nipped at my lips. He pressed his forehead against mine, panting hard. "God help me, I just want you so fucking much…"

I rolled my hips. "You have me. Do something about it." I wasn't sure where the newfound confidence had come from. Possibly seeing Laurie so vulnerable made me want to be more assertive to reassure him. Or maybe it was the pulsing hard-on that was currently straining toward the object of its affection.

Either way, I was over being shy about what I wanted. Without another word, I rolled in his embrace until I was on my stomach, with my ass snug up against his lap. His cock nestled right between my cheeks like it belonged there, and his breath puffed against my nape, warm and rapid.

"But your brother…," he whispered. "He's just across the hall."

"It's a big hall, in a big house. We'll just have to be quiet," I answered breathlessly as I wiggled under him, more desperate with every passing second.

"Think you can?" I heard the smirk in his voice.

I pushed back against him. "Shut up and do me already."

He let out a pained groan before sitting up. The bed dipped and swayed as Laurie reached into the nightstand to get the supplies. I buried my arms underneath the pillows and pressed my face into the cool, crisp-smelling fabric. It was almost hypnotizing, the way he painstakingly slicked me up and worked me with his fingers until the tight muscles were soft and willing. By the end of it, I was groaning into the pillows and pushing back onto his fingers, desperate for more friction.

He pushed down on the small of my back to keep me still, and the tip of his cock nudged at my entrance. I groaned into the pillows as the flared head stretched the tight ring of muscle before it gave way and let him in. He'd prepared me so thoroughly that there was barely any sting to the long, slow thrust that brought his hips flush with my ass.

His body undulated as he lay across my back. We barely even separated with the thrusts, he just rocked his hips, pushing deep each time he bottomed out. It was so sedate compared to how we'd done it in the past, but it was hitting just the perfect spot inside me each time.

"Oh god, oh god, *fuck*, Laurie," I chanted as he pistoned his hips.

"Shh," he warned, though I could hear the smile in his voice. "You'll wake him."

Moaning into the pillow, I rolled my head back and forth. There was no way I could keep quiet with the way he was rubbing my prostate with each thrust. "C-can't... Too good... You're gonna have to make me."

His breath caught, and his head thumped down between my shoulder blades. "Jesus Christ, you're killing me." He wrapped his arm loosely around my neck, and his other hand covered my mouth. I could still breathe easily, but I couldn't move, and any sound I made would be muffled by his hand. Perfect.

Once I was effectively silenced, he started picking up speed, pounding as hard as he could while still holding me down with his arms and the weight of his body. Garbled whimpers and cries spilled from my mouth into the barrier of his skin. My fingers gripped the pillows so hard that I could barely feel them anymore. I was too delirious to bother touching myself, but I pumped my hips in time with his, rubbing my aching cock against the sheets.

It was enough. He pegged my prostate twice more and I screamed into his hand as I came. "Mackenzie," he rasped in my ear as his rhythm stuttered, and he emptied himself into me. "Mackenzie. I love you... Please don't leave me."

There was such a wealth of repressed pain and resignation in those words that it broke my heart. This was a guy that had been locking people out all his life because he was afraid of getting left behind again. In that moment, I wished I could stay with him always...that I could make it so he never had to feel that pain again.

I rolled over and wrapped my arms and legs around him, both of us already drowsy with satiation and lack of sleep. As I rubbed his back and contemplated the pleasant ache in my body from his attention, I began to wonder how in the world I could ever live without this.

I snuck out early, not wanting to meet River in the hallway. I'd come into Laurie's room in my underwear, so I'd pulled on one of his T-shirts—a ratty one with the logo of an obscure band called *Throwback Pilot*—over my boxer-briefs. He had grinned at me from where only his head was poking out from underneath the covers, all rumpled and sexy. Apparently he liked seeing me in his clothes.

It wasn't even light outside yet as I tiptoed past my suite, toward the living room by way of the kitchen. I froze when I rounded the corner and saw River standing at the sink, chugging a glass of water. He startled like he hadn't been expecting to see anyone up this early either. He looked me up and down, raising a brow at my get-up.

"Laundry day," I mumbled, which I hoped explained not only my choice of attire but why I was coming from the hallway that happened to lead to both the suites and the laundry room. He had no way of knowing that it wasn't my shirt…other than the fact that it was quite a bit too big for me.

"Hey," he said.

He looked like he'd gotten as little sleep as I had, but probably not for the same reason. In fact, when I really looked at him, he was too thin, he had shadows under his eyes, and his skin seemed rather pallid underneath his perpetual tan. Not for the first time, I wondered what was going on with my brother.

"Hey. You're up early." I shuffled to the coffee nook and started loading grounds into the filter-lined basket.

"Yeah... Rough night."

"Sorry."

"You shouldn't be. It was all me." He heaved a weary sigh as he turned around and leaned back against the counter. "I wanted to ask you something yesterday but...stuff happened."

"Yeah. Stuff." I frowned. I was on my way to forgiving him, but I also wasn't going to let him off that easily. "What was it?"

"You said you're on break, right? That you get a couple of weeks before the fall term starts?"

"Yeah, so?" I very much wanted him to get to the point.

I heard footsteps just before Laurie appeared in the kitchen, looking more like his usual grumpy, anti-morning self now that we weren't snuggled in bed. He grunted at us as he made a beeline for the cabinet that held the coffee mugs. I couldn't put my finger on it exactly, but something was off. He was moving stiffly, his spine ramrod straight, and he wouldn't make eye contact with me. I wondered what had changed in the fifteen or so minutes since I left the warmth of his bed.

River cleared his throat, bringing my attention back to him. "So what I was gonna ask you yesterday... I thought maybe you'd like to come up to Maine with me for a few days. I hate that I'm not able to stay in town longer and spend some time with you, but I have this pesky deadline. If you came with me, I could get my work done and still hang out with you some. It'd be a great place for you to relax between terms—Rangeley is a really peaceful place. I know I haven't been around as much as I should have lately, but I really want to try and provide you with a little bit of family time—"

"River." I had to cut off his word vomit because I wasn't sure it was going to end on its own. While my instincts jumped at the idea of getting to spend some quality time with my brother, my heart was telling me I belonged here in Baltimore. *With Laurie.* "It's a nice offer, but—"

"You should go," Laurie said in a voice that was all grit and sandpaper. His face was a mask of impassivity as he sipped his coffee. There weren't any traces of the tender smiles and sweet kisses he'd been full of earlier.

"Wait, what?" My voice came out sharp, making me flinch. "You want me to...go?"

He shrugged but didn't meet my eyes. "You should be with your family. I'll be buried in work for the next few days, living off takeout, so you shouldn't give me a second thought."

Why was he...? "B-but I should really..." I trailed off, leaving an opportunity for Laurie to step in and tell me not to go. He wouldn't even look at me.

"Perfect." River gestured between Laurie and me. "See?" He grinned, but his expression wobbled when I remained silent for too long.

I sighed heavily. I didn't like leaving Laurie when I didn't know what was going on with him, but who knew when the next opportunity to hang out with River would come along? "All right, I guess."

"Yes! Awesome. I can book us some plane tickets or rent a car so we can road trip. What's your pleasure?"

"Whatever you want, River." I tried hard not to sound too dejected over being effectively dismissed.

"Road trip it is! On the way, I can try to convince you to take Morrison up on his offer."

"He told you about that?" My voice came out more high-pitched than usual. Since I'd turned Taylor down, I hadn't bothered to tell Laurie.

"What offer?" Laurie demanded.

"It's not a big deal. Taylor's dad is moving, and he offered Taylor the garage apartment in his new house. Taylor asked if I wanted to share it with him. I told him I wanted to sit tight and put away some more savings before I got my own place, so that's why I didn't tell you."

River raised his eyebrows when he heard that part. "Sit tight?

You mean freeload off this rich guy while you put away money you should be spending on rent?"

"Easy," Laurie growled.

"River, you're making me rethink this trip, you know."

River winced while Laurie turned to me. "Maybe you..." He swallowed hard. "Maybe you should think about it. Being with Taylor and his dad... Maybe it would be more like a family."

I stared at him in open-mouthed shock. Did he actually want me to leave, or was this the thing that happened in movies where a character chases away a wild animal so it will go be with its own kind—like it was supposed to be for my own good somehow? Either way, I didn't like it. It made me sad, and being sad about it pissed me off.

I let out a watery sniff, then squared my shoulders. "If that's how you feel, I guess I'll give it some thought."

He nodded, his expression tense but unreadable, and turned away again.

After a beat of awkward silence, River clapped me on the back. "Since you're coming with me, why waste time?" He pushed me toward the hallway. "Go to your room, pack some shit, and let's get on the road!"

"N-now?" I allowed him to guide me, but I looked over my shoulder at Laurie, willing him to say something. *Stop me. Say you don't want me to go. Tell me you love me like you always do.*

His back was to me, but he turned his head just slightly. "Have fun, guys. Mackenzie, see you when you get back."

River shepherded me out of the kitchen while I bent my head to hide the tears that were prickling my eyes. A glance back at Laurie showed him gripping the counter, his head sagging between his shoulders. Everything inside me reached out to him. My body wanted to stop moving and turn around. But it was obvious I had overstayed my welcome.

SEVENTEEN

Over ten hours in an economy rental car with River was, well, awkward. I spent most of the drive obsessing about Laurie's strange behavior. My emotions ran the gamut of angry to hurt to confused and back to angry again, bottoming out into a profound emptiness that settled into my bones about halfway to Maine.

River seemed like he wanted to say something, but he wisely kept his trap shut—he'd said quite enough already. Besides, if he tried to pry into my personal life some more, I had plenty of questions about *his* life just waiting to be fired. He must've sensed it because he mostly stayed quiet beyond a bit of small talk here and there.

We followed I-95 most of the way, and it carried us into Rangeley as the sun was sinking behind the trees.

"Thank god," I said when I saw the sign. "I need to stretch my legs."

"Mmm," River rumbled. "But I'm glad we drove straight through."

I nodded in agreement as we puttered down the main street of the sleepy little town. The town was quiet, though it had a few shops and restaurants dotting the street. The general theme appeared to be fishing and boating, two things I knew nothing about, but the area was pretty with its lush greenery and serene-looking lakes.

"It's pretty nice by the lake this time of year. You wanna maybe camp out?"

He sounded so sincere, but the twist of his lips told me he knew what my reaction would be. I gave him major side-eye and refused to answer, causing him to crack up.

"Right, right, how could I forget? Baby brother doesn't do camping. The inn it is!"

The inn was a homey place, painted a cheerful robin's-egg blue with white dollhouse trim. Though it was a cloudy day, the place seemed to emanate brightness against the backdrop of the gray sky. It looked peaceful, and peaceful was something I didn't know I needed until right in that moment.

River booked a double queen room that overlooked the small pond out back. We were checked in and flopped down on the beds in less than twenty minutes. I'd been sitting in the car for ages, but for some reason, I was completely drained. I rolled my head to look at River, who appeared equally as wrecked.

"So what are we going to do while I'm here?" I asked. River wasn't the type to have a game plan, so I was curious.

"Well, I have to start shooting tomorrow. There are a few main points the editors of the magazine wanted to make sure I hit, but how I go about it is my choice. I thought I'd let you help me pick where to go, and you could tag along while I shoot. There's some nice scenery out here."

I couldn't help but feel a bit disappointed. If I hadn't come and River hadn't left a day early, he'd still be driving tomorrow, yet somehow he supposedly needed to start shooting. I thought we'd do more together than just work, but then again, I hadn't seen River in action in years. He really was a brilliant photographer.

Giving in, I sighed. "Okay. What are our choices?"

He rolled off the bed with a weary groan. "I'll run down to the lobby and get some of the travel brochures so you can have some visual aids."

"All right. I need to give Laurie a call so he doesn't worry."

River had no reaction other than a slight tightening of his jaw. "I'll be back in a few."

I waved him off, already finding Laurie's number in my contacts.

It rang seven times... Seven whole times before it finally went to voicemail, which I didn't make use of. Instead, I fired off a quick text. *Made it to Rangeley. Checked into Rangeley Inn. Call when you can. xo.*

I stared at the text screen, saw the moment it said Read, waited ten more minutes until I realized he wasn't going to answer me. I turned off my phone and tossed it on the bedspread, before lying down and burying my face in the pillows. What had I done to make him push me away like that?

Had he grown tired of me? Did he think I was a freeloader like River had said? No, he'd been acting strangely already before that. Just last night, he'd told me he loved me and asked me not to leave him, and the very next morning he was telling me to do just that. What had changed in such a short amount of time?

I didn't realize I was crying until I felt the damp spot on the pillow case. I couldn't believe how much I *missed* him. Which would've been bad enough if he wasn't blowing me off. What had I done? *What was it?*

The only thing I could think of was...I didn't answer him. When he said he loved me, when he asked me not to leave, I didn't say anything back. I was used to him saying the former, he did it all the time—and he'd been adamant that he didn't expect me to say it back, not unless I truly felt it in time—but the latter... What should I have said?

You should be with your family.

Maybe it would be more like a family.

It kept coming back to family. Did he think he wasn't good enough for me because he was alone? I only had River left, so it wasn't like I had some huge family he was keeping me from. Maybe he felt like he was coming between River and me, but River was totally out of line with all the shit he said, and he knew it. Besides, we were brothers. It'd take more than some harsh words to tear us apart.

My head was full of questions, and no answers were forthcoming. Unfortunately, there was no way to solve whatever was eating at Laurie if he wouldn't even talk to me. I sat up and wiped my eyes before rummaging in my bag to pull out Laurie's shirt. I'd changed before we got on the road, but I'd stuffed the shirt in there on a whim. It still smelled like him—of us, combined.

Back on the bed, I curled up on my side and covered myself with the shirt, burying myself in his scent, imagining he was there with me. My eyes flew open when I realized what I was doing. I was so agonized by being separated from him—someone I lived with and saw *every* day—that I was snuggling his damn T-shirt.

"Jesus, fuck, I *do* love him," I said to the empty room. The realization washed over me in a wave of astonishment. When I thought about it in that context, it was so painfully obvious, yet I hadn't even noticed it was happening. The way he treated me so gently, took care of me, was always worrying about me...and I was the same about him, constantly making sure he ate well and got some sleep once in a damn while, and that nobody—my brother included—fucked with him. He was mine and I was his, and he'd let me go, and I'd *gone*.

"Oh my god," I whispered into the shirt, inhaling deeply of

his spicy, masculine scent. Thoughts of Laurie filled my head as I drifted off to sleep. I never even heard River come back into the room.

I was the worst brother. I'd been following River around to different photo locations for the last couple of days. The scenery was beautiful, the town and the surrounding landscape idyllic, but I was completely miserable. Laurie hadn't called. He hadn't returned my text. I was constantly in my head, worrying about him, missing him, and generally being devastated that now that I'd finally realized how I felt, this thing we had might already be over.

We'd gone rowing on Saddleback Lake—I'd done most of the rowing, while River took shot after shot of the sunrise bouncing off the water. We'd visited the wildlife sanctuary. We'd toured the shops, restaurants, and lodgings in the town. We'd hiked through the lakes and the bog, and even took a fishing charter. It was a perfect vacation for an outdoorsy, nature-loving person—which, sadly, I was not—but I couldn't concentrate on enjoying myself.

Today was the waterfall hike. As I sat on an outcropping, enjoying the cool spray from the tiered, ninety-foot Angel Falls, River finally confronted me. He left his camera on its tripod, pulled two water bottles from his bag, and came to sit next to me. We stared at the rushing water for a minute or two before he finally spoke.

"I'm sorry I dragged you out here, kiddo. I guess I just wanted to give you a little...something of what you've been missing from me the last few years. But as usual, I screwed it up with working too much."

I shrugged a shoulder. "It's really beautiful here. Quiet. Scenic."

He grunted, something that almost sounded like a suppressed laugh. "But it's not your thing. Never has been. I should've taken that into account."

I finally looked at him. "You do you, River. I like that you're so passionate about what you do. Everyone—including you—keeps acting like I should be disappointed in you, like I'm not getting what I need from you. Do I miss you? Of course, all the time, like crazy, because you're my brother and it's just been the two of us for so long now. But if you're doing what you love, then I'm happy. I never wanted you to change anything for me."

"How'd you get so mature?" he said in a gravelly voice. He blinked rapidly a few times before hooking an arm around my neck and pulling me close, touching our temples together. "You're a good brother. The best brother."

In that unguarded moment, I just couldn't keep quiet anymore. I couldn't hide my pain from my brother. "Laurie and I are together, River."

He sighed. "Yeah, I know."

I turned my head sharply, separating us. "*What?* How long have you known?"

"Since the beginning. Since I first met him."

"H-how did you find out?"

He cursed under his breath, and his cheeks colored like he was embarrassed having this conversation with me. "Just... The way that fucking guy looks at you, like you're the goddamn sun... There would've been no way to hide it from me."

My heart gave a painful thump. Laurie looked at me like that? I'd never known. What if he never did again? "Do you...hate me now?

He scowled at me. "Of course not. I'm not that kind of person. Besides, Dad's ghost would come back from beyond the grave and gut me if I gave you shit over something like that."

I huffed out a watery laugh because that was true. Back then, falling in love with a man had never even been on my radar, but

Dad was the most open, loving, accepting person I'd ever met. I was positive he'd have fought tooth and nail against anyone who gave me trouble. I missed him with such a sudden, intense ache, that I doubled over, pressing my fist against my mouth.

River shoulder-checked me gently. "Me too, kiddo."

I nodded, then when I had myself back under control, I narrowed my eyes at my brother and asked him the one thing that was still bothering me. "If you don't hate me, then why did you…" *say all that horrible shit about Laurie.* I didn't want to bring that stuff back between us, not when we were having a brother moment, but he picked up on it. He knew.

His face dissolved into a mask of regret and some much deeper, unvoiced pain. "A lot of reasons. I'm not okay, Mackenzie. Haven't been for a long time now. I think…mostly I was just jealous and lashed out."

"Jealous? Of what?"

"That…this guy, this *stranger*, was giving my baby brother something I was never able to."

I'd never heard this kind of insecurity from my larger-than-life, free-spirit brother. "What?"

"Just… A life. Security. You're just…settled. Comfortable. I've never been settled. *Could* never be. I remember when mom left, did you know that?"

I shook my head. Afraid to speak, to break the spell.

"I remember it, and I think it messed me up more than I ever realized. And I'm more like her than anyone else, and I wish to god I could be different, but…" He raised his hands in a helpless gesture. "I haven't ever found a way to calm my wandering soul. I've always just been so restless. I keep chasing…something. Something out of the corner of my eye. Something I can only ever almost get my fingers around…until it's gone again."

It was all going over my head, but I wanted him to keep talking. "River, I—"

He cut me off with a laugh and ruffled my hair, but his

expression was still sad. "I know I'm not making any sense, but it is what it is. I'll know when I find it."

"I hope you do. I only want you to be happy," I said, linking my arm in his.

"Same here, which is why I'm telling you to get lost."

"*What?*"

"Mackie, you're miserable," he said, using the childhood nickname that made me smile. "You're harshing my vibe."

I shoved him. "You ass."

"Yeah, yeah, but it's true," he replied, finally laughing for real. "You hate outdoorsy stuff as much as I love it, and I don't want to change that about you. I have to go up to the high country for a few days, get some shots of the mountain views. You should go back and settle things with your man."

I felt bad that River had noticed how much I wasn't into the trip. I wanted to be with him, but my heart wasn't in it. "I can go with you. I'll be fine."

He smirked. "I had planned on renting an ATV and camping when I got up there." He cracked up at my horrified expression. "Look, take the rental car back into town or all the way back to Baltimore—unless you want me to buy you a plane ticket. Or, you know I've got the room at the inn booked for two weeks. You could go back there, rest up in the quiet for a day or two, get your shit sorted before going home."

"Yeah… Yeah, that sounds like a good idea. I could use some rest." I hadn't realized I was so emotionally exhausted until right at that moment. My mind going around in circles for days, plus the heavy conversation with River just then had taken its toll on me, body and spirit.

River held out the keys to the rental car and the keycard for the room. "I'll make you a deal. I won't schedule the next stop on the road-trip tour right after this one. I'll come back to Baltimore for a few days, and we can hang out without me having to work. Does that make you feel better about cutting this trip short?"

I leaped at him, enveloping him in a bone-grinding bear hug. "Yes, it does." My words were muffled against his neck.

He squeezed me tight, then set me back. "I want to see you happy, bro. He better make that happen."

His words sounded like a threat of bodily harm, but they made me smile. "I'm gonna miss you, River."

Alone in the dark room, with the heavy drapes drawn, I stared at my phone. I'd already agonized for the past hour about whether I should break down and call Laurie, even though he chose not to answer my text. My conclusion was that he must be feeling uncharacteristically insecure, both about not knowing my true feelings and thinking he couldn't compete with "family."

I knew theoretically, the ball was in his court, but I couldn't shake the feeling that the idiot was trying to do something selfless—like "giving me up" for my own good. That alone was enough to make me want to break the rules and call him again. I'd made up my mind, but when I was unlocking my phone, it rang in my hand, scaring the shit out of me. My heart stopped for a fraction of a second when I thought it might be Laurie, but it was just Taylor. Reluctantly, I accepted the call.

"What did you do to him?" he demanded without preamble.

"Who? River?"

His reply was incredulous and impatient. "What? No, Beaudry."

Cold fear trickled down my spine as I wondered what could be wrong with Laurie. "Ohmygod, did something happen to him?"

"I don't know, that's what I'm asking you."

I pinched the bridge of my nose and forced myself to keep moving air through my lungs. "Taylor, if you don't explain, I'm gonna reach through this phone and strangle you!"

"Jesus, calm down. So savage."

"*Goddamnit, what about Laurie?*"

"I don't know, man, he had to come into the office to get something, and he looked like microwaved death. Did his dog die or something? Wait, did he even have a d—"

I hung up the phone.

So Laurie was miserable too. That was something at least. *Enough stalling.* I thumbed through my recent calls and pressed the button to redial Laurie. Of course, there was still no guarantee he'd answer this time.

He picked up on the second ring.

"Mackenzie? Are you okay? I-I'm sorry I didn't answer your text. Work stuff got crazy busy, and after...then I wasn't sure you'd want to hear from me."

Hearing his voice after so long choked me up, constricting my throat so I couldn't speak. I barely managed a pained whimper.

"Mackenzie! Say something!"

I had to pull it together. He sounded really worried. "I... I'll be coming home—*back*, a little earlier than expected." I couldn't contain the soft sniffle. "If... If you want me to live with Taylor, c-can I just stay for a few more days until I get things sorted out with him?"

When no answer was forthcoming, my heart sank. I had thought that even if he didn't want to live together, staying with him while I set up the move would give me a little more time with him. But maybe that wasn't what he wanted. I backtracked quickly. "Or, you know, not. It's fine. I can move right away. I don't want to be a bother..." I trailed off, barely muffling a sob as my heart continued to shatter.

"Mackenzie." His voice sounded as awful as I felt. "Are you crying?"

Crap. Apparently I hadn't muffled it enough. "No!" *Sniffle.*

Fuck. *"You're* crying!"

His soft chuckle gave me life, even as it twisted the knife in my heart at the same time.

"Are you still at the Rangeley Inn?"

I sniffled again. It was very undignified. "Yes."

"Good. Stay there." There were muffled sounds over the line, like he was moving around, tossing things about. "I mean it, don't go anywhere. I'm coming to you."

Wait. "What?"

The line went dead.

EIGHTEEN

A loud knock woke me sometime during the night. I'd put on Laurie's T-shirt, gone to bed in it, and cried some more. Once I started, I always had trouble stopping. Taylor would probably laugh and say I was such a woman, but he'd always been really supportive of my emotional sensitivity.

I realized I'd spaced out in my cocoon of Laurie's scent when the knock came again. I thought it might've been a dream or River coming back to check on me because I didn't think I believed Laurie would actually come.

So when I saw him on the other side of the door, looking haggard and adorable, I rubbed the sleep from my eyes in case it was a mirage. His fingers flexed at his sides, like he wanted to reach for me but was resisting the urge. His eyes widened and his nostrils flared when he took in what I was wearing—nothing but his shirt, black boxer-briefs, and white socks.

He cleared his throat but his voice still came out gritty. "May I come in?"

"Y-yeah, okay." I stepped back to allow him to enter. Then I turned on a dim-bulbed floor lamp so I could see him properly, even though it probably illuminated my blotchy skin and puffy eyes.

Suddenly weary, I plopped down on my bed and watched him pace like a caged animal. His clothes, ripped jeans and a crisp white undershirt, were unusually casual for him, suggesting he'd dressed in a hurry. He was shaking his head and muttering to himself while he paced, but then he stopped abruptly and turned to face me, like he'd come to some kind of decision.

"Listen… You can't—I've decided I'm not letting you go."

"Huh?" I squeaked.

"I was trying to do the right thing, to not hold you back from living your own 'Mackenzie' life, but I just…can't. I don't think I can live without you."

"You can't?" My heart constricted, as if resisting the urge to hope. I was so confused. Wasn't this the same man who had told me to leave not a week ago?

He began pacing again. "I know I seem like some lecherous old bachelor or some lonely orphaned rich-boy, or both, to the outside world, but I'd like to think you've been happy with me…"

"Of course I have." I blinked up at him. This little speech was definitely snowballing fast.

He didn't even seem to hear my response, he was on such a roll. "So yeah. I've decided I'm not giving you up. I'm going to fight. Morrison, your brother, whoever. Because I really cannot see my life without you—not to mention I almost blew up the microwave while you were gone. Twice."

"*What?*" I was beginning to sound like a broken record but just…what the fuck was happening?

He stopped in front of me and sank to his knees at my feet. Grabbing my hands, he looked up at me, his pleading eyes so naked with his need.

The way that fucking guy looks at you, like you're the goddamn sun... There it was, right in front of me. How had I not seen it in this light before?

"So I know you're younger than me, and you've really just started living your life, and I'm kind of a horror to live with, and even though you don't love me back...yet, I—"

"But I do." My heart soared because I realized he still wanted me, and his neurotic babbling was adorable.

"Yeah, so that's why I—wait, what? What did you say?"

God, he looked so hopeful but guarded at the same time, I just wanted to kiss the doubt off of his face.

"I said I do. Love you, I mean. I—sorry, do I get to talk now?" I asked with a slight smirk. I couldn't resist yanking his chain for all he'd put me through in the last week. I laughed when he nodded frantically.

"When you told me to leave...," I began again.

He winced.

"I started realizing how much I didn't want to. I couldn't stand the thought of not being with you. I was inconsolable this whole time, you can ask River."

"Not gonna ask River about anything," he grumped, making me smile.

"So when I found myself spooning your damn shirt because it smelled like you and obsessing over why you hadn't called, I realized that of *course*, I love you. I just didn't realize that was what this feeling was, you know? I've never been in love before. But... I don't think I can live without you either."

He stared at me with a dazed expression for a few seconds before he pounced.

Wrapping his arms around my waist, he forced my thighs apart to make room for him. He nuzzled my stomach, rooting around until he got to skin. I started to take the shirt off, but he grabbed my wrist to stop me.

"Uh-uh. I'm gonna fuck you while you're wearing my shirt."

"Oh, Jesus," I breathed. My belly twitched as he ran his tongue along the skin there, tracing my ab muscles.

My cock went from half-hard to full mast as he continued his path downward, stretching the fabric of my briefs to strain toward him. He wrapped his hand around my shaft through the thin cotton, giving me a few teasing strokes. I let my head fall back with a groan. It wasn't enough, not nearly enough. He lapped at my cock until the fabric began to grow wet around it. When he sucked hard on the tip, the muted, warm-wet feeling was enough to drive me out of my mind.

My hips bucked of their own accord, seeking more of…just more. Anything to get closer to him. He applied so much suction to the head of my cock that stars burst behind my eyelids. "Please," I moaned.

"Please, what? What do you need?"

"More… Skin… I need you!"

He slid my briefs off, then pushed me so I flopped on my back with my legs hanging off the bed. Standing, he fit his hips between my thighs. More than happy to lay back and let him do whatever he wanted, I extended my arms out past my head and arched my back in a languid stretch. I saw his throat bob with a swallow before he continued to run his hands all over my body.

He rucked the shirt up around my armpits so he could tease my nipples until I was wild with need.

"More," I muttered again, almost incoherent.

His concentration was evident in the line between his brows and the set of his jaw. "You're so beautiful," he said as he rolled his hips, rubbing his cock over my balls and behind them. "I can't believe I get to have you."

I let out a near hysterical laugh. "If you don't get to having me soon, I'm going to explode."

The sound he made was something between a laugh and a moan, which turned into a hiss when I reached for him. He twisted away from my questing fingers.

J.K. HOGAN

"If you touch me right now, *I'll* explode."

He reached for a bottle of complimentary lotion that had been placed on the nightstand, squirted some on his hand, and dipped two fingers from his other hand into the dollop. The slick left hand glided over his cock in loose, slippery strokes while he thrust the slick fingers inside me with very little warning.

"Ah!" I gasped at the sting and ache of the intrusion, heat quickly giving way to pulsing pleasure.

"Life lesson, Mackenzie..." He broke off to groan as I clenched my muscles around his fingers. "You should never have unprotected sex, except with a long-term partner, whom you know is faithful. So..." He crooked his fingers, brushing my prostate, and my hips surged up off the bed. "So what do you want?"

I tried to slow my panting so I could answer. "I want you to fuck me while I'm wearing your shirt."

I couldn't even clock the speed of his movements as he pulled out his fingers and replaced them with the full length of his cock. All I registered was him filling up all of my empty spaces. He pushed my right knee out to the side, while pulling my left leg straight up and hugging it to his chest as he slowly thrust.

His steady rhythm left me breathless and dazed, so all I could do was watch him—the way his long hair fell across his brow and curled at his ears; the way sweat rolled down his neck and pooled in the hollow of his throat; the way his meaty abs rippled as he flexed. His heavy-lidded gaze stayed on me the entire time as he began to nuzzle and kiss my ankle and calf.

"Mackenzie," he whispered, rolling his hips. "I love you."

He held my leg out to the side as he snapped his hips. It changed the angle so he pegged my prostate dead on. I yelled out an incomprehensible sound that came out something like "Hnnngh!"

His cocky grin went straight to my dick. "Yeah?" he asked, out of breath. "Right there?"

222

"Yeah." The word came out as a moan as I gripped the covers above my head and held on for dear life.

He began pounding me at that angle relentlessly, and all I could do was thrash and writhe on his dick. My body twitched and jolted while he ran his hands over any patch of my skin he could reach, pausing to tease and tug my nipples. My orgasm was building exponentially with each second that passed, but I couldn't quite crest that hill until Laurie wrapped his long fingers around my cock. Just the faintest stroke and I detonated, splashing my chest, all the way up to my chin.

Laurie hiked his knee up on the bed so he could fold over me, smearing the cum between us and lapping it from my chin. When he took my mouth in a kiss as rough and brutal as his thrusts, I tasted myself on his tongue. Then he buried his face in my hair and came with a shout. The sensation of his seed filling me up was new and strange, but it gave me this alien sense of possessiveness. I wrapped my arms around his broad back, hooked my legs around his hips, and held on tight, not letting him pull out. Not yet.

"I love you too," I whispered in his ear, still marveling at the rightness of it.

"Say it again." His voice broke on the last syllable, so I squeezed him tighter.

"I love you."

EPILOGUE

Six months later...

This is our happy ending. Our swan song. Well, it isn't actually the *end*, but it's the conclusion of the "How Mackenzie and Laurie got together" story.

Today is Laurie's birthday and I'm throwing him a surprise party. I know, sounds like a good idea, right? Yeah, it doesn't to me either, but I had to do something—it's his first birthday since we've been together. Because Laurie works from home and doesn't leave the house much, I had River take him out under the guise of some boyfriend-brother bonding time. I'm still not sure how good of an idea that was.

"I'm not convinced they haven't killed each other," I say to Taylor as he joins me in the kitchen where I'm putting last minute touches on the buffet-style refreshments.

"Could've just let me kill River and take Beaudry out myself."

I glare at him, still hating the fact that he and my brother can't get along. "Just help me set out the food."

I set the dishes out on the bar that separates the kitchen from the living room and on the small breakfast table in the corner, as Laurie and I never use the formal dining room. The guests I invited are congregating in the living room, among them are Shayna, Brian, and a couple of other people from Mindstream, whom I don't know as well, Charles and Emily from school, Toru Atami, Taylor's moms, Sierra and Lane, his sister, Erinn, and his dad, Chris.

Laurie and I spent Thanksgiving and Christmas with the Morrisons, so I want to keep up that familial relationship. I don't know Chris very well, though that is slowly changing now that Taylor lives with him. Chris feels almost more like a big brother to Taylor, as he is barely past forty, having been just eighteen when he donated sperm to his sister, Lane, to have a child with her partner.

Conspicuously absent at the party are Henry *and* Karla, both now being exes. While Taylor's family has come around about the change in his future plans, Karla did not. Taylor has been messed up about it for a while now, but fighting with River actually seems to be distracting him at least.

Toru hands me a steaming bowl of pancit, a Filipino dish he told me he learned to make for an ex.

"Hey, Tor. Thanks for bringing food!"

He casts questioning glances behind him. "Uh, what's up with your friend?" he asks, nodding In Taylor's direction. "He asked what I made, and when I told him, he looked like he might either cry or puke."

"His ex is Filipina. It's still...fresh."

Toru winces, then heads across the room to engage Chris in conversation. I watch them thoughtfully for a moment until I get a text from River.

"They're pulling in! Quick, everyone in the kitchen. Duck

behind the counter!" I shout.

I hear the front door open, followed by the sound of—mostly—good-natured bickering.

"I still don't know what you expected to see at the botanical gardens in February," Laurie grouses.

I shake my head at River's choice of diversionary tactics. When I step into the foyer, Laurie's whole face lights up. He pulls me into his arms and kisses me, slow and deep, right in front of River. When it goes on just a touch too long and Laurie's hands start to wander, River clears his throat.

"You can leave any time now," Laurie growls against my lips.

Laughing, I take a step back before I get lost in him like I usually do. "Actually, I need you both to come into the kitchen for a minute."

Laurie follows me through the open entryway that leads into the combined kitchen-living room suite.

"Hey, what's with all the food?" he asks. "And the pres—"

"*Surprise!*" everyone in the kitchen jumps up and yells.

Laurie staggers back in shock, but River's hands on his shoulders steady him. "What is...?" He turns to me, eyes round as saucers. When he sees that I'm *not* surprised, it starts to sink in, and he huffs out a breathless laugh. "You did this?"

I nod and smile as our friends all come over to wish him happy birthday, surrounding him in a cloud of hugs and cheerful chatter. River sidles up next to me, watching me as I watch the love of my life and contemplate how I got to be so lucky.

"You're really happy, aren't you." It's not even a question.

Laurie grins and raises a glass to me as he talks with Toru. I smile and wave in return. "Yeah." I turn to my brother. "He's the sun."

Hours later, as we cling to one another in the dark, sweaty and sated from a marathon of lovemaking, Laurie strokes a hand down my cheek. His eyes glitter in the moonlight from the windows—these days, the drapes stay open more often than not.

"Thank you," he says.

"For what? The party?"

He kisses my forehead. "For choosing me. And for giving me something I never realized I needed so badly until you came along."

"What's that?" I ask, brushing the hair off his forehead.

"Someone to be my family."

TRADEMARK ACKNOWLEDGEMENT

The author acknowledges the trademarked status and trademark owners of the following wordmarks mentioned in this work of fiction:

Mercedes – Daimler Automotive Group
Angry Birds – Rovio Entertainment Ltd
Lagavulin – Diageo Scotland Limited
Batman/Bruce Wayne/Batmobile – DC Comics
Toyota – Toyota Jidosha Kabushiki Kaisha
Lotus (Esprit) – GROUP LOTUS, PLC
Michelin Star – MICHELIN NORTH AMERICA, INC.
Sub-Zero – The Sub-Zero Freezer Corporation, Inc.
Harlequin – HARLEQUIN ENTERPRISES LIMITED
Thor – MARVEL CHARACTERS, INC.
Dom Pérignon – MOET HENNESSY USA, INC.
Under Armour – UNDER ARMOUR, INC.
National Geographic – National Geographic Society
Ferragamo – SALVATORE FERRAGAMO S.P.A.
Gucci – GUCCI AMERICA, INC.
Perry Ellis – PEI LICENSING, INC.
Harrow – HARROW SPORTS, INC.
Men In Black – COLUMBIA PICTURES INDUSTRIES, INC.
Kenzo Murasaki – Kenzo Estate, Inc.
Born Gold Junmai Daiginjo – Goushi Kaisha Katoukichibee Shouten
Cambridge Culinary School – The Cambridge School of Culinary Arts
MIT – MASSACHUSETTS INSTITUTE OF TECHNOLOGY
Lincoln – FORD MOTOR COMPANY
Finding Nemo – DISNEY ENTERPRISES, INC.
Baltimore and Ohio Railroad Museum – Baltimore & Ohio Railroad Museum
Captain America – MARVEL CHARACTERS, INC.
Pikachu – NINTENDO OF AMERICA INC.
SpongeBob – VIACOM INTERNATIONAL INC.
YouTube – GOOGLE INC.
Tylenol – Johnson & Johnson
Gatorade – STOKELY-VAN CAMP, INC.

ABOUT J.K. HOGAN

J.K. Hogan has been telling stories for as long as she can remember, beginning with writing cast lists and storylines for her toys growing up. When she finally decided to put pen to paper, magic happened. She is greatly inspired by all kinds of music and often creates a "soundtrack" for her stories as she writes them. J.K. is hoping to one day have a little something for everyone, so she's branched out from m/f paranormal romance and added m/m contemporary romance. Who knows what's next?

J.K. resides in North Carolina, where she was born and raised. A true southern girl at heart, she lives in the country with her husband and two sons, a cat, and two champion agility dogs. If she isn't on the agility field, J.K. can often be found chasing waterfalls in the mountains with her husband, or down in front at a blues concert. In addition to writing, she enjoys training and competing in dog sports, spending time with her large southern family, camping, boating and, of course, reading! For more information, please visit www.jkhogan.com.

ALSO BY J.K. HOGAN

Strong Medicine
Shadows Fall
I Survived Seattle – Coming About, Book 1
Love and the Real Boy – Coming About, Book 2
Unbreak Broken – Coming About, Book 3
Force of Nature – Coming About, Book 4 (Coming June 2017)
Fire on the Island (Vigilati, Book 1)
Blood in the Valley (Vigilati, Book 2)
The Serpent's Fate (Vigilati, Book 3)

Made in the USA
Monee, IL
18 March 2022